STILL
WATERS

"Patricia Johns's *Still Waters* is a tender journey that explores friendship, second chances, and finding unexpected love. It reminds us God's grace and mercy are ever present, especially when we're uncertain of His plan for us. This story will delight readers who love the Amish culture and an endearing romance."

Amy Clipston, bestselling author of *The Heart's Shelter*

"Patricia Johns beautifully captures the struggles of three sisters trying to fit their dreams into the expectations of Amish life. You'll find yourself rooting for each of them as they navigate love, faith, work, and the push and pull of tradition."

Susanne Woods Fisher on *Green Pastures*

"Amanda Schrock had my heart from the minute she paid a call on the most ineligible bachelor in town. The multiple storylines were fresh, well-written, and simply adorable. *Green Pastures* is yet another example of why Patricia Johns is a true fan favorite."

Shelley Shepard Gray on *Green Pastures*

"*Green Pastures* explores the ties that bind a community as three sisters navigate their way through romance, heartbreak, and marriage. Patricia Johns tackles tough topics, resulting in a poignant story of hope, faith, and love that shines a bright light on the Amish—and human—experience."

Leslie Gould on Green Pastures

"*Green Pastures* by novelist Patricia Johns is a skillfully crafted and original story that is as inherently fascinating as it is emotionally engaging for the reader."

Midwest Book Review on *Green Pastures*

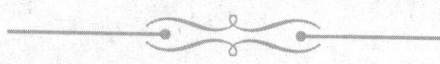

STILL
WATERS

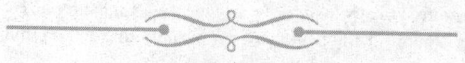

THE AMISH OF
SHEPHERD'S HILL 2

PATRICIA JOHNS

BETHANYHOUSE

a division of Baker Publishing Group
Minneapolis, Minnesota

Published by Bethany House Publishers
Minneapolis, Minnesota
BethanyHouse.com

Bethany House Publishers is a division of
Baker Publishing Group, Grand Rapids, Michigan

Printed in the United States of America

Library of Congress Cataloging-in-Publication Data
Names: Johns, Patricia (Romance writer) author
Title: Still waters / Patricia Johns.
Description: Minneapolis, Minnesota : Bethany House, a division of Baker
  Publishing Group, 2025. | Series: The Amish of Shepherd's Hill ; 2
Identifiers: LCCN 2025004882 | ISBN 9780764244186 paperback | ISBN
  9780764245633 casebound | ISBN 9781493451241 ebook
Subjects: LCGFT: Romance fiction | Christian fiction | Novels
Classification: LCC PR9199.4.J6364226 S75 2025 | DDC
  813/.6—dc23/eng/20250502

LC record available at https://lccn.loc.gov/2025004882

Scripture quotations are from the King James Version of the Bible.

Cover design by James Hall

Cover image of Amish woman by Laura Klynstra / BPG

The Author is represented by the literary agency of Liza Dawson Associates, LLC.

Baker Publishing Group publications use paper produced from sustainable forestry
practices and postconsumer waste whenever possible.

25   26   27   28   29   30   31   7   6   5   4   3   2   1

1

Friesen Lake was still and deep, nestled with the quietness of a prayer in the middle of treed hill country. It shimmered on the far edge of Shepherd's Hill, a Pennsylvanian Amish church district. Chilly water lapped the rocky shore, and the pebbled lake bottom sank in quick decline down into the water, disappearing into crystal depths. With its deepest point at ninety feet, where an underground spring fed the lake, even the summer heat never completely warmed the water. But that vast, sparkling expanse was tempting all the same, and Beth Peachy longed to swim.

In her many visits to see her grandmother in Shepherd's Hill, Beth had never been permitted to swim in this lake. Not when the weather was sweltering hot in the middle of August. Not when the *Englischers* in the cabins farther down the lakeshore were paddling around by the dock, their laughter surfing the breeze. Mammi had forbidden swimming in this lake. Beth's *daet* had supported the rule, though no one in her family explained the reasons behind it.

But that was what her family did—they kept secrets. Daet had never spoken about his childhood here, and there was no explanation for that either. Beth had been plying her mother with questions since Daet's death, though her mother knew very little. But *why*? That question had plagued Beth since her father's passing last year. Why all the silence and secrecy surrounding their family history?

Farther along the lakeshore, there was another Amish home nestled in next to the old ice house. Decades ago, that ice house used to provide ice for local Amish iceboxes. They would harvest the ice in the winter and keep it in the insulated ice house all summer. But those days were past, and their community now used propane-powered refrigerators and freezers for their families' needs. The Lapp family owned those cabins beside the lake, where *Englischers* liked to stay, and they had recently renovated the old ice house into an attractive little cottage too. Beth could make out both the Lapps' two-story house and the newly painted cottage from here.

She shaded her eyes. Did Danny Lapp still live there with his parents? He had been her friend long ago, but she hadn't been to Shepherd's Hill in about three years—Mammi had come to visit her family in Strasburg instead—and a lot could change in that amount of time.

Goldie barked hoarsely from the yard behind her. She was a twelve-year-old golden Lab. Her face was white, and her torso was thick. She plodded around the property with the gait of a regal old woman.

"Beth?"

Beth turned back to wave at her grandmother, who bustled out the back door of her house. Mammi was as portly as Goldie and often said that at their ages, neither of them could be expected to have waistlines anymore. Mammi had a round face and eyes that squinted so they almost disappeared when she smiled. But she wasn't smiling now.

"Beth!" Mammi puttered over the grassy lawn, beckoning. "Come away from the water, Elizabeth. Come away. Come, come."

Mammi flapped her hands at Beth as if she were one of the chickens. She grinned but cooperated all the same. She'd arrived this morning to help with housework and chores while they prepared Mammi's house for sale later that summer. Now in her late seventies, Mammi was starting to struggle with more than just the physical work. She'd been getting more forgetful lately and having bouts of confusion. Beth's mother wanted Mammi to move in with them, and when they started looking for a young person to help Mammi get the big house ready to sell, Beth had volunteered for the task. It would provide Beth with some space and time to make her own decisions too.

"Mammi, I'm twenty-one," Beth said, crossing the rocky shore and heading back up to the grass. "I'm not a little girl anymore."

Mammi had always had strict rules regarding the water at her own house, but she wouldn't try to enforce those when she moved in with Beth's family, would she?

"The lake doesn't care how old you are," Mammi responded. "Come sit on a chair on the lawn. You can see the water from there. It's a very nice view."

As Beth's feet touched the grass, a smile returned to her grandmother's weathered face, and the old woman turned around and bustled past a pair of white Adirondack chairs that sat in the shade of two cherry trees. Mammi had a large garden, too, and her rows of vegetables were already flourishing even though it was only the beginning of June.

"I'm a strong swimmer, you know," Beth said. "You don't need to worry about me."

She'd brought her homemade bathing dress with her. It

had a high neckline, short sleeves, and shorts underneath the knee-length skirt, so she was modestly covered. Her bishop back home in Strasburg had permitted her to wear it as long as boys and girls weren't swimming together. Besides, no one from the Lapps' section of the beach would see what she was wearing once she was in the water.

"It's not safe," Mammi said.

"That's all you've ever said about it. But my *daet* taught me to swim."

Mammi silently met her gaze for a moment. "There are people who have drowned in that lake and were never found." Mammi pursed her lips. "That lake holds more secrets than you can imagine. While you are here, Beth, you need to listen to me, or I will send you straight home. If you really are so grown up, then you'll understand that life is fragile, and it's prideful to take unnecessary risks. You are not less mortal than anyone else."

Beth looked at her grandmother in surprise. That was the most her grandmother had said about the lake in Beth's hearing. Ever.

"You'd send me home?"

"If I have to." Mammi crossed her arms over her chest.

Beth cast the glistening lake one last look of longing, then put an accommodating smile on her face. She was here to help Mammi, not upset her.

"All right, Mammi. I won't swim."

"*Danke.*"

She followed her grandmother in through the side door of the big three-story house. Goldie plodded after them, her back legs looking stiff. The dog stopped a couple of yards from the door, and when Beth bent down to give her a pet, Goldie yipped and shied away.

10

"Careful with her back end," Mammi said. "The poor girl is awfully sore these days."

"I'm sorry, Goldie," Beth whispered. She held out a hand to the dog, but Goldie wouldn't come close again. Beth straightened. She'd have to regain Goldie's affections. On her last visit three years ago, they'd had a lot of fun together. Now, the dog padded stiffly over to Mammi's side.

This house was big enough to accommodate a large family, but in recent years, it had only housed Mammi and Beth's *daet*, Mose, when he was a boy. Which bedroom had belonged to Beth's father? She didn't even know that. Had he slept on the second floor or the third? What had they done in this big rambling house, just the two of them? No one had ever shared any stories.

The side door led into a spacious kitchen. The windows were propped open today to let in the cool air coming from across the water. The wooden floors were polished to a glow with linseed oil, and the cupboards were freshly painted a bright white. The counters were a little cluttered, but Beth could help with that. Goldie stopped at her water bowl and took a slow drink.

A plate of glazed donuts waited on the counter, but Mammi went to a cupboard and pulled it open. Beth looked over her grandmother's shoulder. There were mugs and plates with a single black walking shoe sitting on top of them.

"Mammi, why is that shoe in the cupboard?" Beth asked.

Her grandmother blinked at the shoe in confusion. "I don't know."

"Here, I'll take care of it." Beth pulled out the shoe and tucked it under her arm, then pulled out the dishes too. "I'll wash these for you."

"You should eat something first," Mammi said, her cheeks

growing pink with embarrassment, and she gestured toward the plate of donuts.

"Of course, Mammi. I'd love one." Beth put the dishes in the sink, then brought the shoe over to the rack by the door. She didn't see its mate, but she put it into a free space all the same. Then she went back to the sink and washed her hands.

"These are very good donuts," Mammi said. "Aent Mary made them. She wanted you to have something special when you arrived."

Aent Mary was actually Mammi's niece and Beth's father's first cousin, but in a large family like theirs, sometimes people who were more distantly related were lovingly given closer titles, and so they'd dubbed her *Aent*. The donuts did look delicious. Beth picked up a plump pastry and took a bite. She chewed slowly and nodded her appreciation.

"Good?" Mammi asked with a hopeful smile.

Beth nodded again. "Delicious."

"Aent Mary will come by soon to say hello," Mammi said. "She was so happy you were coming."

"That will be nice," Beth replied. Aent Mary was more open and talkative than most of Beth's family on her father's side. She was always fun to visit with, and she was full of news from all corners of the family, which was why Beth liked her so much.

"I'm so glad you came too," Mammi said. "I've missed you, Elizabeth."

"I've missed you too, Mammi. It was so nice when you came to see us, but I missed this house and Goldie and your good cooking."

Mammi smiled in response.

"I was hoping you'd tell me stories about my *daet* while I'm here," Beth added. "When Daet passed away, I realized

I don't know much about when he was little. I should have pestered him more to tell me stories."

Daet had died six months ago, and too late Beth had realized just how little she knew about her father's childhood and upbringing. It was also time for Beth to make a choice for the church and get baptized, but she'd been holding back. She had a few hopes and dreams of her own that couldn't be fulfilled in the Amish world. Maybe if Daet had lived, he could have passed along some wisdom to help her make her decision. No one understood her quite so well as Daet had.

"You miss your father," Mammi said softly.

"I do. And I wish I knew more about him."

"What do you want to know?"

"What was my *daet* like as a *kind*?" Beth asked. That was an easy enough question to answer, wasn't it?

"He was a sweet boy," Mammi said, tears misting her eyes. "He was kind to everyone. To animals, to friends, to me . . . He was a very gentle child."

"What about when he was a baby?" Beth asked.

Mammi didn't answer. Was that her confusion or the old refusal to speak of the past? Beth wasn't sure.

"What was his first word?" she pressed.

The old woman pushed herself to her feet and went over to the fridge. "I'll get you some milk to go with your donuts."

Evasion. It seemed like everyone except Aent Mary was so used to keeping secrets that they forgot how to talk about ordinary things.

"Daet was like this too, you know," Beth said. "I don't understand it. Why does no one talk about the past?"

"There's nothing to tell about your father as a baby," Mammi said, returning with a pitcher of milk. "Every

13

mother thinks her baby is wonderful. The stories don't get interesting until the *kinner* are older."

That answer felt like more evasion to Beth, but she'd given this some serious thought over the years, and she had a theory. Mammi seemed to have raised her son alone. There wasn't a *dawdie* in the picture—at least none that had ever been mentioned. Had Mammi ever had a husband? Had he died? Had he abandoned her? Beth didn't know because no one spoke about that, and when Beth asked questions, she was hushed. Apparently, Mammi didn't have a husband that anyone had ever met, and Daet had never mentioned his father. But Mammi did have a son. If Mammi had had her son out of wedlock, that would have been a deep disappointment to her conservative Amish family. Had Mammi been a single mother? Was that the big secret?

"I want to hear about you," Mammi said. "Tell me how you've been doing, Elizabeth."

"I've been working at the flour mill, and I've been learning some new quilting blocks. I'm making a Star of Bethlehem quilt to sell at the next mud sale."

"Very nice," Mammi said. "Are you making it alone?"

"My *mamm* is helping me get everything pinned, and my sister-in-law is doing some edging for me. But the hard work—that's mine."

"It's important to know how to quilt." Mammi fixed her with a fond look. "One day, you'll be making quilts for your own home with your husband and *kinner*."

"One day." Although if she married an *Englischer*, her homemaking duties would be a whole lot lighter.

"Is there a young man who's caught your eye?" Mammi asked coyly. "Your secret would be safe with me."

"There was a boy I liked a lot," Beth said. "His name is

Luke. I thought he liked me, too, but he ended up courting my friend Mary-Anne and marrying her."

"I'm sorry."

"It's okay."

They both fell into silence, and Beth took another bite of the donut. Luke marrying Mary-Anne had been heartbreaking. Daet had told her that Gott must have someone else in mind for her, and that disappointments opened doors to new opportunities. Daet's insight had helped. She'd spent that summer swimming at their own local lake, getting stronger and faster, and praying.

"Did you ever get disappointed like that?" Beth asked.

"Me?" Mammi blinked a couple of times and then looked away. "Oh . . . that was a long time ago. I hardly remember."

Beth would never forget the pain of seeing Luke driving Mary-Anne home from Singing. Or the distinct agony of watching them take their wedding vows. She'd been one of Mary-Anne's *newehockers* too. But maybe Mammi's dementia had stolen her memories from that time already.

Mammi pushed the plate of donuts closer still. "Have another one. It's been a long time since I've had a young person to feed."

Beth shook her head. "I've had enough. *Danke.*"

Everyone back home wanted her to get baptized, to make her decision for the church once and for all. During her lengthy *rumspringa*, Beth had made several *Englisch* friends from town, and she had an *Englisch* neighbor she was particularly good friends with too. Those *Englischers* were much more open about their family stories. They knew the good, the bad, and the embarrassing about their family histories. It was refreshing how open and honest *Englischers* seemed to be about those things. It didn't matter to Beth if Mammi had been a single mother—she just wanted her family to trust her with the truth.

Beth had a big choice to make about her own future, and she felt stuck on the fence, sometimes leaning toward her heritage, other times leaning toward *Englischer* freedom with opportunities she'd never have access to if she stayed Amish. And even with this monumental choice before her, her family was still closely guarding the truth about the past.

"Mammi, can I ask you something?"

Her grandmother raised gray eyebrows. Again there was that hesitant air. "*Yah.*"

"What bedroom belonged to my *daet* when he was a boy?"

Every time they'd visited, the *kinner* would play outside or hang out together in the kitchen, and the adults would chat. If they did ask a question, Daet used to joke around. He'd say something like *"Me? I slept in the barn,"* or *"Your mammi gave me a mat to curl up on next to the dog."* And Mammi would playfully swat his arm and shake her head, and the conversation would move on.

But now Mammi pointed directly above them. "That one."

"The bedroom above the kitchen?"

"*Yah*, that was his."

Finally, a fragment of information. It was a start. Beth was here for the summer to help Mammi, and that gave her three months to wheedle out more details. The time for secrets was past. Mammi was becoming more confused and muddled, and there might come a time rather soon when she wouldn't be able to tell those stories anymore. They'd be lost, and as heartbreaking as Mammi's decline was, Beth didn't want to waste a moment of this summer with her grandmother.

Daet had had both a childhood and a father, and he was gone now. Maybe the stories were going to be hard for Mammi to tell, but Beth was determined to find out about both of them.

2

The bedroom above the kitchen, the one that used to belong to her father, had a window overlooking the lake. Beth leaned the heels of her hands against the wooden windowsill, looking out across the backyard, down the grassy hill that turned more and more sparse until it faded into rocky beach. The far side of Friesen Lake was wild—trees and shrubbery growing almost to the shore, and thick forested hills beyond. Late-afternoon sunlight slanted low across the water, giving it a golden sparkle. Some geese paddled across, leaving a visible trail through the calm water.

Beth's pulse slowed to the pace of the geese's easy glide. Still waters ran deep. That was something she'd been told since she was a little girl, paddling around in the stock tank her father had filled up to teach her and her brothers how to swim. Their mother had never fully agreed with those swimming lessons. It seemed unnecessary to her. The Amish didn't tend to learn how to swim because it brought up modesty issues with bathing suits. Sometimes boys would learn to swim at the pond, but it wasn't common to learn more than some basic strokes and kicks to stay afloat. There were plenty of things the Amish simply didn't bother themselves with. Their focus was on Gott, family, and farming, mostly. Or whatever other skill a man needed to make a Plain living. But then some teens had fallen out of a fishing boat and would have drowned if there hadn't been another boat close by to rescue them. Daet had talked to the bishop himself about wanting to teach swimming lessons, explained how he'd make sure all the requirements were met. He insisted that it was a survival skill, and Bishop Mark had agreed, with conditions, of course. Daet was an earnest Amish man. He met all of them.

"You never know if you'll fall in," Daet told his children. *"If you do, you need to be able to swim. That's what I care about—you getting to shore and not drowning."*

That had been one bit of advice, and the second had been *"Notice how still the water is. If the surface is like glass, the water is deep. Don't be fooled. Lakes can seem almost bottomless."*

And Friesen Lake was smooth tonight, disturbed only by the geese's silent trek. Since he grew up next to this body of water, she understood her father's caution. But he'd taught them all well, and Beth could do much more than get herself to shore if she fell out of a boat—she could probably even get another person to shore with her. The Amish people Beth knew enjoyed boating, fishing, and being by the water. She might have started swimming in a stock tank, but Daet had found some lakes in their area and taken Beth to swim longer distances because she enjoyed it so much. For a long time, he made her stay where she could touch the bottom, but eventually he eased off when he was sure she was strong enough, and they'd swim side by side through clear, cold water.

He allowed her to remove the skirt that went with her bathing outfit, and she'd put it back on while still in the water before they got out. But leaving the skirt behind made swimming much easier.

"Don't over tire yourself," he'd tell her. *"If you're getting tired, head back for shore."*

A woman had stopped Daet once and suggested that Beth was such a strong swimmer, she could compete in a swim club, but Daet had refused to listen to that.

"We don't compete," Daet said. *"We do well for the moral value of doing well. But we do not compete. Is she fast?* Yah. *Is she strong? Very. Is she faster and stronger than some other girls her age? Who cares? My daughter swims—she doesn't race."*

If something was worth doing, it was worth doing well. If a young woman swam long enough, she'd end up being very good indeed. And that was enough for Daet. It had been enough for Beth, too, but a tiny part of her had warmed at those words praising her abilities. Was she really that good? She hadn't realized it before the woman mentioned it to Daet.

So Mammi might worry about the dangers of Friesen Lake, but Daet had worried first, and he'd made sure his children could swim.

Beth turned away from the window and looked around the spacious bedroom that used to belong to her father. The bed was made up with a thin, worn quilt. A rag rug was on the floor next to the bed, and a bedside table held a ticking clock and a vase of violets that spread a sweet scent throughout the room. The floor was swept, and the closet was neatly organized with extra bedding, a few bolts of cloth, and what looked like an old tackle box.

Mammi was normally very meticulous in her organizing, and Beth was reminded of the shoe in the cupboard. She'd found a few more instances of Mammi's confusion around the house. Knitting needles in the cutlery drawer, a half-finished sewing project underneath the couch—which arguably could have been tucked there for a reason—and an opened jar of jam sitting on her grandmother's dresser. Mammi might be more confused than people realized, and it was a good thing she'd be going back to Strasburg with Beth. She shouldn't continue on by herself in this big old house.

Downstairs, Beth heard the front door bang and cheerful voices filter up through the floorboards. Someone was visiting, and Beth headed out of the bedroom and down the wooden staircase that led to the kitchen. There were two staircases that led down to the first floor—one leading to the sitting room and one leading to the kitchen. As she emerged into the kitchen, she spotted Aent Mary and her cousin Jonas. Jonas was a grown man of thirty, so he wasn't near her age, but she'd always liked him. He told funny jokes that he laughed at harder than anyone else, and he always brought her chocolate bars from town when she was visiting.

"Elizabeth!" Aent Mary bustled over and threw her arms around Beth, giving her a squeeze. "Oh, it's good to see you! It's been too long, sweet girl. Too long."

Aent Mary released her, and Jonas gave her a smile.

"How was the bus ride?" he asked.

"It was long, but there was a lot of pretty scenery," she said.

The bus ride between Strasburg and Shepherd's Hill was two hours including the rest stops. She'd been thinking seriously for most of the ride, though. There was a baptismal class starting in the fall, and Mamm wanted her to join it. She had several friends who would be taking part too, and everyone seemed to expect Beth to be there. It was time to make a decision, but this choice wasn't a simple one for Beth. Maybe it should be. It seemed to be for other Amish people, but it wasn't for her.

She wanted to take swimming lessons—real ones. She could become a lifeguard or a swimming teacher, but there was no way the bishop would allow it. As a lifeguard, she'd have to wear shorts and a T-shirt as her uniform, and that would be entirely inappropriate for an Amish woman. Plus, she'd have to swim with men and women in a pool at the same time, which was utterly forbidden.

There were more opportunities than swimming in the *Englisch* world, though. There was further education that led to interesting jobs. She'd been particularly good at math and science in school, and she'd finished all the math up through the eighth grade, so the teacher had gotten her a math textbook for ninth grade and then tenth, just to keep her occupied while the other scholars were studying. She liked the idea of working with numbers. She'd even looked into a job as a bank teller but had been told she needed her high school diploma. She was also interested in learning more about computers, but that would pose a problem in her conservative community.

Beth had scanned the courses at her local community college, and there were other options that had appealed to her—an X-ray technician, for example. That would be a job in which she could learn more science and then help others. There was more out there—so much more than she would ever see if she took that vow and settled into Amish life in earnest. Something inside of her was tugging toward the edges of her safe community. When she looked out the window, her eyes immediately turned toward the hills, toward the sunset, and toward that cold, deep lake.

She'd been seriously considering finishing high school and joining a swim club to start. Her *daet* hadn't wanted her to compete, but she'd watched videos of races online at the library, and they were thrilling. Was she too old to train? Maybe, but maybe not. Maybe she'd be an Amish prodigy who amazed the world when they let her compete. She'd gotten to be very fast and strong using her Amish bathing suit that was quite restrictive. How fast could she swim in an *Englisch* bathing suit? Beth had never swum in Olympic-sized pools or learned how to flip and push off the wall for another lap. But she had swum in lakes and pushed herself to her limits of endurance and speed. And there were open-water swim races.

The *Englisch* world held so many exciting opportunities, and once she was baptized, those doors would be closed for good if she didn't want to be shunned.

"How is your *mamm*? How are your brothers?" Jonas asked.

"Mamm is good. She's still really sad since Daet passed, but we all are. Violet and Adam just had a baby, and Andy just graduated school, so he's going to be home full-time now to work the farm. How have you been, Jonas?"

"I can't complain."

"Have you found another girl yet?" she asked with a teasing smile. "Because that's what everyone wants to know about you. Mamm will ask me, for sure and for certain."

"No, not yet." He chuckled. "You can tell your *mamm* that I'm waiting for the right woman, and when I find her, you'll all be invited to the wedding. But not a minute sooner."

Beth laughed. "That's a good answer."

"*Danke.*"

Goldie pushed herself up from her spot by Mammi's chair

and started toward her food bowl but then lay back down again.

"Oh, Goldie," Jonas said. He grabbed the food and water bowls and brought them over to the dog. "How are you, old girl?"

He took some pieces of kibble in his hand and fed them to Goldie, who ate them up readily enough. While the other animals such as Mammi's horse and milk cow would be sold, Goldie was going to make the move with Mammi to Strasburg.

"She's got a sore back end, Mammi says," Beth told him.

"*Yah*, she's getting older," Jonas said, then he raised his voice a little louder. "Aent Iris, has Goldie been getting worse?"

"*Yah*, she's getting slower and more sore," Mammi replied. "But we all get that way when we're old, and I'm not putting her down. So don't even suggest it."

"I'm not suggesting that," Jonas said. "I'm suggesting you bring in the vet."

"The new girl?" Mammi squinted.

Beth's interest piqued at those words. There was a female veterinarian? *Englischer* women could do anything, it seemed.

"She's a very good veterinarian," Jonas explained. "She's worked on our animals, and she's excellent."

Mammi sighed. "Can she really do something for an old dog?"

"She might have some medication that can help Goldie have less pain," he said. "That's all I was thinking."

"Who is this female vet?" Beth asked.

Mammi and Aent Mary exchanged a look. It was the same kind of look she'd been getting when she asked too many questions about family history lately.

"Tabitha Schrock," Jonas replied as he stroked the top of Goldie's head. He didn't seem to have noticed the women's hesitation. "She jumped the fence ten years ago, became a vet, and came back home. So she's our local veterinarian now."

"She's a full vet?" Beth asked. "An Amish veterinarian?"

"*Yah*. She's good too." Jonas caught the look from his aunt at long last, and he blinked. "What, Aent Iris?"

"Tabitha had a very painful time of it beyond the fence," Mammi said meaningfully. "She came home again for good reason."

"What happened?" Beth asked.

Mary turned toward Beth. "She left the faith when she was about eighteen and married an *Englischer* boy she fell in love with. He wasn't a good man. He was flagrantly unfaithful to her, and she left him. She didn't have a lot of choice—he wasn't going to choose her, and he wasn't going to stop seeing the other woman. After she divorced him, he married the woman he was cheating on her with, and Tabitha came home to be Amish again."

"She's divorced?" Beth asked in surprise.

"*Yah*."

"Oh . . ." She'd heard of people jumping the fence and marrying *Englischers* before, but she'd never heard of those marriages ending. If Tabitha Schrock had come back to the Amish faith, then she couldn't marry again while her ex-husband lived. Divorce might mean something to *Englischers*, but it made little difference for the Amish. Marriage vows were stronger than legal dissolutions. That was the nature of a vow before Gott. That was why Beth's baptismal choice was so deeply important too. Vows were forever.

"So should I ask her to come take a look at Goldie for you?" Jonas offered.

Mammi nodded slowly. "Yes, please, Jonas. I would appreciate that."

Beth would meet this Tabitha Schrock, and she was already storing up questions to ask her when she had the chance. An Amish woman had left, gotten more education, lived *Englisch* for a decade, and returned. What was it like out there? And if Tabitha could become a veterinarian, what other options were available for a girl who'd been raised Amish?

"They're friends," Mary told her quietly.

Beth hadn't noticed her aunt's approach, and she looked up in mild surprise. "What's that?"

"Jonas and Tabitha know each other from their school years," Mary said.

"And they're friends still?" Beth asked.

Mary nodded. "She's a nice young woman. She's very likable, and she's smart as a whip, they say. But like your *mammi* said, she came home for a reason. She saw what all that freedom offered her, and it was nothing but pain. We're thanking Gott that she returned."

Tabitha's story was meant to be a warning, but Beth was still curious. What had happened out there, exactly? And what had brought her home again? Because most people who jumped the fence never returned.

3

Danny Lapp tossed the used linens into a pile by the door of the ice house cottage. He shook out the fresh white sheet in a billow and set about remaking the bed. The sound of a scrub brush whisked from the direction of the bathroom as Mamm cleaned. This was their routine when a guest left. Danny stretched the fitted sheet over the corners of the mattress. He liked the smell of fresh laundry—bleach and sunshine.

This cottage was more popular than the rental cabins. Sometimes the cabins would be empty if the weather wasn't fair, but the ice house cottage tended to stay booked up rain or shine, summer or winter. People liked the historic and spacious interior and the big windows that Danny and his brother Zach had installed together before Zach jumped the fence. They also liked the big potbellied stove and the beautiful view of the lake.

Danny glanced out the window toward the water. The afternoon was cloudy, and the water took on a moody gray cast. He enjoyed helping his parents run the rental business, but he had plans of his own to open a store in town once he had enough money saved up. He wanted to sell handcrafts, bird-houses, wood carvings, and some painted Amish scenes that he was sure would be popular with the tourists who passed through. The guests they entertained often asked about where they could buy souvenirs, which sparked the idea. So every extra dollar he made was going to his bank account now that he had a clear vision of what he wanted to do.

Outside, the sound of an engine drew Danny to another window, and the scrubbing sound stopped as his mother appeared in the doorway. Danny opened the door and spotted his brother's familiar rusted red pickup truck.

"It's Zach," Danny said.

"Oh." His mother peeled off her rubber gloves and joined Danny at the window.

Zach got out of the truck and stood there for a moment, looking a little deflated. He wore a pair of blue jeans and running shoes, and his T-shirt pictured a band of some sort that Danny didn't recognize. These visits were never easy on any of them. Zach had left home almost a year ago, and he hadn't been baptized yet, so he could still come back and see them. But his visits were filled with disagreements and frustration most of the time. Zach wanted them to "see the light," as he put it, that the Amish faith was backward and harmful. They wanted him to see that he was turning his back on the only parts of his life he could actually count on—family, community, and faith. They hadn't come to an agreement on any of it yet.

"I guess we'd best go see what he wants," Mamm said, and she straightened her shoulders and headed out the door first.

Danny picked up the laundry from the floor and followed his mother outside into the cool afternoon. When Zach spotted them, he headed in their direction.

"Hi, Danny. Hi, Mamm."

"Hi, Zach." Danny paused in front of his brother and adjusted the laundry in his arms. "Did you come to help clean the cottage?"

He was joking, but Zach only gave him a wan smile.

"Are you hungry, dear?" Mamm asked.

"I could eat," Zach replied.

Mamm brightened then. "I made a fresh cherry pie out of the last of the canned cherries this morning. It's your favorite."

Zach did seem more excited at the offer, and they all headed toward the house together.

"Where are Anne and Tobias?" Zach asked about their younger siblings.

"At Aent Lydia's place, helping paint fences," Danny replied.

"And Daet?"

"Went into town for some errands."

"Huh."

Zach marched along beside Danny, but then stepped back and let Danny go inside first. Danny took the laundry down to the basement and tossed it into the hamper next to the wringer washer. Most Amish families in their district did laundry on Mondays, but here they did laundry every time a guest checked out. Danny came back up the stairs and emerged into the kitchen just as his mother served a thick wedge of pie onto a plate in front of Zach.

Zach pulled out his phone and took a picture of the food, then pocketed the phone again. Mamm eyed Zach uncertainly.

"Why did you do that?" Mamm asked. Cameras were against their *Ordnung*, and using a cell phone camera in their home was more than against the rules that Mamm and Daet had raised them to keep, it was rude as well.

"So when I tell people later about my mother's amazing cherry pie, I can show them what I am talking about," Zach said with a grin. He picked up the fork and sank it into the flaky crust. Mamm looked like she might argue, but then she gave Danny a faint smile.

"Did you want pie too, Danny?" Mamm asked.

Danny shook his head. His stomach was in a knot anyway. He'd have pie later after he knew what this visit was all about.

"Do you use lard in your crust still?" Zach asked.

"You know I do," Mamm said, pulling out a chair to take a seat next to her son. "It makes the tastiest crusts."

"But I told you about vegetable shortening," Zach said. "Even margarine. Lard is full of really unhealthy fat. It causes heart problems. My girlfriend, Meghan, bakes with margarine all the time, and it's much better for your heart health."

Right. Meghan. Zach had been quoting her a lot lately when he popped by for these little visits.

"I make pie the way my mother and my grandmother made pie," Mamm replied. "It's delicious. If you'd rather eat a carrot, I have plenty."

Danny smothered a smile.

"Mamm, I'm just saying that you should watch how you eat," Zach said.

"*Danke* for the advice, *sohn*, but I'm not changing a recipe that works," Mamm responded. "So how are things going with Meghan? You mention her a lot. Is it serious?"

"Not in the way that you're thinking," Zach replied. "We're getting to know each other, and I really like her. But I'm not planning a wedding or anything." Zach pulled out his phone again and then lifted it to face Mamm.

Mamm pressed her lips together in a thin line. "Are you making a video of me, Zachariah?"

"No."

"Put that down, please."

Zach lowered his phone. "Mamm, I just want a picture of you."

"You know how your father and I feel about that," she replied. "It's against the *Ordnung*. It's fancy, and we've lived easily enough without pictures in the past. There is no reason to break with tradition now."

"You know, your son wanting a photo of you because he loves you might be reason enough to break with tradition."

Mamm rose from the table and headed for the stairs. Her footsteps echoed up the staircase, a door shut, and then there was silence.

"She cries when you leave, you know," Danny said, lowering his voice. "You do this stuff, and when you go, I can hear her crying up there."

"Because I point out facts?" Zach put his phone down in front of him. "It's just the truth! Danny, we were raised seeing the world through one particular lens, and that's the way you see it. But all these things you've taken for granted aren't true, you know. We aren't going to lose our salvation because we stop being Amish. There is no moral reason why we shouldn't be driving cars or using electricity. God doesn't expect us to stay uneducated to please him, and the rest of the world is not out to get us."

"Are you done?" Danny asked.

"Do you ever wonder what you could do with yourself besides this?" Zach asked, leaning closer.

"No."

"Really? Haven't you ever watched a truck pass on the

street and wondered what it would feel like to drive one? Have you ever considered how much easier it would be to get into your own car on a snowy morning and drive out to a job that pays you better?"

Of course he'd considered those things. He wasn't blind to the ease of *Englischer* life.

"I'm Amish, Zach," Danny said quietly. "I'm baptized into the church. If I left, I'd be shunned and I'd never see my family again. But it's not just that. I believe in this life. I know you don't—you've made that very clear. But there is value in a life lived close to the earth and close to our neighbors. I believe Gott created us for more than just ease and comfort, and I want to live that out."

Zach's gaze moved toward the staircase, his eyes clouding. "Why does Mamm cry?"

"Because you're rejecting everything she gave you," Danny said. "You're telling her that everything she believed to be true and taught you so carefully was just a load of garbage. She makes pie, and all you see is a heart attack."

"I care about my parents' health!" Zach countered.

Danny shrugged. "And they care about your soul. You're coming at cross purposes."

"I'm not going to hell because I attend a church in town," Zach said.

"I didn't say you were. I'm saying, you're going to keep trying to convince Mamm and Daet to change how they live, and they won't do that. And they'll keep trying to convince you to come back and be Amish again. Why can't you just come and visit and eat some pie and stop trying to video us or take our pictures?"

"Pictures aren't vanity either," Zach said. He looked down at his phone, touched the screen a few times, and then lifted it up so that Danny could see it. On the screen was a photo of their mother. Her eyes were a little wary, and she held the pie server in one hand. "One day Mamm is going to get old, and when that happens, don't you want to remember her like this? Younger and full of energy and making her cherry pies?"

Danny looked at the photo a moment longer. "You took that without her permission," he said at last. "She didn't want a photo taken of her, and you took it anyway. That's what I'll remember when I see that picture again."

Zach shoved his phone into his pocket and stood up from the table.

"You are a self-righteous twig, you know that?" Zach moved toward the door. "Do you remember what Mammi looked like?"

Danny blinked. "What?"

"Mammi and Dawdie. Do you remember what they looked like? Do you remember their faces? Tell me honestly. Do you?"

Danny sifted through his mind for memories of their late grandparents. They had passed away when Danny and Zach were young teens. He remembered his grandfather's pipe smoke and his grandmother's soft hands. He remembered Mammi's apron and the way she used to scoop up mashed potatoes with this big, wood-handled spoon. Strange little details that swirled together. He remembered his grandfather ruffling his hair, and his grandmother giving him cookies hot from the oven. But their faces were blurred. He could remember something of them—Mammi's eyes when she laughed, Dawdie's beard—but not whole faces.

How had he forgotten?

"Well?" Zach pressed.

33

"I remember what matters," Danny hedged.

"When you have *kinner* of your own, will you even know if they look like our grandparents at all?" Zach asked. "Because I won't. And I want to know those things. I wish I could see pictures of Mamm and Daet when they were young like us, but we'll never see any of that. So if I get a picture now and again of our mother, you might find yourself grateful at some point in the future. You might even change your mind about this stuff."

Growing up, Danny and Zach had done everything together, but so much had changed.

"If I changed my mind, I'd be shunned," Danny said.

"Don't get me started on shunning. You owe it to yourself to look around and see what you're missing out on."

They changed topics and chatted for a bit longer. Danny filled him in on some family news—a cousin who got a new job, another cousin who had a new baby. They talked about the ice house renovations and how they'd helped make the rental business more profitable. Then Zach took his leave, and Danny leaned against the door frame and watched as his brother started the truck and backed out. Zach waved once, then rumbled up the drive.

Zach thought Danny should look around at the outside world. Well, Danny was equally convinced that Zach should look inside himself. Sure, the Amish life might not offer many options to a man. It didn't go wide, but it did push its roots down deep into the soil. It brought stability, safety, family, and depth of character.

So Zach might have options available to him that Danny would never experience, but Danny had discipline that Zach lacked. And Danny would never regret joining the Amish church.

He heard the squeak of the third stair and looked up to see his mother coming back down. Her eyes were red-rimmed, but she forced a smile.

"Zach left," Danny said.

"I saw him go from the upstairs window." Her gaze moved toward his plate on the table. "Did he say anything different than usual?"

"No, just the same old things."

Mamm nodded. "I'm still praying."

And Mamm would continue to pray. Zach could make fun of her, insult her, hurt her feelings, but he couldn't stop her from praying. And when Mamm prayed, she was handing him over to a much higher power.

Out the door, Danny could see the ice house cottage and the lakeshore as it wound around toward the Peachy house. Part of the shoreline was pebbled, providing a small beach, and then it melted into brush that went right to the water's edge. Another beach emerged farther down, and a woman stood on the rocky stretch. He thought he recognized something in her stance, in the way she put her weight on one foot. He hadn't seen her in three years. But he'd seen her every summer before that. . . .

"Mamm, is that Beth Peachy?" Danny asked.

His mother joined him at the door and leaned outside to get a better look.

"*Yah*, that's her," she said. "I heard she was staying with her *mammi* for the summer. Not a moment too soon either. Iris needs the help."

"I didn't know she was back," he said.

He'd thought about Beth a lot the last three years, and he'd wondered what she'd been up to. Did she think about him? She hadn't written, but then, he was a terrible letter writer himself.

His mother shot him a smile. "Now you know. Let's go finish cleaning the cottage."

They headed back out toward the cottage once more, and Danny's gaze stayed locked on that woman on the beach. Beth Peachy. He'd harbored a crush on her for years, but nothing ever came of it. He'd been an awkward kid, and she just hadn't seen him that way. As he crossed the yard, he raised his hand in a wave over his head, and she did the same in return.

Danny smiled to himself. Beth Peachy was back. How much had she changed in three years? He'd find out.

4

Tabitha Schrock carefully stitched two pieces of fabric together. When she was done, it would be an eight-pointed star quilt block. But she wasn't done yet. She sat at the kitchen table in a pool of early evening sunlight from the nearby window. The June day was warm, and even with the window cranked open, Tabitha would have rather been outside in a field somewhere. Her younger sister Rose stood over her shoulder, watching her work. Rose had volunteered to teach Tabitha what she could about proper quilting before the upcoming quilting bee.

Most Amish women knew how to quilt, but Tabitha had never been very good at it or applied herself to getting better. When she was young, she was more focused on acquiring her high school diploma—the very education that would lure her out of the Amish fold. But after ten years away, Tabitha had returned from an *Englischer* life, and she was now the large animal veterinarian for Shepherd's Hill. But coming home came with its own challenges. She now had little in common with the women she'd grown up with. They were wives and mothers; Tabitha was an unmarried vet. They could quilt; she was struggling.

"You should have learned this years ago," Rose muttered.

Tabitha winced as the needle connected with her fingertip. She stuck her finger into her mouth and tasted a drop of blood. "Ouch," she muttered. "I tried, but I wasn't much good at it back then either."

She'd been particularly good at academics, not handcrafts or cooking. And when she'd gotten her high school diploma after her mother's untimely death, she'd received some enthusiastic encouragement from the teachers to follow her natural talents. That had been a huge relief. To simply do what came easily? It was a pleasure, to be sure. Following her natural abilities had left her highly educated and in possession of a career she loved, but outside of the social framework of her Amish community.

"I don't think anyone actually expects you to quilt," Rose said, cocking her head to one side and inspecting Tabitha's work.

Tabitha looked at the quilt block. It wasn't straight. This wouldn't be square in the end.

"They don't expect me to quilt," she agreed. "I know that. But quilting is where women talk and build friendships. I'm outside of those circles, and I want friends, Rose."

"Rip out those stitches and start over." Rose handed her the seam ripper.

Tabitha sighed. Her sister was right, of course. Something had gone wrong, and all she could do was start the seam over again. Much like her life. She'd had to do some seam ripping of her own when she divorced her cheating ex-husband and came home to her Amish life again. And now, in many ways, she was starting all over. No one really knew her anymore. No one really understood her. And Tabitha now worked a job that was not only considered *Englisch*, but also in the male sphere. So even if Tabitha was not very good at handcrafts, she was determined to work on her quilting skills so that she could at least sit down with a roomful of women and join in on a group task. They made quilts to be sold at auction to collect money for their community medical fund. This was the *Ordnung*-approved form of insurance, where everyone helped raise money for a fund that could be used for any member's medical bills. They didn't rely upon an insurance company. They relied on each other. And Tabitha would chat, and listen, and hopefully prove to the other women that she wasn't quite as different as they'd thought.

Tabitha picked the last of the thread out of the fabric and rolled it up into a little ball, then flicked it across the table. Rose shot her an amused smile.

"You'll get better with practice," Rose said.

"I know."

"You don't have to be so miserable about it."

"Do I look miserable?" Tabitha glanced at her sister. "Rose, not everyone is as talented as you are when it comes to homemaking. Your home is spotless, your bread is fluffy and rises like a cloud, and your quilts are flawless."

"Not flawless."

"Pretty close," Tabitha retorted. "You're good at this. I'm not. But I'll do my best."

Tabitha started the seam again, focusing on small, straight stitches. Her sister leaned over her shoulder.

"Those stitches are too big," Rose said.

"What?" Tabitha sighed.

"If you were stitching up an incision, those would be

39

perfect," Rose said. "But you aren't doing surgery. You're quilting."

Tabitha bit her bottom lip in concentration as she worked. Rose was right. If this were surgery, she'd have already saved an animal's life. Instead, she was butchering a quilt block. She slowly worked her way up the seam, then folded the fabric back and looked at it.

"Better," Rose said. "It'll do. Tie off your thread, and you can do the next seam."

That was high praise at the moment, and Tabitha did as her sister instructed.

"So what's the gossip these days?" Tabitha asked. When Rose came over, she always came with community news. If there was something going on, Rose would know about it.

"Iris Peachy's granddaughter is visiting from Strasburg," Rose said.

Iris only had one son, and out of his *kinner*, only one granddaughter.

"That's nice. How long is she staying?"

"Not sure," Rose replied. "But Iris is very pleased to have her come visit. I think Iris gets lonely in that big house by herself. Apparently, Mose kept inviting her to live with his family in Strasburg, but she wouldn't budge. And now that Mose has passed, it's a bit late."

"She could stay with Mose's wife and *kinner*."

"She might yet."

"Can you imagine us getting Daet out of this house when he's old and grumpy?" Tabitha asked with a chuckle.

"He's already old and grumpy," Rose joked. "But you're right. People get set in their ways."

"Luckily for him, I won't be going anywhere," Tabitha said. She picked up her spool of thread and unwound a length of it to rethread her needle. "I'll be the old woman who ends up alone in her house."

The thought was a dismal one, and she licked the thread and got it through the eye on her first attempt. She glanced up to see her sister looking at her with sadness in her eyes.

"Oh, stop that," Tabitha said. "That's why I need friends, though. That's why all of us need friends, Rose. What about women who outlive their husbands? Someone always ends up on their own. It's how this works."

"That's a very sad thought," Rose said.

"'And even to your old age I am he; and even to hoar hairs will I carry you: I have made, and I will bear; even I will carry, and will deliver you,'" Tabitha said, quoting the verse from Isaiah. "And I found one 'hoar hair' in my braid last night. Can you believe that?"

"Going gray already?" Rose laughed. "It better be the stress, because I don't want to turn gray at thirty."

"It better be the stress," Tabitha muttered. It had been a reminder that she was getting older. Time was marching forward.

Rose went to the big wood stove out on the summer porch and put on an oven mitt before she attached a handle to a heated iron and pulled it off the heat. They had an ironing board set up next to the table, and when Tabitha finished the next seam, she handed the partially finished quilt block to her sister, who ironed it flat. It was easier to see where the next piece belonged once it had been properly ironed.

"Maybe I can just be the one at the ironing board during the quilting bee," Tabitha said.

"You could. But the hostess normally irons."

Outside, hooves and buggy wheels sounded on the gravel

drive, and Tabitha got up and went to the window. "It's Jonas."

"I've heard you two spend quite a bit of time together," Rose commented.

"Heard from who?"

"From . . . people. They notice. I heard you and Jonas are rather good friends."

Good friends was a term that could mean two different things. It could mean two buddies, or it could mean a dating couple. What someone meant by the term was relayed in tone and position of eyebrows. The higher the eyebrows, the more likely they meant a dating relationship.

"We are friends," Tabitha said. She felt a little bit defensive when it came to Jonas. "And it's only friendship. I can't marry again. There is absolutely no confusion there."

Tabitha couldn't marry again while her ex-husband was alive, at least. It was the Amish way. She'd made her choices, and they would affect the rest of her life. She'd made her own peace with that fact.

"I know that," Rose said. "I'm just letting you know what I heard."

People were wondering what was happening between them. Should she be more careful about being seen with Jonas? Reputations mattered, especially for a woman wanting to make more female friends.

Jonas reined in, then hopped out of his buggy. He tied his horse to the hitching post and headed over toward the screen door. Tabitha pushed it open for him in welcome, and he jogged up the steps.

"Hi," Tabitha greeted him. "Come on in. How are your folks?"

"Good, good." Jonas gave her his familiar smile. "I took

my mother to see Aent Iris today. My cousin is visiting from Strasburg."

"Right. Elizabeth. I heard."

"Already?" Jonas walked into the kitchen. "She just arrived."

Rose shot him a demure little smile. "I heard from someone."

"You are very well connected, Rose," Jonas said. "How is Aaron?"

"He's good." Rose put the iron down on the ironing board. "I should be getting home to him pretty soon."

"Rose is helping me improve in my quilting," Tabitha said, and Rose held up the half-finished quilt block as proof.

"Do you need to quilt?" Jonas turned back to Tabitha quizzically.

"*Yah*, I need to quilt," Tabitha said. "Even if it's frustrating, I need to know how to do it. This is what Amish women do."

"It's what other women do," Jonas countered. "You're a vet. You do other things that are very useful in the area."

"I want to quilt." Tabitha looked down at her pricked finger. "There are things women do together, and quilting is a big one. I can't live my life on the fringes all the time, being 'different and unique.'" She used air quotes around the last three words. "It's time to fit in."

If it wasn't too late. Her stomach tightened at the thought. She'd come home for many reasons—Gott's prodding, her conviction that this was where Gott wanted her, and for the community. She'd missed these people, *her* people.

"Maybe you could take up knitting instead?" He looked at the fabric dubiously.

"Oh, hush, it'll look fine when it's done." Tabitha took

back her quilt square. "Everything looks raggedy before it's finished."

Jonas shot her a teasing grin, and she rolled her eyes.

Daet's boots sounded on the step outside. He was back from evening chores. Jonas sobered immediately. The door opened and shut, and the tap on the mudroom sink turned on.

"I actually came about my Aent Iris," Jonas said. "She is wondering if you'll come take a look at her elderly golden Lab. The dog's getting old, and the arthritis is bad. She's in quite a bit of pain. Aent Iris was wondering if there is any treatment."

"*Yah*, there are a few treatments, actually," Tabitha said.

"Would you be willing to go by and take a look at Goldie?"

"Gladly." Tabitha smiled.

The water turned off, and Daet appeared in the doorway with a jovial smile.

"Hello, Jonas," he said. "Good to see you. How is your family?"

This was a big step forward from a few months back when Daet and Jonas's father could hardly stand being in the same room together. They still preferred to avoid each other, but they'd started up some social niceties now. And manners were an important step toward mending those fences. Tabitha was proud of her father for tackling his own hard feelings so honestly.

"My parents are doing well," Jonas said. "*Danke* for asking. My *daet* will pass along his greetings, I'm sure. I'd better get back and help with the rest of the work tonight. *Danke*, Tabitha. Take care, Rose, Abram."

Jonas headed for the door, and Daet watched him go.

"What's his hurry?" Daet asked after Jonas climbed into his buggy.

"He only stopped by to get me to look at his *aent's* dog," Tabitha replied. "Did you know that Mose's daughter is visiting?"

This was how news passed. People talked—about themselves, about each other. They passed along news. It wasn't really gossip. Gossip could be mean-spirited and wished the worst in others. News was simply what was happening in other people's lives. And it was important, because without it, no one would know when someone needed help or might be struggling and trying to keep up appearances. Amish communities were built and nurtured by curious neighbors who passed along news.

"Mose Peachy was a good man," Daet said quietly. "A very good man. Mose was a Christian in every sense."

This community had loved Mose well, and they would do whatever they could for his daughter.

5

The next morning, Beth milked Mammi's cow, Bessie. Normally the neighbor came by and did it, but she was sure that they'd be happy to have one less chore. She didn't know how much milk this cow normally produced, but the milk she got only half filled the bucket. When she finished, she gave Bessie some water, then carried the milk into the kitchen for Mammi to deal with. Then she went through the chicken coop, collecting eggs into a wire mesh basket. She gathered the eggs carefully—most in the nesting boxes, but a few were laid in sneaky places like in the corner on the floor. The hens clucked peacefully. One put up a token fight as Beth reached underneath her to retrieve a warm egg.

Beth put the last egg into her basket and headed out of the coop. There was a chain link fence that surrounded the chicken yard, and she locked that gate behind her. She stopped in the warm morning sun, the basket over one arm, her gaze turned toward the lake. She could hear the distant *thunk* and *crack* of someone chopping wood, the sound carried on the morning breeze to where she stood.

Sunlight sparkled on the water, and she ambled down in that direction. There was another *thunk, crack. Thunk, crack.* Mammi didn't like her being by the water, but while Beth would abide by Mammi's rules and not swim, she wasn't willing to completely shun the beautiful Friesen Lake either.

A brown rabbit bounded across the lawn and vanished into the trees, and Beth carried on toward the pebble beach. She glanced back at the house once, but Mammi must have been preoccupied with her knitting. She was making blankets for some new babies in their district. That was something Mammi did for every baby born, and she took her private obligation very seriously.

But to be honest, Beth wasn't as interested in the water as she was in the ice house around the side of the lake. She'd spotted Danny here yesterday, but he hadn't come up to see her, even though she'd been hoping he would. Maybe he was courting a girl and it wouldn't be appropriate?

Now, she spotted Danny at the woodpile on the near side of their property. He had an ax over one shoulder, and he brought it down. A heartbeat later, the crack of ax meeting wood reached her ears. He seemed to sense her presence, because he looked over then, and she waved. He waved back. He looked toward his family's house, then put down the ax and started in her direction.

Beth's breath caught. He was coming to say hello, after all. Suddenly, her bravado disappeared, because she hadn't seen him in three years and had no idea what she'd even say to him. But he loped along at a steady pace, making his way over the path that led through shrubbery and long grass, around the lakeside toward her.

She held the basket of eggs in front of her, feeling foolish just standing there, but her feet were bare, and so she waited until he emerged onto their pebble beach. Then she started toward him, and they met in the center.

Danny had grown taller since she'd seen him last, and his face was more angular, a little more rugged. He was truly a grown man now—the gangly teenaged boy was gone. His brown eyes were the same, though, and he cast her a familiar, lopsided smile. Her stomach fluttered in response. Having his attention focused so directly on her made her feel a little bashful.

"Beth," he said, "I saw you yesterday."

And she'd seen him. She'd almost questioned if it really was Danny—he looked so much bigger, stronger, broader. But it was. She'd known it the minute he waved.

"Why didn't you come by?" she asked.

"I could ask you the same thing," he replied.

She'd wanted him to come to her to see if he cared enough. It was a silly pattern of hers. She'd also wanted him to write her letters, once upon a time, and that hadn't exactly worked out the way she'd wanted either.

"I'm here to help my grandmother get the house ready to sell at the end of the summer," she said. "So I'll be here for a little while."

"Iris will be moving away?" he asked.

"She needs extra help these days. We don't think she can stay on her own any longer."

"I can see that." He nodded, then his warm gaze met hers. "It's been so long since I've seen you. You look really different."

"Do I?" She looked down at her dress, but she knew what he meant. She couldn't see the maturing in herself, but she certainly saw it in Danny. Three years had changed a lot.

"*Yah*," he said. "You look . . . wonderful."

Her cheeks warmed. "*Danke*. You look like a grown man. Yesterday, I wasn't sure if it was you or some adult friend."

He smiled, but it wasn't the boyish grin she remembered. There was some deeper humor in his eyes, a little more maturity.

"I heard your family renovated the ice house and are renting it out," she went on, feeling a little flustered. "It looks nice from here."

"*Yah*, it's more popular than the cabins."

"You're running the place with your *mamm* and *daet*?" she asked.

He nodded. "For now. My brother Zach left the community last year, so I'm helping my parents with the rentals. It's a lot of cleaning. I'm working toward my own plans, though."

"He jumped the fence?" That was news!

Danny told her about how his brother decided he didn't want the Amish life after all, how he left the faith and moved to town, and now visited just often enough to rattle their parents all over again. She told him about working at the flour mill and how she'd been asked to come help Mammi for the summer.

"But you said you have your own plans?" she asked.

"A goal. I'm still saving to open up a store in town to cater to tourists."

She eyed him thoughtfully. "Danny Lapp, the shopkeeper. I like it."

"Daniel Lapp, the shop *owner*." He winked, and she felt some heat touch her face.

"All grown up . . ." She nodded.

"Do you have plans for the future?" he asked.

"I'm trying to sort them out. My *daet* died, and I'm giving my next steps a lot of thought this summer."

"Right. I'm really sorry. That's a terrible loss."

"*Danke*." The loss had been more difficult to process than she'd expected too.

A distant *thunk-crack* drew both of their gazes back toward the Lapp woodpile. Danny's *daet* was there, taking over the wood chopping that Danny had abandoned to come say hello.

"It's busy this time of year," Danny said. "We've got a new couple coming to stay at the cottage, and I think there are a couple of families coming for the cabins too. So there's a lot of work to get done."

"Does that mean you need to get back?" she asked.

"I probably should." He met her gaze for a moment, then shook his head. "You grew up, Beth Peachy."

"It was bound to happen eventually." She adjusted the egg basket in her hands. "I should get back to my *mammi* too. She's just terrified of me being anywhere near the water, so I'm trying not to upset her."

Danny pulled off his straw hat and wiped his forehead. The day was already heating up. His posture was hesitant, like he didn't want their conversation to end. "It's really nice to see you again, Beth," he said.

"Same." She smiled, then lifted her basket of eggs. "I'd better bring these inside. You should come by and get a slice of pie later."

"Is that an official invitation?" he asked.

Her cheeks warmed at the question. As teens, they couldn't really have a serious relationship. Even if something sparked, nine months apart would douse it again. She'd only seen him in the summers, and teenagers could be fickle with their feelings when they spent long months apart. But at this age, his question felt like less of a joke.

"Of course." Beth lifted her chin and held his gaze. Those dark eyes sparkled as he smiled, and she found herself rather taken with this handsome new version of her adolescent friend.

"All right," he said. "I will, then. I'll see you later."

Gone were the days when they'd have to ask permission. He was a man now, and he could do what he liked with his free time.

Danny headed back the way he'd come, and she couldn't help but notice a bit more bounce in his step. She was glad he planned to come by the house. Mammi would probably enjoy the company too, and she could get the rest of the story about his brother's fence-jumping. There was another fence jumper besides the returned veterinarian, it seemed. So much drama around here.

Beth turned her steps back up toward the lawn, and she carried the eggs inside through the side door. "Mammi?" she called.

She poked her head into the kitchen, but it was empty. The door to the basement stood partially open, and Beth opened it the rest of the way, the faint, cool scent of cold storage rising up to meet her. "Mammi? Are you down there?"

Mammi didn't answer, but Beth heard some rustling. Was it the dog? She hadn't seen Goldie in a while either.

"Goldie, come!" Beth ordered. Nothing happened. Maybe it was Mammi, then.

"Are you all right?" Beth came down the stairs. The basement had high, narrow windows that let in a little bit of light along one side. Shelves of canned food were a little sparse this time of year. A few jars left in each section—meat, carrots, pickles, green beans, cherries, apples, peaches—which would be refilled again this summer and fall when Mammi processed her garden's and fruit trees' bounty.

Goldie wasn't down here, but Mammi stood at the shelf, poking around at the peaches.

"Mose likes pears," Mammi said. "I know I have pears, I know it! Where are my pears? Mose will be so disappointed if he gets back tonight and I didn't make the pear cake."

Beth's throat choked up in a wash of fresh grief. Mammi thought she was making pear cake for her son. And Daet had loved pears. He loved them any way Mammi made them. They were his favorite.

"Mammi?" Beth prodded.

Mammi turned around, her face pale and her eyes frantic. "I have pears!"

"Mammi . . . it's okay. My *daet* isn't coming tonight," Beth said quietly.

Mammi stilled, sucking in a breath as if to argue her point, and then she frowned. Was she remembering now? Beth slipped an arm around her grandmother's shoulders. Daet wasn't coming back to visit his mother ever again, and that thought left Beth's throat feeling raw.

"I thought I had pears," Mammi said feebly.

"It's okay. Come upstairs," Beth said. "Is Goldie with you?"

"Goldie?" Mammi looked around. "No, she went outside to do her business."

"Well, come upstairs with me," Beth said. "The vet is coming this morning to check Goldie, remember?"

"The vet. *Yah*, that's right. Tabitha Schrock," Mammi said.

She was back in the present, it seemed. That was a relief. That had been a little scary to see Mammi so confused—was that what people were talking about? What had Mammi been thinking about when she'd put the jam on her dresser or the shoe in the cupboard with the plates? What little part of the past had been uppermost in her mind?

"Elizabeth?" Mammi said as they mounted the narrow staircase together.

"*Yah*, Mammi?"

"I really thought I needed pears." Mammi's voice quavered.

"It's okay, Mammi," Beth said. "I really miss him too."

They emerged into the kitchen, and Beth shut the basement door firmly behind them. The kitchen was bright with late-morning sunlight splashing in through the windows. Outside the window, Beth could see Goldie nosing through the garden. She seemed to have spotted something in the row of radishes.

Mammi looked at Beth hopefully, her watery gaze begging for some understanding. Gone was the *mammi* who was in control, who made the rules, who guarded the secrets. In her place was this vulnerable old woman.

"Sometimes I wake up early in the morning, and I think I hear Daet's boots downstairs. I think I have to get up to help him with chores," Beth said quietly.

Mammi nodded, but she didn't say anything more. Maybe she didn't know how to explain her confusion. Maybe she'd already forgotten.

Mammi went over to the side door and pushed open the screen. "Goldie! Come inside!"

Just a forgetful old lady . . . but Mammi had never done this before. She'd come to visit them in Strasburg for Daet's funeral, and she'd never forgotten that Daet had indeed died. Not once. Something had changed.

The dog came inside, and Beth heard the sound of a buggy pulling up next to the house. Mammi stayed at the door, holding the screen open.

"Is that the vet?" Beth asked.

"*Yah*, Jonas brought her," Mammi replied. Goldie stopped at Mammi's side, her tail low.

Beth went to the window. An Amish woman was sitting next to Jonas in the buggy. She seemed ordinary enough—brown hair, a blue dress. She was older than Beth, but she didn't look old, exactly. Maybe thirty. When Jonas reined in the horse, they exchanged a few words, then she hopped down from the buggy and went around the back. Jonas got out too, and he waved at Mammi in the doorway—he didn't see Beth in the window—and carried on around to tend to the horse. The Amish woman came from the back of the buggy, carrying a brown leather medical bag in one hand, and she had a cordial smile on her face.

"Hello, Iris," she said. "It's nice to see you. How are you doing these days?"

Footsteps echoed on the stairs, the screen door bounced shut, and the veterinarian emerged into the kitchen. She crouched down next to Goldie and reached out to touch her. Goldie backed away.

"It's her back end that's sore," Beth said.

The woman looked up at her. "Good morning. You must be Beth. I heard you're visiting."

"Good morning," Beth said. "*Yah*, I arrived from Strasburg a couple of days ago."

"It's nice to meet you. I'm Tabitha Schrock. I'm the vet."

"I heard." Beth smiled. "I've never seen an Amish vet before. Especially not an Amish woman vet."

"There's always a first." Tabitha smiled. "I'm just glad to be home again." Then she turned back to Mammi. "How old is Goldie now?"

"She's twelve," Mammi said. "Her arthritis is getting bad,

but I don't want you to recommend I put her down, because I won't do it. She's a good dog."

"Of course not," Tabitha said. "There are a few different treatments that can make Goldie a lot more comfortable. I'll need to examine her just to make sure that's the only problem, though."

"Come, Goldie," Mammi said, leaning down. "Stay."

Goldie did as Mammi told her, but she trembled when Tabitha reached toward her. Tabitha didn't seem daunted, and her touch was gentle. She stroked Goldie's head and ran a hand down her back.

"You're a good girl, Goldie," Tabitha murmured. "A very good girl. You'll be all right, won't you?"

Beth watched as Tabitha worked. She ran her hands down Goldie's limbs, but she seemed to know how to touch the old dog so as not to cause additional pain. When Goldie yipped once, Tabitha crooned apologies and gave her a little treat from her pocket. She took a stethoscope from her bag and listened to the dog's chest—the front, the sides. She checked in her ears with a lighted tool and then in her mouth. When she finished, she stood up, and Goldie padded stiffly over to her blanket and lay down.

"I could do some blood tests and the like and see if there are any other illnesses to be treated," Tabitha said. "Or I can just give you some medication that will help with joint inflammation."

Beth looked anxiously toward her grandmother.

"We all go at some point," Mammi said, her gaze clouding. "All we can do is pray we are right with Gott when the time comes."

"Would you like me to do further tests?" Tabitha put the stethoscope back in her bag.

There was a tap on the door, and Jonas came into the house. He and Tabitha exchanged a friendly look.

They seem very comfortable together, Beth thought.

"No more tests," Mammi said. "The length of our days is in Gott's hands. I don't go to the doctor looking for trouble for myself, and I'm not about to do it on Goldie's behalf either. We're two old girls who are getting creaky. That's all."

"That's fair." Tabitha nodded. "I have some medication on hand."

6

Jonas stood back as Tabitha talked with Aent Iris about the medication options. He learned a lot just listening to Tabitha work. There was a glucosamine chew and an injectable anti-inflammatory that would need to be done monthly, but Tabitha assured Iris that she had seen great results in other dogs with that combination.

Beth crossed her arms over her stomach. She was watching Tabitha, her expression filled with admiration. *Yah*, he knew that feeling. Tabitha was impressive. She walked into a room looking like every other Amish woman, and by the time she left, it was evident that she was in a category all by herself. Today she was only doing a quick examination of a dog, but he'd seen her working in other vet cases. She was smart, educated, knowledgeable, and had a way of giving people complete confidence in her abilities. And with her being so young, people couldn't help but be impressed.

Tabitha stood talking with Iris, listening to her concerns and nodding sympathetically. She gave her clients one hundred percent of her attention, which made them feel heard. It also gave Jonas a chance to watch Tabitha without her noticing his scrutiny. She had a few wisps of hair that fell down her neck, but she wouldn't notice. She hardly ever did. She also had the faintest of freckles across her nose, and one freckle on her neck. He'd never tell anyone he noticed those things, though.

She was prettier now than ten years ago when she married her ex-husband and left the community. Jonas had thought that the difficulties she endured with the *Englischers* might dim her shine, but they didn't. Instead, Tabitha had become more thoughtful, more compassionate, and a whole lot wiser. Her beauty went deeper now, like polished hardwood over time. She'd grown more nuanced, and maybe he was a little smitten with her too.

His *mamm* had received a letter from Beth's *mamm*, and apparently there was some worry that Beth wouldn't choose to join the faith. She wasn't baptized yet, and while all of her friends had made their decision for an Amish life, Beth was still holding back. His *mamm* said she hoped that meeting Tabitha wouldn't give Beth any ideas about going *Englisch*. And looking at Beth's face, he could understand her concern now.

"Will you need any help getting the house in order?" Jonas asked, raising his voice so his cousin could hear him.

Beth startled. "Oh! Um, I definitely will need extra help. So far I'm packing up some old clothes and linens, trying to see what we can donate to charities and what needs to be thrown away. And I'll be doing some deep cleaning. My job is to get the house ready to show. The packing up to move will be a whole other challenge—that's for later."

"That's probably a job for the rest of us," he said with a shrug. "But many hands make light work, right?"

Beth moved over to where he stood by the window. "Will you miss having my grandmother here?"

"For sure," he replied. "But we'll worry a bit less too. At

her age, we're worried about a fall or a broken bone. It's good that you're here."

"Your *mamm* said you and Tabitha have been friends for a long time?"

Jonas glanced over to where Tabitha was petting the dog.

"*Yah*, we were in the same grade in school," he said. "I think she liked me less back then. I used to put grasshoppers in her desk."

Beth laughed, but then she lowered her voice further. "Are you allowed to be friends?"

"What do you mean?" he asked.

"I mean, no one is pressuring you to get married or anything?"

"Oh." Jonas nodded. "She's divorced, remember? Tabitha can't get married. She's going to stay single. That's just the way it is. And she needs friends too."

Beth nodded slowly. "Is she sad about that?"

Jonas shrugged. "Not really. Her marriage was really hard, so I think she's just enjoying some peace."

"Are *you* sad about that?" Beth asked.

"Me?"

"That she can't get married?"

His younger cousin seemed a little too insightful for his comfort. Maybe he was. If Tabitha had just jumped the fence and hadn't married Michael, would he be considering more with her?

He watched as Tabitha filled a syringe and crouched down next to Goldie. She was gentle and confident, and he'd been thinking lately that she had pretty hands. Another silly thing for him to notice.

"No, no," Jonas said. "It's not like that, Beth. We're only friends."

"Just as well, I suppose," she replied.

"*Yah*, just as well." He shot her a wry smile. "Are you feeling the pressure to get married now too?"

Beth shook her head. "First they want me baptized."

"First things first," he said.

She angled her head to the side in thought.

Tabitha packed up her bag and peeled off a pair of rubber gloves, turning them into a little inside-out ball that she tucked into her bag.

"It was really nice to meet you, Beth," Tabitha said with a smile.

"How did you become a veterinarian?" Beth asked, falling into step next to Tabitha as she headed for the door.

Jonas let them move on ahead and looked back at Aent Iris. Her lips were pursed in thought.

"It looks like Goldie will be okay," Jonas offered, pulling his aunt out of her thoughts.

"*Yah*, it looks like it," Iris said. "I'm more concerned about Elizabeth right now. She's awfully interested in the *Englisch* world these days."

"She has to learn about it," Jonas said. "When she gets baptized, she'll have to make her own informed decision."

"How much does a young woman need to know?" she asked.

"I don't know. I certainly considered my own options before I got baptized. I thought about the kind of life I could have, and the kinds of jobs I could do. . . . I mean, she owes it to herself to think it all through. Then when she decides to get baptized, she'll be completely sure."

His aunt gave him a thoughtful look. "If she decides to stay."

"Aent Iris . . ."

"It happens, Jonas," she said. "And the *Englisch* world isn't all freedom and daisies. There are dangerous things out there, and a vulnerable young woman has no idea."

Did his elderly aunt really know about all those *Englischer* dangers? She'd spent her entire life in the Amish fold. Sure, they'd all heard stories from time to time about the problems people out there had, and they thanked Gott above that they lived the way they did. But Aent Iris was talking like she had some kind of inside knowledge.

"Are you really worried she'll leave?" Jonas asked, lowering his voice. "Did she say something?"

The old woman nodded. "*Yah*, I am. And so is her mother. She's rather keen on her swimming, and I never agreed with Mose about teaching her. She's not satisfied with a quiet Amish life with a good man. She wants more—but more isn't always better. You remember that. I've seen things that you haven't."

Again, a hint at more life experience. "Aent Iris, haven't you been Amish all your life?"

"Me?" She looked mildly offended. "Of course. But there is wisdom that comes with age, young man. We might be old and start slowing down, but we have a store of experience that can be of use to you, if you care to use it."

"And we appreciate your wisdom, Aent Iris," he said.

"Would you care to hear my advice for you?" she asked, and her smiling eyes took on a teasing cast. Jonas had a feeling he knew exactly what advice she had. It would be the same advice the entire community was tossing his way these days.

"Wash behind my ears?" he joked. "Sew up that tear in my pants before it's unmendable?"

"Get married already!" Her eyes twinkled as she smiled up

at him. "You are a charmer, Jonas, but don't waste it on me. Find yourself a sweetheart and make an honest wife of her."

"You're in on this too?" Jonas asked. "My parents are telling me to do the same thing."

"You should listen to them," she replied. "As the Good Book says, 'A wise son heareth his father's instruction.'"

"*Danke*, Aent Iris." It was easier to just agree at this point.

"Oh, and one other thing," Iris said, her smile slipping. "You will find it much easier to meet a nice, available woman when you aren't spending quite so much time with another woman. If you catch my meaning."

The last few months, he and Tabitha had been spending more time together. They enjoyed each other's company, and when couples were off going for buggy rides together or sitting side by side during a corn roast, it was nice to have a friend so he felt less isolated in the midst of people in various stages of falling in love. There weren't any other women he felt drawn to like he was to Tabitha. Most of the unmarried girls around here were five or ten years younger than he was, but it was more than that. Tabitha had a way of drawing him in without even trying.

"We're only friends," he said.

"I know. It's all you can possibly be. But women don't like to share a man's attention. So if you know what's good for you, you'll spend more time with your male friends and look around at the single women in these parts."

Yah, he'd looked around already, and Tabitha was the first woman in a long time to draw his interest.

They headed out the door and into the summer sunlight. A bee buzzed past his head, and he angled his own steps toward the buggy. Tabitha stowed her bag into the back while he untied the horse, and they both got inside.

Jonas waved to his *aent* and cousin, and they both waved back.

"That was the most enthusiastic meeting I've had with someone who's heard where I've been and that I'm the vet," Tabitha said as the buggy started forward with a soft creak.

"*Yah*?" He glanced over at her. Tabitha smoothed her skirt over her thighs and settled back into the seat. "What was Beth asking about?"

"Oh, how I got the education. How long it took. Who helped me." Her gaze clouded and flicked over at him uneasily. "She's not thinking of leaving, is she?"

"Aent Iris thinks she might be," he replied. "Her *mamm* is worried about the same thing. She's been really holding back on making her decision."

Tabitha pressed her lips together. "I wonder how I can help."

"Make it seem less glamorous out there?"

"I'm divorced! How much less glamorous can I make it?" she asked, shaking her head. "I had a husband who flagrantly cheated on me!"

Jonas sighed. "Sorry. You're right. I think it's your job that has her attention."

"I think so too," she agreed. "But in order to achieve this, I sacrificed everything else."

"Would you do it again?" he asked.

She was silent, and he looked over at her to find her gaze turned out the side window.

"Tabby?" he prodded.

She glanced back. "I can't undo the past. I don't have that choice. This is my life."

"*Yah*, but if you could . . ." he said. "Do you regret it?"

"Here's the difficulty," she said quietly. "My time away

63

from here . . . it made me who I am today. It gave me a chance to use my talents in a way I never would have if I'd stayed. It let me do this job—and I *love* this job, Jonas."

She was very good at it too. He could see how she relaxed into the work—and if nothing else, Amish people could appreciate joy found in work.

He nodded. "I guess I can understand that. Do you wish you hadn't married Michael?"

She sucked in a breath and looked away. "The ironic part is, I wouldn't have left if it weren't for him. So . . ." She shook her head. "This is my life. This is how it all shook out. I'm really glad to be back."

When Tabitha married Michael, she flaunted her *Englischer* status every time she came back to visit. Not having been baptized yet, she was not shunned. But she and her husband hadn't even tried to blend in. It was like they took pride in being as different as possible. Jonas hadn't liked her husband either. There was something about him that hadn't sat right with Jonas—a certain cockiness, like he was a rooster and the whole world was his henhouse. So when Tabitha returned home after her divorce, contrite and determined to live Amish, he hadn't believed she'd be successful in living Amish again. He'd given her six months.

But Jonas had since changed his mind about that. Tabitha was finding her place, and she had set aside those prideful ways. She was well and truly back. But he didn't like that she didn't regret having left at all. That was her mistake, wasn't it? She'd fixed her mistake by returning. So to have her not regret her time away—

He pushed back the uncomfortable feelings. It shouldn't matter. She had come back. She couldn't turn back time—it was ridiculous to be upset by a what-if.

"What would you tell Beth about leaving?" he asked.

"That it's not easy out there. And that there are pitfalls you don't even see coming."

"Would you tell her to stay home?" he asked.

"She wouldn't ask me that," Tabitha said. "Who am I to her?"

"That's a dodge," Jonas said. "You don't want to answer."

"I can't tell her what to do," Tabitha said. "And I doubt she'd ask my opinion about her choices."

And how could Jonas argue with that? But he wanted to. This should be simple. Leaving was a mistake, and staying was the right choice. Why couldn't she just say that?

7

Danny stood outside the Peachy side door that evening. The screen was closed, but the thick wooden door stood open, and he could hear cupboard doors bouncing shut and the quiet tones of Iris and Beth talking to each other. The chickens in their coop were clucking softly too. He knocked on the screen door, and the voices stopped, then Beth appeared.

"Danny!" she said with a smile. "You came. I'm glad."

She pushed open the door, and he stepped out of the low, golden light and into the dimmer kitchen. There was a selection of serving bowls and platters stacked up on the kitchen table, and Beth had two cardboard boxes on the floor alongside some old linens. Some sort of organizing and packing was going on here.

"Danny?" Iris said. "Danny who?"

Didn't Iris recognize him? Granted, he didn't come up this way personally very often, but his *mamm* came by every few weeks with a little bit of baking or some sort of treat for the old woman.

"I'm Danny Lapp, Iris," he said. "From around the lake,

at the ice house. My *mamm* says to say hello. She said she's going to send some bread for you in a couple of days."

"The ice house," Iris repeated, shaking her head. "I do not like that place. There are parties and drunkenness over there, and I do not abide that kind of behavior."

Right. She could get stuck in the past sometimes, and his *mamm* said she couldn't always see it coming. The ice house used to be a spot where the more wild Amish young people went to have parties. He'd heard the stories too.

"Not anymore," Danny said. "Not since my parents took over the cabins. We renovated the ice house, and it's a rental cottage now. No one comes to party there. My *daet* makes sure of that."

"It's okay, Mammi," Beth said. "Danny came by to visit me. We used to fish together off the dock, remember? Back when I'd visit with my parents?"

Iris's gaze moved between them uncertainly.

"He's here to visit me, Mammi," Beth repeated.

"Oh . . ." Iris nodded a couple of times. "Right. Yes. Right."

She didn't look like she fully remembered him, but she shuffled off toward the sitting room, murmuring something he couldn't make out.

"Is she okay?" Danny asked, lowering his voice.

"I think she is," Beth replied softly. "She's been getting more confused lately. In a few minutes she should come out of it, and she'll remember you."

Beth went to the doorway of the sitting room, then came back into the kitchen.

"She's knitting," Beth said. She got out two plates, forks, and a pie server and set about dishing them each up a piece of cherry pie. She handed him a slice on a plate, and they leaned against the counter to eat, the kitchen table being too full to use.

"Did you make it?" Danny asked. He halfway hoped she had.

"No, this is Mammi's."

"It's been a long time since you last visited." Danny sank his fork into the flaky crust. "Didn't we say we'd write to each other last time?"

"We did," she said, shooting him a rueful smile. "And I did write. You answered me with one paragraph about Dutch elm disease, and I didn't write you back. And you didn't try again."

Had he really? He remembered writing her back and not being very sure what to say, but somehow he'd been certain she'd hear his voice between the lines. But apparently she hadn't.

"I wasn't a very smooth guy." Danny shook his head. "Sorry."

"It's okay. I thought you didn't really want to talk to me." She shrugged. She'd put on a little weight since he last saw her. He liked it—it softened and rounded her in a way that seemed more mature. She reached up and wound a wisp of hair that had come free from her *kapp* around her finger, tucking it behind her ear.

"I did want to write. I guess I didn't have anything interesting to report. I do remember that Dutch elm disease was a problem that year, and the farmers were trying to band together to treat it."

Danny watched as she took a bite of pie. She was pretty—rosy cheeks, pink lips, and she had a speck of cherry filling on her lip until she licked it off. He dropped his gaze again. He hadn't realized he was such a terrible letter writer. Maybe he didn't blame her for not writing back.

"So how are you doing, really?" Danny asked when she hadn't said anything for a while.

"I'm doing pretty well." She raised her gaze to meet his, and his heart skipped a beat. "I'm missing out on babysitting my new nephew. That's my brother Adam's baby. He got married two years ago. Baby Moses—he's named after my *daet*."

"That's special," he said.

"It is. And he's my *mamm*'s first *kinnskind*, so he's a very big deal. We all spoil him rotten."

Danny grinned. "That's great."

"So . . . what happened with Zach?" She turned her attention to taking another bite of pie. "You said he jumped the fence."

"*Yah* . . . He's being really difficult. He thinks everything we were raised with is backward and wrong. He argues about everything. You could tell him that the Amish believe the sky is blue, and he'd call us ignorant and declare it was purple. He's just like that these days."

"Where does he live?" she asked.

"In Delton. He's working at a grocery store as a shelf stocker, and he's renting a room in a house with a bunch of students. He's got this girlfriend named Meghan that he's enamored with."

"She's *Englisch*?"

"*Yah*."

Beth nodded. "But he wasn't baptized, so he's not shunned?"

"Exactly. We kind of knew something was up when he refused to join the church. He'd been asking a lot of questions and arguing about why we do what we do. But my parents thought he just needed more time. Then he said he was leaving the Amish life completely, and it's been really hard on my parents ever since."

Danny had gotten baptized when he was eighteen with the rest of his friends. Two of his friends from his school years were married already. "When did you get baptized?" he asked.

"I haven't yet."

"Oh." He winced. He'd probably misspoken, then, about his brother's choice to hold off. "Sorry, I didn't mean to imply—"

"No, it's okay," she said. "Everyone wants me to just join the church already."

"Why haven't you?" he asked.

She took another bite of pie and chewed thoughtfully. "I haven't decided if I'll stay."

Danny stilled, and he rolled her words over in his mind. "You might go *Englisch*?"

"I don't know." She shrugged and shook her head. "When I think about actually leaving everything I know and love, it's hard to imagine. But then I think about taking vows to the church, and it's equally difficult. I feel stuck in the middle."

"You don't want to live Amish?" he asked.

"It's not that, exactly. It's . . ." She pushed her plate away. "Danny, does your family treat you like a child still?"

"I help my parents run the business," he said. "I do everything my *daet* does, and I'm taking over some of the management just so I'll understand it. So, I guess no, they don't."

"Do they ever just go silent on you when you come into the room?" she asked. "You know how when you're a little *kind*, and you walk into the room, and the adults stop talking about whatever it was they were discussing? Do they do that still?"

Danny thought for a moment. "Not really. If my parents are talking about something private they might, but I have better hearing than they think, so I normally hear it anyway."

"Do they let you know about money?" she asked.

"*Yah.* I mean, I'd better know about it. If I'm managing the place, I need to know how it all works. Plus, it's good experience for when I open my own shop."

She sighed. Maybe he wasn't giving her the answers she was expecting. "So . . . your family still hides adult things from you?" he guessed.

"*Yah.* They do. And they always have. That's a big thing for me. They want me to make this choice for the church, but they treat me like a *kind* still. I ask questions, and I get nothing back. I realized that I know absolutely nothing about my father's childhood. Nothing at all. In fact, during this visit, I just found out which bedroom was his in this house. I didn't even know that before this! And I know anger might seem like an overreaction, but all this secrecy does make me angry."

"Why do they do it?"

"I think part of it is that they're on eggshells with me, wanting me to stay Amish."

"Why would you leave?" he asked.

She was silent for a moment. "The things I'm good at aren't really valued here. I'm good at math—really good at it! I finished through tenth-grade math in school, and I'd kind of like to finish up through twelfth grade, just for the fun of it. But the jobs available to an Amish woman don't really include math. I'd love to work at a bank, but I'd need my high school diploma for that."

"There might be some other job you'd enjoy."

"I'd like to take proper swimming lessons too, so I could be a lifeguard."

He nodded. "I think I get it. That wouldn't be allowed here either."

"Not in a million years." She sucked in a breath. "So I'm really having to think seriously, and my *mamm* has been pressuring me for two years to get baptized, but I can't do it. Then add in that I feel like they're hiding something from me."

"They must have a reason," he said feebly. He had no idea why they wouldn't tell her more. It certainly seemed strange to him, but he couldn't speak badly about her family just because he didn't understand.

"My *Englischer* friend Cadence tells me stories from her family," Beth said. "She tells me about her alcoholic grandfather who tried to beat her grandmother, and her grandmother locked him outside in the winter when he was drunk and raging, and he slept in a snowbank and lost his little toe to frostbite."

Danny blinked. "What?"

"*Yah.* This is a story that she tells with no shame, no worry about my opinion. It's just . . . a story! Now, Cadence is a bit more extreme of an example, and I'm not saying that every *Englischer* family is like hers, but the point is, they don't seem to have the same sense of shame that we do."

"Where did you meet her?"

"She's my neighbor. I've known her for years. But these are her family stories," Beth said. "It's just information that everyone knows. She likes that her grandmother fought back against abuse. With *Englischers*, they don't get shamed because a relative behaves badly. They simply learn a lesson from their mistakes and carry on. There is no big secret."

"Amazing," he murmured.

Because Zach had jumped the fence, every once in a while

someone would say they saw him in town, and they would all wince, waiting to see what embarrassing things he'd said or done that would reflect badly on their family. Danny couldn't imagine that kind of nonchalance around a family member's misbehavior. There was a reason why they had family meetings to deal with a problematic family member. They all reflected on each other.

"So, that kind of freedom of information is something I find very interesting," she said.

"You'd leave for that?"

Beth seemed to be thinking about that for a moment because she didn't answer for a few beats. "I want to drive too. It looks fun and convenient. I want to wear jeans. Is that too scandalous? They seem so much warmer in the winter than a dress."

His heart sank. She had a lot pulling her away.

Beth seemed to notice a change in him, because she cast him an apologetic look. "I know I'm probably freaking you out."

"No, it's okay," he replied. What else could he say?

"Plus, I can't just join the church without my family trusting me as an adult. Knowing about my *daet* is really important to me right now."

Danny sighed. His brother had left for less. Their parents had been preparing them to take over the family business, but Zach wasn't interested. He'd said he wanted to learn some carpentry, so Daet had been trying to find a place where Zach could start learning and contribute meaningfully. Then Zach changed his mind again and said he was leaving.

"I'm not sure I like how the *Englischers* do things, though," Danny said.

"No?" she asked. "Why?"

73

"They might be willing to tell stories, *yah*, but do they take responsibility for each other?"

"Sometimes there's nothing you can do," she said.

"We're still our brother's keepers," he said. "Maybe we can stop them before they go too far."

"But what happens when we can't?"

That was when a family sealed shut their vault of stories, it seemed, and they stopped speaking of whatever it was they couldn't fix. No, things in the Amish faith weren't perfect, but Danny still deeply believed in their efforts. He had a brother he hadn't given up on yet.

"I didn't mean to unload all of that onto you," Beth said.

"No, it's okay. We're friends. You should be able to say what you really think, right?"

"It's been a while since I've been able to just talk openly," she said. "So . . . *danke*."

Even with her strong pull away from the People, Beth's open vulnerability when she talked to him tangled him into a knot. It was like there was a part of his heart from his teenaged years that just wouldn't let go of her, no matter how much he was likely to get hurt.

"Another piece of pie?" Beth asked.

He nodded, and she pulled the pie pan over so she could dish him up another slice.

Beth chatted away about teaching her younger brother new skills in the water, and Danny ate his pie, happy to listen to her talk. In some ways, she was still the girl who used to make his heart patter in his chest because she was so pretty, but she'd grown up, and she was different in a lot of ways now too.

It was like they'd picked up where they'd left off—talking, enjoying each other's company, opening up about their lives

. . . Beth's hopes for her future might have changed a whole lot over the last few years, but their honest connection hadn't, and it was that ability to open up to each other that had always been special between them. He hadn't found it with any other girl either.

And she was still distractingly pretty. Her blond hair had darkened just a shade since he'd seen her last, but her blue eyes hadn't.

"What?" she asked suddenly, and he realized he'd been staring at her.

"I just—" He shrugged, and some warmth touched his face. "I guess I missed you."

She smiled then, and her cheeks pinked too.

"I'm really glad you came by, Danny," she said. "It's going to be a nice summer, isn't it?"

A summer of seeing Beth Peachy. *Yah*, it would be a very nice summer, indeed. But he couldn't let himself get too attached. She wasn't sure if she wanted to stay Amish, and that detail mattered for a man who longed for deep roots. She might not be sure, but he'd gotten a good view of what leaving their faith did to someone . . . what it did to a whole family.

When one person went *Englisch*, it broke a lot of hearts. It shook up a whole family, and it left people frustrated and aching. Roots mattered, because when you tore them up, a lot of damage was done. But when they continued to push deeper into the ground, they found everything they needed— nourishment, comfort, meaning, belonging. That choice for the church wasn't a game. It was everything that mattered.

8

As soon as they'd finished their pie, Mammi came out of the sitting room and gave Danny a very pointed look. Beth understood—Mammi was letting Danny know it was time for him to go.

"*Danke* for the pie, Iris," Danny said. "It was really good."

"My pleasure," Mammi said. "Say hello to your *mamm* for me."

"I will."

Mammi went over to one of the boxes Beth had been filling to give items away for charity and pulled out a dish wrapped in an old cloth. She unwrapped it, and Beth grimaced. Getting Mammi to part with anything was turning out to be a chore. They didn't have room for all of these dishes in their kitchen at home. But the downsizing was hard on Mammi too.

Beth followed Danny out, and they circled around to the back of the house and ambled slowly down to the beach.

The evening was cooling off, and the breeze from the water brought a trail of goosebumps on Beth's arms. Danny walked beside her, his gaze directed down at the ground and his hands shoved into his pockets.

"Mammi is protective," Beth said. "I'm sorry about that."

"It's okay," Danny replied. "That's not a bad thing."

They walked down onto the beach, and Beth put her bare toes into the cool water. Goldie woofed from the steps, and Beth glanced back to see her grandmother at the door, watching her.

"She's losing her memories," Beth said, turning back toward Danny. "She's not herself anymore. She used to be so strong and sure of everything."

"That happens," Danny said.

"It happens to other people's grandmothers," Beth said with a sad smile. "It wasn't supposed to happen to mine."

"I'm glad you decided to come lend a hand," Danny said. "She obviously needs the help. And who knows? Maybe you'll see something worth staying Amish for while you're here. Then everyone will stop bugging you about it."

"Not you too, Danny," Beth said, shaking her head. "I told you—I need answers first, and I need to think things through for myself. This is a big decision."

"Maybe your grandmother will be able to fill you in on the missing details," Danny said.

"So far, she doesn't seem to want to."

Danny shrugged. "You've got the whole summer. Try again. Ask her straight what you want to know. You're not a child anymore. Maybe she'll see that."

"*Yah*, I think I will," Beth said.

Danny angled his head toward his home. "I'd better get back."

"Okay." She moved her foot through the shallow water, watching rippled sunlight reflect on her skin.

Danny headed off across the beach.

"Danny?" she called.

He looked back, and she liked the way he looked at her—dark eyes locked on her in a way that gave her a shiver.

"Find some excuse to come back," she said.

That was bold of her, she knew. But if she was about to start saying things straight, maybe she'd practice on Danny Lapp. What were friends for?

Danny grinned, those dark eyes of his glittering with sudden mirth. "I'll try. You do the same."

That sounded like a challenge, and something to add a little excitement to the long, warm days ahead. She couldn't help but smile to herself as she headed back up the rocky beach toward the grass once more.

Goldie barked again, coming out into the yard with slow, stiff steps.

"I'm coming, Goldie!" Beth called.

Goldie was as much of a worrywart as her grandmother. And like Danny said, maybe that wasn't a bad thing. It meant she was loved. But at this stage of her life, Beth needed more than worry and affection. She needed her family to allow her to know their secrets.

Later that evening, Beth stood behind a chair in Mammi's bedroom and carefully combed her grandmother's long, freshly washed hair. Mammi's bedroom faced away from the lake and toward the stable, beyond which stretched a cattle-dotted pasture. It wasn't Mammi's pasture—it belonged to the neighbors.

This bedroom got the morning sun, so at this time of day, the light in the room was muted, and it was warm, like a nest. Outside the window, the soft lowing of cows calling for calves filtered through evening birdsong.

Mammi's hair was thin with age, but when it hung free, the wispiest white ends were down to her knees. The shoulders of Mammi's faded pink cape dress were wet from her hair, and Beth slid the comb gently over Mammi's scalp and then down through her long hair. She had to take a couple of steps back to get the comb all the way to the ends.

Mammi's bedroom would be the hardest to clean out. She had accumulated a lot of personal items over the years—handcrafts that had been given to her by friends and family, linens and blankets, books, a collection of calendars. That was just what was within sight from where Beth stood. But if there were going to be people looking at the house to purchase it, they'd have to clean out this room.

"I think Danny Lapp likes you a great deal," Mammi said quietly.

"Danny? I mean, we're friends. You don't have to worry about anything when he comes by."

"You're both single and quite old enough to do something about it," Mammi said. "You will be supervised."

That might be a valid point if they were both baptized, of course. Many people fell in love, and that was the push toward making their decision. Marriages in the Amish faith weren't permitted before baptism.

"I suppose we did both grow up while I was away." Danny especially. She felt a little flustered when she thought about him now—tall, muscular, manly.

"That happens," Mammi agreed.

Beth took out a bottle of hair oil and poured a small amount into her palm. She rubbed the oil between her palms and then began to smooth it through her grandmother's hair down to the tips that were already dry.

"Danny's brother Zach leaving the community is a big challenge in the Lapp home right now," Beth said, smoothing her grandmother's long hair in steady strokes.

"*Yah*, it's heartbreaking," Mammi agreed.

"It's hard on Danny in particular," Beth said. "But I think it's easier when the family can talk about it, instead of trying to hide it."

This was her broad hint, and she wondered if her grandmother would understand what she was getting at.

"Well, Zach doesn't exactly hide his choices when he comes back to visit," Mammi said with a wry chuckle. "I doubt they could hide it, even if they tried."

"But I think that being open and honest about things makes a hard time easier for a family," Beth offered, her hands working methodically as she smoothed the oil down the lengths of her grandmother's damp hair. When she finished, she laid a towel on the bed and then spread her grandmother's hair over it to air dry.

Mammi didn't answer.

"It's just that sometimes families hide things," Beth went on. "And that might be easier for some, but I don't think it's good for the family."

"I'm sure that doesn't apply to us," Mammi said. "And what another family does is their business, not ours."

This wasn't going in the direction Beth had hoped. She moved around to the front of the chair her grandmother was sitting in, then she sank down onto the edge of the bed.

"Mammi, what about my *daet*?"

Her grandmother looked straight ahead.

"I want to know about him," Beth said, and unexpected

tears stung her eyes. "He's dead now. What harm can be done by me knowing the truth? He would never tell me about his childhood. And you wouldn't talk about it either."

"Like I said—" her grandmother began.

"There's nothing to tell?" Beth finished for her.

Mammi turned her head to face Beth.

"I think I know what all the secrecy is about," Beth said. "And I want you to know that I don't judge you for even a second."

"What do you think you know?" Mammi asked, her faded blue eyes locking on to Beth's with a forcefulness that almost made her lean back.

She could let this go—she knew her grandmother would much prefer that she did. But when Mammi's memory went, so would any chance at getting answers. Daet had died without breathing a word about his childhood or his birth, and maybe Beth even understood. If he was protecting his *mamm's* reputation, or trying to protect his young *kinner* from knowing too much about a painful subject, she could understand a father keeping a few secrets. But Beth was no longer underage. She was a grown woman, and while people deserved their privacy, a family deserved to know its history too.

"Were you married, Mammi?" Beth asked quietly.

Her grandmother didn't answer, but her cheeks pinked.

"You never mention Daet's *daet*," Beth went on. "Did he die?"

Silence.

"Did you not marry him?" Beth's voice shook.

"What are you suggesting, Beth?" Mammi asked tartly. "I think you should stop there and leave it be."

Beth was tempted, honestly. There was nothing comfortable about this conversation. Maybe she just needed to voice her theory out in the open—say it out loud. It wasn't so bad. It had been over fifty years since her father's birth!

"Mammi, I think that you had my *daet* out of wedlock, and that's why you won't talk about it. I know it must have been very difficult for you, and maybe you were even trying to protect my *daet's* father—"

"I was not pregnant out of wedlock," Mammi retorted. "That's what you think?"

"*Yah.*" Beth wasn't sure what else to say. It was exactly what she thought. "Mammi, I have an Amish friend who got pregnant, and she got married very quickly. My *mamm's* youngest sister ended up pregnant and quickly married too. It isn't unheard of, and no one asks a single question once that marriage happens. People just put it behind them. What does it matter at that point? I think attitudes have changed."

"I wasn't an unwed mother."

"Who was my *dawdie*, then? Who did you marry? Why won't you talk about him?"

Mammi sighed. "In my day, youngsters didn't ask unnecessary questions."

"I'm not a youngster anymore, Mammi."

"Beth, stop!" Mammi said. "You don't need to know everyone else's heartbreak."

"Can't you just tell me who my *daet's* father was?"

Her grandmother pressed her lips together and gave her a no-nonsense look.

"I'm not a child, Mammi," Beth said again.

"I know," Mammi said, her tone gentle now. "But neither is it your business. Your father was a good Amish man who lived a good Amish life. Who he was born to, who fathered him—none of that was his choice, was it? Remember him for the good man and the loving *daet* that he was. Let the rest go."

But Beth couldn't. She needed something—some signal that her grandmother trusted her with the truth about their family history, because while this was her grandmother's personal story, it was also part of Beth's family legacy.

"Were you married, Mammi?" she asked once again, determination in her tone.

Tears misted her grandmother's eyes, and her chin trembled. "No, dear, I was not."

And that was all the information Beth would get tonight, it seemed. But her grandmother had most certainly become pregnant out of wedlock, and that thought made Beth's heart squeeze in sympathy. Who had broken Mammi's heart and abandoned her with her son? Who had been thoughtless enough?

And had he been Amish or *Englisch*?

9

Tabitha had an appointment to check on some goats that had a severe case of lungworm, which she'd been treating with a deworming medication, but before she got on to her day's work, she had decided to drop off the glucosamine chews for Iris's old dog.

Settling into the rhythms in Shepherd's Hill again was an ongoing challenge. She'd hoped that coming home would make her life easier—at least she wouldn't be going against Gott's whisper in her heart. And when she came back, her community forgave her mistakes, but the closeness she'd enjoyed in old friendships was now gone. An Amish woman could forgive because Jesus commanded it, but it was harder to demand the intimacies of a real friendship after Tabitha had gone *Englisch* for ten years. An honest connection came with time . . . or not at all. That was the risk, wasn't it?

Somehow, Tabitha had hoped that people would be more excited to see her, but she also understood their trepidation. Unbeknownst to Tabitha, while she was still married to Michael, he had been trying to convince other young people to jump the fence. And he'd been flirting with some of Tabitha's cousins as well. It was a mess. Tabitha hadn't meant to, but she'd caused trouble with every visit home, and people were still wary of her.

Would it have been better to stay *Englisch*? Not really. She'd never fully fit into her *Englischer* life either. So Tabitha could be the odd one out with *Englischers* who'd never really understand her way of seeing the world, or she could be the odd one out here at home. At least here in Shepherd's Hill, she felt certainty that she was where Gott wanted her, even if she was still struggling to find some honest female friendships.

Jonas had turned out to be a surprisingly loyal friend, though. Their fathers had been at odds for years, and they were now trying to mend fences. And while Jonas also had been wary of her at first, she could now count him as someone she trusted. But he was a man, and that meant that whatever their connection was, it was temporary. Because one day he'd get married, and their friendship would never be the same after that. Tabitha had been married before, so she fully understood it. That was why she needed to find female friends—women she could count on, who she could connect with, and who would stay her friends for years.

Tabitha reined in Fritz at a four-way stop and waited while a pickup truck turned. Then she flicked the reins and they started off again. Fritz was a special horse to Tabitha. He was a big, strong workhorse, and he was well trained. But he had a finicky stomach, so he couldn't eat just anything, and because of his dietary requirements, she didn't take him when she had a long day ahead of her. He stayed in the field most days, and Tabitha could tell his mood was declining because of it. One couldn't take work away from a workhorse and expect him to be fine. Horses were emotionally complicated.

So when she had lighter days, Tabitha hitched Fritz up to her buggy, and his big, liquid eyes would be filled with such gratitude that she got choked up. Making friends again in the community might be difficult, but there were some friendships that didn't require the same careful work, like her connection with Fritz.

Tabitha could see the sparkle of Friesen Lake through the trees long before she turned down the Peachy drive. Iris's three-story house looked like it needed paint. The front porch had some dried leaves scattered over it, and the garden was functional but looked like it could use a good weeding.

Beth was pushing a manual lawn mower with a spinning blade that sent up a spray of grass clippings as she passed through the front yard. She stopped when she spotted the buggy and shaded her eyes with one hand.

"Good morning!" Tabitha called as she reined in Fritz.

"Good morning!" Beth called back.

Tabitha picked up the package of medicinal chews and hopped down from the buggy. She circled around to tie Fritz at the hitching post, then gave him an affectionate pat on his neck.

"How are you doing?" Beth asked, leaving her mower and heading over to where Tabitha stood.

"I can't complain," Tabitha said. "I just wanted to drop off these chews for Goldie before I head off to another call. How are you?"

Tabitha glanced around again. It looked like Beth had been busy in the front yard. The flower garden had been weeded, and there was a mound of brush sitting to one side that looked like it was ready to be hauled over to the burn pile.

"I'm trying to catch up on a few chores for Mammi," Beth

said. "She says Jonas normally does the grass for her, but my organizing inside has been starting to upset her, so I thought I'd do something outside today instead."

"You're getting the house ready to sell?" Tabitha asked.

Beth shrugged. "There's no other choice. It's time."

Tabitha had seen how frail Iris was getting, so it made sense. It was time for Iris to live with family who could care for her.

"How is Goldie?" Tabitha asked.

"She seems a little sprier since you gave her that shot."

"Well, add in these chews, and she'll be more limber yet," Tabitha replied. "How is your *mammi*?"

The side door opened, and Iris came outside. She was wearing her black shoes and had a cloth bag over one arm. She pulled out a key.

"Mammi, don't lock the door!" Beth called. "I'm here."

Iris looked at Beth with a faint frown. Then her gaze moved to Tabitha.

"Can I help you?" Iris asked uncertainly.

"Hi, Iris," Tabitha said with a smile. "I came with the glucosamine chews I was telling you about yesterday."

"Oh?" Iris shook her head. "I don't remember that."

"They're for Goldie. For your dog." Tabitha gave her another encouraging smile.

Iris shook her head. "I have to go. I don't have time. I'm sorry."

"Where are you going, Mammi?" Beth asked.

"I have to bring a lunch to Mose." Iris headed across the grass in the direction of the stable. Mose—Iris's late son. Tabitha hadn't really known him. He was twenty years her senior, after all, but she'd known who he was when he came back to visit. And he'd had a good reputation.

Tabitha looked over at Beth, and the younger woman sighed. She brushed an errant hair away from her face. "Mammi's been doing this lately. She gets lost in the past."

Tabitha watched as Iris marched purposefully into the stable, and Beth jogged across the grass and opened the stable door.

"Mammi, come back." Beth's voice filtered back toward her. "Mose doesn't need a lunch."

Iris stepped back outside. "I need my horse hitched up. Where is my Nellie?"

"Mammi, you don't need to bring Mose a lunch." Beth's voice shook.

"I didn't give him his lunch this morning. I forgot. He'll be famished," Iris said. "He's a growing boy."

Arguing with an old woman who was stuck in the past, a woman who thought her son needed her, was downright impossible. Was it better to tell Iris that she was wrong, that her son was dead, or was it better to distract her?

"I brought Mose a lunch already," Tabitha said, raising her voice.

Iris and Beth both turned. Iris frowned, cocking her head to one side. Beth looked hopefully back at her grandmother.

"I dropped it off already," Tabitha went on. "Don't you remember, Iris? You'd never leave Mose without a lunch."

"No, I wouldn't. . . ." Iris smiled then. "I would never do that."

"Exactly," Tabitha agreed. "It's fine. No need to worry. You don't have to hitch up. He has his lunch already. I dropped it off."

"Oh, that's a relief. . . ." Iris nodded a couple of times. "Are you sure?"

"Positive," Tabitha said.

Iris started back toward the house. "I was worried that he would be hungry. That boy could out-eat a wolf."

"Can't they all," Tabitha said, and she cast Beth a re-assuring smile. "How is your dog doing, Iris?"

"My dog?" Iris looked back.

"Goldie, Mammi," Beth said.

"Oh, Goldie. *Yah*, she's fine. She's . . . She's . . ." Iris paused, her gaze flicking back toward Tabitha, then toward the stable again. Tabitha could see the present coming back to her now, sliding into place. "Oh . . ."

"It's okay, Mammi," Beth said softly.

"I thought—" Iris's voice quavered. "I really thought I needed to—"

"It's okay, Iris," Tabitha added. "All's well that ends well. I came with some medication for Goldie. I was here yester-day, and I gave her a shot, remember? And I told you that I'd bring by a second medication that Goldie can take that will help her feel a lot better."

"*Yah*. Goldie's medication," Iris repeated.

Iris opened the door, and the dog came padding out to meet them. Tabitha could see that Goldie was moving much more easily today than she had been yesterday, which was a good sign.

Tabitha followed Iris and Beth back into the house, and she noted the worry on Beth's face.

"I'm sorry I lied," Tabitha said softly to Beth once Iris was puttering around in the kitchen again.

"It's hard to know what to do." Beth heaved a sigh. "It did seem to help, though."

"She was a loving mother," Tabitha said. "And I only wanted to remind her that she'd already been a very good mother to her son. That's all."

Tears welled in Beth's eyes. "*Danke*, Tabitha. We're all just doing our best."

Tabitha showed Iris and Beth how to give Goldie a chew each morning. Iris picked up her knitting project again and headed into the other room, and Beth followed Tabitha to the door.

"I'll let Jonas know that Iris is getting worse," Tabitha said quietly.

"*Danke*. I appreciate that," Beth said. "I told Jonas I'd be okay, but I might need some extra help around here after all."

Tabitha headed back out to her buggy. As she untied Fritz from the hitching post, she glanced back at the house. Iris was going to need more than a granddaughter helping with the cooking and cleaning, that was for sure and for certain.

But that was what family was for. That was why communities pulled together to take care of one another. Life wasn't easy, and Gott had given them each other for such a time as this.

10

The Shepherd's Hill Farmers Market was located on the far edge of town in an old airplane hangar that had been repurposed for the market. A lot of Amish families sold their wares here, and Jonas nodded at Verna Yoder, who was sitting with her arms crossed next to shelves that displayed her needlework in her stall. Next to her was Amos Mast, who sold frozen beef out of a big upright freezer with a transparent door, and then next to him was Elizabeth Froese, who sold ready-made pierogi on paper plates, slathered in butter, sauteed onions, and a dollop of sour cream. The smell of those pierogis made his stomach growl, but Mamm was cooking dinner at home, so he didn't dare buy himself a plate.

Music played overhead, though Jonas never recognized any of the songs. They were from the local radio station. The hum of voices reverberated around the big building, and both *Englisch* and Amish meandered down the aisles, doing their shopping and browsing. The scents from different food booths collided in a mouthwatering frenzy that always seemed to have the undertone of sweet cotton candy from the cotton candy booth at the far back.

Jonas walked through the market next to his father.

"Daet, we'd be the first ones to own sheep," Jonas pointed out, keeping his voice low. "Look around here. There's chicken, pork, beef—but no mutton! And no sheep dairy products. Sheep products are getting popular these days in Pennsylvania. Plus, there is the wool that we can sell to spinners for yarn."

Jonas's father slowly shook his head. "We know nothing about sheep."

"We'll learn," Jonas countered. "And we can start small. Maybe ten or twelve sheep to start. We'd make sure we get a ram to breed them. But if we're the first in our area, we can set the price for mutton going forward. There will be a learning curve, that's for sure and for certain, but I think it's worth it."

Jonas had been giving this a lot of thought. First of all, he liked sheep. He'd chatted with some *Englischer* sheep farmers who'd brought sheep in for the mutton-busting show, where young children rode them like broncos. It was a fun event—one that Jonas thought the Amish *kinner* would enjoy. Jonas had taken the time to talk with the sheep farmers and get some information. Sheep farming was different from cattle ranching, to be sure, but it would be new and interesting. More than that, Jonas needed something that was his own—his own project, his own herd, his own success as a man.

"I don't know . . . I mean, how much could we even make?"

They passed the Weaver stall—Menno Weaver sold pork products, but the stall was manned today by his new wife, Amanda. Amanda was Tabitha's sister, and she was busy talking to some customers, a clipboard in hand as she made notes.

"Think of the meat stalls," Jonas said. "They don't just sell from their freezers on-site, they take orders too. It's a great way to get your product in front of potential customers."

"I'm thinking about our actual farming," his father said. "We're using our pasture for horses and cattle."

"There's room to adjust," Jonas shot back. "What about the western field we haven't sown in three years? It's almost grown over. It could be a pasture if we wanted it to be."

"That's wasting a field."

"Not if it's making us money with sheep." He could nearly feel his father's defenses going up. "Daet, this is a good idea. And I need something that's for me. I need something I can work on and grow myself. Can't you understand that?"

"You might start with a family," his father said with a wry little smile. "A wife and *kinner*. They'd be yours."

Jonas wasn't going to be baited. "This would be good for you too. This would be expanding the farm, growing a broader customer base. If we were the first ones to start raising sheep, our products could be in real demand in this district. Think of how much our business could grow."

Jonas looked back at Amanda Weaver while she bid her customers farewell and tucked a credit card receipt into an envelope. Her husband, Menno, worked a farm by himself and had grown a very solid reputation for his pork. Now that he was married, he had Amanda to help out too, and at a recent auction, Jonas had noticed Menno buying two more sire boars. He must be doing well. Menno had that happy, satisfied look about him that came with success whenever Jonas saw him on Service Sunday or around town.

It could also be the newly married look, Jonas thought.

"I'm not coming at this idea cold." Jonas turned back to his father. "I've done some research, and I really think we can do this."

"But it is still my farm, and I don't want sheep," his father retorted.

Jonas tamped down his irritation. He'd expected some resistance from his father—Daet could be like that. But Jonas wasn't some *kind* without any sense of the real world. He was thirty years old, and while he respected everything his father had built, he could contribute more around the farm. And sheep could be his own personal challenge, something he needed right now. Besides, growing the farm would make more money for his father too.

A young Amish man brushed past Jonas and then looked up in surprise. It was Danny Lapp.

"Sorry about that," Danny said. "I didn't see you." He had some papers folded over in his hands.

"No problem. How are you doing?" Jonas asked.

Jonas's father headed over to Agnes Byler's stall. She brought in all different kinds of yarn, and he'd be picking up Mamm's order from last week. Agnes would be an excellent customer for sheep's wool once they had some.

Jonas and Danny chatted for a couple of minutes about nothing in particular—the weather and how their families were doing. Then Jonas noticed one of the papers in Danny's hand looked like an application for a stall here at the market.

"Are you planning on opening a stall?" Jonas asked.

"I'm thinking on it," Danny said. "It would be a place to start. I want to open a store of my own, but it occurred to me that I could start a bit smaller."

"*Yah?*" Jonas's interest was piqued. "What are you thinking of selling?"

"I'm not ready to say anything just yet," Danny replied with a grin. "I'm keeping it private for now, but ideas are stirring, I can say that much."

"Understandable," Jonas said. He hadn't told anyone else about his sheep idea either. A good idea for them could end up being a good idea for someone else too. "I hope it goes well for you."

His father returned then with a paper bag filled with Mamm's yarn order, and after Jonas said farewell to Danny, they headed out toward the buggy parking.

"If we don't grow, we'll be left behind, Daet," Jonas said. "That's all I'll say for now."

"And I think you should start with getting yourself married," his father replied, then mimed locking his lips. Always getting the last word.

Jonas laughed and rolled his eyes. Arguing with Daet was like trying to hold a balloon under water. You might think you were getting ahead, but it would always pop back up to the surface.

Gott, please let him think this over, he prayed as he got into the buggy and picked up the reins.

Soon after they arrived back home, another buggy turned down their drive, and Jonas turned to see who it was.

"It's that Schrock girl," Daet said. That was what Daet called Tabitha Schrock. "I wonder what she wants. Are our animals in good health?"

Daet still seemed to forget that Tabitha wasn't just the vet, she was also Jonas's friend.

"*Yah*, Daet. There are no veterinarian issues here."

"That's a small comfort," he muttered.

Jonas waited as Tabitha reined in and then hopped down from her buggy. It was nice to see her, even though he was stewing with irritation at his stubborn *daet*. Sheep would be an excellent investment if Daet would just give it a chance.

"Is that Fritz?" Jonas asked of the horse pulling her open-top buggy.

"*Yah*, he needed to get out and feel useful," Tabitha said.

Jonas knew the feeling.

"I hope I'm not interrupting anything," Tabitha went on, "but I dropped by Iris's house today."

"How's the dog?"

"Doing better. The treatment is working. I'm not here about Goldie, though. It's Iris."

"Is this visit going to be expensive?" Daet asked gruffly.

"*Nee*, not at all," Tabitha replied with an amused smile. At least she could see Daet's dry humor. That was helpful.

"I'll tend to the horse," Daet said.

Jonas opened the screen door and nodded her inside. "Better come in, then."

"*Danke*," Tabitha said.

Tabitha had a little piece of straw in her hair, but he didn't dare touch it with his mother staring at Tabitha in mild surprise.

"Hello." Tabitha gave Mamm a polite nod. "I hope I'm not interrupting dinner yet."

"No, no, I'm still cooking," Mamm said, chopping up a potato. "How are you, Tabitha?"

"I went by Iris's place this morning to bring her some medication for the dog," Tabitha said, "and I saw something that was . . . well, I'll be honest, it was a little upsetting."

Mamm's chopping stopped. "What happened?"

Tabitha described what she'd seen.

"She was making Mose a lunch?" Tears misted Mamm's eyes. "Oh, Iris . . . When Mose died it nearly killed her. Her only child."

"Beth is doing a good job over there," Tabitha said. "She's working very hard on all the chores, but she seems a bit overwhelmed when Iris gets lost in her memories like that."

"Of course," Mamm murmured. "She's going to need help."

"I told Beth I'd come by and let you know about it," Tabitha said.

"*Danke* for doing that," Jonas put in. "We appreciate it."

"I'll head up there after supper and see how I can help," Mamm said. "*Danke*, Tabitha."

Tabitha turned for the door, and Jonas followed her outside. He reached out and plucked the piece of straw from her hair. She put her hand up to her *kapp* in surprise, and he held up the straw in silent explanation.

"Oh." She smiled.

"I'll go with my *mamm* tonight to see Aent Iris," he said. "I'll see what chores I can get done for her. I normally go by once a week at least, but I can pitch in a bit more."

"I'm sure both Iris and Beth would appreciate it," Tabitha said.

"You'd be wrong there. Aent Iris gets offended when I try to help too much. But maybe times have changed."

"Offended or not, she needs help."

He nodded. "Understood."

Jonas followed her to her buggy and waited while she untied Fritz. Tabitha had a sure way about her, but he'd started to see that the confident demeanor was a protective shell. She wasn't really as confident as she pretended.

"How are you doing, Tabitha?" he asked.

"I'm fine." She shot him another smile.

"Really?"

She paused, her hand on Fritz's strong shoulder, and she deflated just a little. "Things are getting better. I'm going to the quilting bee, and maybe the women will get more used to me being around."

"What about Katherine Blank?" he asked. "I thought you were getting to be friends again."

"We are," she said. "But it takes time, and she's busy with her little ones and her in-laws. She'll be at the quilting bee, though."

So Tabitha had plans to sort out her situation. He wanted her insight into his as well. She was smart, and she knew animals and animal husbandry.

"Tabby, can I ask you something?"

Her expression relaxed at the old nickname. "Sure."

"What would you think of someone starting up a small sheep herd here in Shepherd's Hill?"

"I think it would be applicable to the name. Some sheep in Shepherd's Hill." She laughed at her own word play.

"Right." He grinned. "But beyond the poetic bit, what would you think about a farmer's chance of success with sheep around here?"

"Well . . ." She frowned. "Currently, there aren't any sheep farmers in our area. I think it would add some interesting options at the Amish Market. You might even find someone in your family who wants to work with the wool, dye it, and turn it into knitting wool. A quality homespun wool is worth a great deal to the right knitter."

"How finicky is a herd of sheep?"

"I've never farmed sheep myself," she said, "but I do have

some experience working with sheep in a veterinarian ca-
pacity. And medically, they aren't complicated. Sheep are
surprisingly accident prone, though. They can get stuck on
their backs if they fall over. So the kinds of accidents they
encounter are different than cattle or horses. They spook
easily, too, and will trample each other or all run over a cliff
if they get scared. So they need a lot of supervision."

They did sound like a lot of work, he had to admit.

"I'm thinking of starting up a small flock of sheep," he
told her. "Would you have any advice for me?"

"I mean, talking to an experienced sheep farmer would be
a must," she said. "But I can go over the vaccines they need,
and the typical veterinarian issues to look out for. You'll have
to be prepared to do shearing and crutching, dehorning, tail
docking . . . There's some overlap with cattle in castration
and hoof care, and the dehorning, of course. Sheep tend to
need a lot of help giving birth, and they also tend to have
multiples. So I guess they require a lot of intervention, but
that said, I like sheep. Are you really going to do it?"

"I'm thinking about it." He nodded toward the small side
pasture where his father was just sending their horse out to
graze. "I'm trying to convince my *daet* that it's a good idea.
He's not in agreement at the moment."

"That's the challenge, then," she said.

"That's always the challenge."

Tabitha hoisted herself up into the buggy and wrapped
the reins around her hands. "I have to get back home and
start supper," she said.

Right. She had her *daet* to cook for too. Jonas's father
headed on past them toward the house.

"*Danke* for coming by and telling us about Iris," Jonas
said. "I'll see you around."

She gave a little wave. "See you later."

Jonas stepped back, the piece of straw from her hair still between his fingers, as Tabitha flicked the reins and Fritz started forward. It was then he spotted his *mamm* in the doorway and his *daet* on the step, and for some reason, he felt uncomfortable about that piece of straw, so he flicked it into the grass.

"You know, *sohn*," Mamm said as he came back up the steps, "I know of a matchmaker in Ohio who has been responsible for some very good marriages. Verena Lapp's sister-in-law was talking about her. She says that she's got a list of quality women looking for husbands."

"Is that what we've come to now?" Jonas joked. "You want to get some professional help in finding me a wife?"

"It might be time." Her gaze slid over his shoulder, following the sight of Tabitha's retreating buggy, then snapped back to his face. "Tabitha can't marry again, Jonas."

His mother's voice was quiet and compassionate, and somehow that irritated him. He didn't need her pity. He'd been talking to a friend—that was all.

"I know that, Mamm."

"I thought you might need reminding, is all."

Jonas headed back inside, and his father followed him in. They washed up, and when they went into the kitchen, his father picked up *The Budget* newspaper. He flipped it open and tapped an article.

"Right here," Daet said. "It says Harold Byler of Intercourse, Pennsylvania, married Loretta Hochstetler of Sugarcreek, Ohio. They were introduced by matchmaker Nellie Stoltzfus, who resides in Sugarcreek and communicated by letter. The couple will live in Intercourse, Pennsylvania."

"Another one?" Mamm came around behind Daet's chair

and leaned over to read the announcement. "She is having so much success."

"Congratulations to the happy couple," Jonas muttered without much enthusiasm.

"Indeed," Daet said, lowering his gaze back to the newspaper again. "I'm always happy to hear about a wedding. The parents must be so pleased."

Yah, yah. Jonas got the hint loud and clear. They wanted him to settle down already. And truth be told, Jonas had been praying for a wife. He wanted to find the right woman, though—the one Gott had especially for him.

And Jonas had looked seriously at the local women, but none had really interested him. He was waiting on Gott to bring him the right one.

But explain that to his parents. Explain it to the bishop, even. Everyone believed in listening to Gott's voice until Gott's voice went against their ideas of what was best for Jonas.

When the right woman came along, Gott would let him know. He was sure of it.

11

The next week was a busy one for Danny, but not only because of the summer guests arriving. He found reasons to stop by Iris's home. He brought his mother's baking one day, and another evening he went over to borrow some vanilla. His mother hadn't sent him, but he figured it was a good reason to come by, and then he had an excuse to go back the next day when he returned it.

Beth came for a walk in the direction of his house a few times, and one afternoon, she stood on the lakeshore in front of the cabins, watching some *Englischers* swimming. They were just paddling around—their *kinner* had life jackets on. But he could see a wistfulness in her eyes while she watched them.

"You said you swim at home," he asked her. "Why not here?"

"I don't know that your bishop would allow it," she said.

"I guess we'd find out. And who would tell? It's just me and my family here, and the *Englischer* guests. You're a visitor too."

102

"Mammi would panic. She has a real fear of this lake. I promised her I wouldn't swim, so I'll keep my word."

Danny's younger siblings, Anne and Toby, sat on the edge of the dock, bare feet dangling over the water. Anne was tearing up some leaves and tossing them into the lake, and Toby just looked distant and brooding. At fourteen, Toby had turned melancholy and introverted. He was probably still upset about Zach moving away, Danny guessed. But Toby wouldn't talk about it.

Honestly, Danny found himself a little moody lately too. Having Beth back was like spring returning after a long winter, but he had to be realistic. If she didn't want to stay Amish, they didn't have a future together, and he had a heart to protect too. But somehow, he felt like he knew her on a deeper level than most. Maybe it was only wishful thinking—he was logical enough to allow for that—but while she was questioning everything she ever knew, he sensed that she did want to believe in their Amish roots. And *wanting* to believe in something was a big part of conviction. Danny wanted to believe that this community of people mattered both on earth and to Gott. He wanted to believe in something bigger than himself, and he wanted to be part of it.

So maybe this summer Beth would find a reason to stay. And some foolish part of him hoped that he could be that reason. Her own faith had to come first, of course, but couldn't this warm relationship they shared factor in too? He had never had this kind of connection with another woman, and he was relatively certain it was a rarity in her life too. They had something special.

And he was willing to work for the life he wanted. He wanted her to be able to see the life he imagined together, too, because it was a beautiful one.

"I might get things moving a little faster with my plans to open my own shop," he told her now. "Instead of starting out with the shop in town, I think I might open a stall in the Amish Market first."

"*Yah?*" Beth's eyebrows rose. "What's the hurry?"

"I want to start my life. I want to get things moving . . . make some room in my life for a family of my own."

Beth stilled. "Do you have a girl you're driving?"

That was how they courted—driving in buggies on the back roads and going home together from Singings.

"*Nee.*" He laughed softly. "But that doesn't mean I can't get ready, does it? I know what I want."

"Then you should do it." She looked hesitant, though.

"My parents will still need my help around here with the rentals too."

"But you need to think about your own future," she countered.

"*Yah*, but I can do both." He leaned forward. "Not everything is all or nothing, you know. I can make room in my life for more while keeping a tether to the past. So can you."

"Some things are all or nothing." She sobered, and he knew she was thinking about the choice ahead of her.

"I hope you stay," he said, and a lump rose in his throat. "I really do."

Beth reached over and squeezed his hand—a spontaneous gesture that took him by surprise. He squeezed her fingers back and glanced in the direction of the house around the lake. He spotted Iris standing on the edge of the beach, Goldie at her side. Even from this distance, he could feel the old woman's tension.

He was silent for a moment, wishing that his time with Beth wasn't always so short, but it couldn't be helped.

"Are you coming to service tomorrow?" he asked.

"Of course."

"In the evening, there's going to be a Singing for the *youngie*. Are you . . . interested?"

She nodded. "I'd like that, but I'd have to get someone to come stay with Mammi while I'm gone."

"My *mamm* might," he offered.

"My *aent* probably will too," she replied. "If I can get that sorted out, and if you'll drive me, I'd like to go."

Was that just because she didn't know the area well enough, or did she want him beside her? He wished he knew.

"I'll drive you." Danny looked back toward Iris again, and Beth turned to look too. She straightened. "I think your *mammi* needs you," he told her.

There was something deeply beautiful about Beth when she focused like that. He'd noticed it when they were *kinner* playing together. When Beth stopped and looked at someone, he'd hold his breath. It was like he could feel all of her thoughts tumbling around inside of her, and he longed to know what some of them were. Now that they were both grown, he found that he still held his breath.

"It looks like she's waiting for me," Beth said. "I should get back."

"Okay. I'll see you tomorrow."

A truck turned into their drive, and Danny recognized it as Zach's. So his brother was back for a visit now too. Great.

"Is that Zach?" Beth asked.

"*Yah*, that's him."

"I wish I could say hello, but I'd better get back to Mammi."

Danny nodded. It was better that way, anyway. He might

have told her the truth about his brother's choices lately, but that didn't mean Danny wasn't embarrassed. He'd rather not have Beth see his brother's abrasive ways in person. Danny cared what she thought about his family, and if he could keep some of her good opinion about them intact, that would be nice.

Beth headed back along the lakeshore path, and Danny headed in his brother's direction. He'd brought someone with him—an *Englischer* young woman. This must be the Meghan he'd been talking about all this time. She looked nice enough, with a hesitant smile on her face, but she wore a sundress that left her shoulders bare. It wasn't decent. Danny tried not to look at that bare skin. Daet came out of the stable with a pair of work gloves tucked under his arm, and a moment later, Toby and Anne appeared around the side of the house.

"Hi," Zach said. "This is Meghan."

For half a beat no one moved, then Daet stepped forward with a smile. "Nice to meet you, Meghan. We've heard a lot about you."

Danny shot Meghan a smile too. "It's nice you could come by. I'm Danny, Zach's brother."

"Right!" Meghan put her hand out to shake, and Danny hesitated. Amish women didn't shake hands. But Meghan wasn't Amish, and he didn't want to make a scene, so he shook her hand. "You have a beautiful farm. Zach's shown me the pictures, and I'm glad to finally see it in person."

Pictures? Danny looked at his brother in surprise, and Zach refused to meet his gaze.

"I wanted to come by for dinner. I hope it's not too short of notice," Zach said, switching to Pennsylvania Dutch.

"It's fine," Daet replied in *Deutsch*. "Come inside." Then

Daet switched back to English. "Please come inside, both of you. There is always room at the table for our son. Always."

Zach's visits home never ended up being simple or even enjoyable these days. But this was still a chance to see Zach again and maybe rebuild some of those bridges between him and the family.

Toby cast Danny a rueful look.

"A nice family dinner?" Toby said in Pennsylvania Dutch.

"Be nice," Danny muttered.

"Isn't she vegan?" Anne asked. "What are we supposed to feed her?"

"Quinoa," Toby said, and he and Anne burst into a peal of laughter. It was probably a joke between the two of them, because Danny didn't get it.

"Be nice," Danny repeated. "I'm sure we'll find something. Remember, I don't care how complicated this is, we're all still Christians. We'd better act like it."

That sobered his younger siblings, and they all headed into the house together.

Mamm was slicing a beef roast on a cutting board, and she looked up with a surprised, then mildly anxious, smile on her face when she saw Zach and Meghan. Anne went to help Mamm with the rest of dinner, and Toby headed into the sitting room to grab the extra kitchen chairs that they lined up along one wall.

"Maybe you could help my mother in the kitchen," Zach said quietly to Meghan.

"Why me and not you?" Meghan asked, her voice pitched low.

"Because it's how we do things," Zach whispered back.

Danny tried to look like he couldn't hear them, and he headed over to the cupboard to grab water glasses. Zach and Meghan whispered together, and Toby returned with two chairs.

"She's vegan, remember?" Danny said to his mother.

"Right!" Mamm wiped her hands on her apron and looked at the roast beef dinner she had prepared. "Anne, run downstairs and bring up a jar of beans. I'll leave some potatoes out so we don't mash them with butter—that will keep those vegan. And the pickles and sauerkraut will be fine. I have some vegetarian cabbage rolls in the freezer too. . . ."

The meal was delicious, and everyone chatted about ordinary things as they ate. Meghan asked questions about the horses and buggies, and Zach told them about his job at the grocery store. He had some funny stories about his coworkers.

"So, Toby, you've finished eighth grade?" Meghan asked.

Toby had to swallow a mouthful of food before he answered. "*Yah*, I finished this year."

"Have you thought about what you want to do now?" Meghan asked.

Toby shook his head. "I'm still thinking about it."

"That's okay." Meghan smiled. "You know, my mother is a high school teacher, and there are actually some different ways you can get your high school diploma."

"There's a GED program in town too," Zach added. "That's where Tabitha Schrock went to school."

"Toby will decide what he wants to do, but there is no pressure at this time," Daet said firmly.

"You might want to keep studying, though," Meghan said. "Once a student drops out, the chances of him going back are very low."

"It isn't dropping out," Danny said. "It's finishing up."

"Eighth grade isn't finishing up," Zach said. "Twelfth

grade is finishing. Having only an eighth-grade education is holding us back."

Silence descended around the table, and Daet cleared his throat.

"We are Amish. We have our own way of doing things. Toby has no need of finishing a high school diploma."

"I don't know," Zach said. "Look at Tabitha Schrock. She's Amish, but she's also the local veterinarian. Her education has made her incredibly valuable to the community. Normally a vet would be an *Englischer*, right? So what's so wrong with an Amish person getting the education and holding a position like that? It's good for everyone."

"Because we don't do things that way," Daet replied.

"I can be a teacher, if I want," Anne said.

And Anne could. Most teachers in their schools had no more than an eighth-grade education themselves.

"But why can't Anne and Toby be more?" Zach pressed. "What if Toby wants to make better money? He's really good at math. That's valuable. If he went on for more education in mathematics or science, he could do well for himself."

Toby's gaze whipped between Daet and Zach, and Danny could feel this visit getting out of control quickly. It was one thing for Zach to question everything the Amish believed in, but it was quite another to drag their younger siblings into it.

"Zach, just leave it alone," Danny said in *Deutsch*.

"Just tell me this"—Zach held his hands up—"Why is it perfectly acceptable for Tabitha Schrock to be highly educated and no one else? Huh? Why?"

"That's a complicated situation," Mamm said quietly.

"Not really."

Zach wasn't about to be distracted from his point, and

Danny watched as Meghan picked up a piece of bread and took a bite.

"That bread has milk in it," Danny said. He'd watched his mother make bread every Saturday for his entire life. He knew the ingredients and measurements by memory. If he was ever forced, he could probably bake the family's bread.

Meghan's gaze snapped back to Danny, and she froze. For a moment, she didn't move, then she picked up her napkin and spat the bread out into it. Her face blazed red, and she looked ready to cry.

"Sorry," Danny said. "Thought I'd warn you."

She nodded. "I didn't mean to start an argument. I'm sorry. I should have kept my mouth shut."

The meal and the debating continued, mostly because Zach just wouldn't let it drop. Mamm didn't bother bringing any pie to the table once they had cleared it, and Danny's head started to hurt.

"We should probably get home," Meghan said at last.

There was something in the way she said it that made Mamm's shoulders tighten.

"Home . . . separate homes?" Mamm asked.

"No, Mamm," Zach said with a sigh. "I didn't mean to tell you this way, but Meghan and I moved in together."

"Oh . . ." Mamm said weakly. "Are you getting married?"

"No."

"So you're living together like husband and wife without being actually wed?" Daet asked in English.

Meghan looked up at Zach, her cheeks blazing again.

"*Yah*, we are," Zach said. "Look, other people do things differently. They don't need to get married right away. They can think things through."

"You don't just have a trial run at these things," Daet said.

110

"I'm sorry to say this so plainly, Meghan, but we raised Zach to get married first. We believe that a woman is worth the commitment. A man, too, for that matter. Starting out without that commitment is trouble, for sure and for certain."

Meghan just stood there rigidly, and Danny had to wonder if that was what Meghan really wanted—Zach as her boyfriend but nothing more?

"Daet, we're making our own choices. I'm not living Amish." Zach was speaking in Pennsylvania Dutch again. "But I'm giving you the respect of telling you what I'm doing with my life."

Meghan slipped out the side door, and Danny saw her go stand next to the truck.

"You're really living together?" Mamm asked sadly. "What if children come along? Would you marry her then?"

The discussion continued, and Danny looked out the screen door toward Meghan. Her shoulders were hitched up and she was facing away from the house. She wanted out of here—that was clear enough.

"Look, I'm going home now. But I wanted to tell you the truth and not lie to you. That has to count for something."

Tears misted Mamm's eyes, but she didn't say anything.

"And, Toby, just so you know, you're really smart," Zach said. "And if you want to know what else is out there for guys as smart as you are, you can come stay with me for a bit."

"Enough!" Daet's voice boomed, and even Mamm startled. "Zachariah, I know you spit on everything I raised you for, but you will not try and lure your brother and sister off into the sinful life you are leading. Do you understand me? This is my house. You're a man now yourself, and you are welcome to live your life the way you want to live it, but you will abide by my rules under my roof!"

111

Zach's eyes blazed in response, but he didn't argue.

"Thanks for supper, Mamm," Zach said. "And if you have anything to say about me and Meghan and how we choose to live, I ask that you address it with me and don't talk to Meghan about it."

Zach headed out the door and stomped down the steps. Danny watched as his brother and Meghan got into the truck and the vehicle started. Then he turned back to see Toby and Anne staring at him.

"Why isn't Zach marrying her if he's living with her?" Anne asked.

"I don't know," Danny said. "I guess they don't want to."

"How much does he make at his job?" Toby asked.

"It doesn't matter," Daet said. "Gott won't bless disobedience. If you go against Gott's will, you can make all the money in the world, and it won't buy happiness or contentment. Gott gives sleep to those he loves."

Toby nodded, but Danny saw an unsettled glimmer in his younger brother's eyes. That wasn't a good sign.

12

Service Sunday was a cheerful day in Beth's home community, and it was no different here in Shepherd's Hill. Beth and Mammi put on their best dresses, and Beth helped her grandmother pin her apron. Outside, the third buggy that morning went trotting past the house on its way to church. With the bright summer sunlight warming the dew-laden grass outside the open back door, Beth couldn't help but feel the refreshing Sunday glow.

She loved Service Sundays in her Amish life. The day when the whole community came together to worship was both holy and celebratory. Beth had gone to church with Cadence a few times over the last couple of years, and while Cadence really loved her church, it didn't have the same feeling to Beth. If Beth did choose to go *Englisch*, she'd have to find a church to attend, and that thought was daunting. She believed that she could find Gott there, and even if she took the wings of the morning and dwelt in the uttermost parts of the sea, Gott would be with her, as Psalms said. Still, she'd miss Amish church.

Beth hitched up the buggy, Mammi gathered up her Bible,

and before long, they'd joined the line of Shepherd's Hill Amish heading to the service being held at one of the district farms.

They arrived at the same time as Aent Mary, Onkel Nathaniel, and Jonas, and Jonas walked with Mammi up toward the house, where the furniture would have been cleared to the side to make room for the church benches.

Other women quickly came to gather up Mammi into their midst, and Beth let her steps slow, feeling the relief of being "off duty" with her grandmother.

"Are you doing okay, Beth?" Aent Mary put a hand on her arm.

"I'm fine." Somehow the smile that normally came so easily to Beth's lips faltered.

"*Yah?*" Mary didn't sound convinced, and suddenly Beth desperately missed her own *mamm*. Mamm could always see right through her too.

"It's just nice to have people come take care of Mammi for a while," Beth said.

"I'll come by and help you out more often," Aent Mary offered.

"Danny wants me to go to the *Youngie* Singing tonight. Do you think you could come by and stay with Mammi?"

"Of course. I think it's a good idea. You should get out with people your own age."

"*Danke.*" Beth felt some of the pressure coming off her shoulders. "You know, I wanted to catch you alone because I had some questions that I didn't want to ask in front of other people."

"Like what?" Her *aent* hooked her arm through Beth's and guided her toward the parked buggies, away from others who might overhear. Children's chatter came from the direction of the stable, where some boys were catching up after not seeing each other for two weeks.

"It's about my father." A warm breeze plucked at Beth's dress. "About his childhood. I realized after he died that I didn't know any stories about him from before he was an adult. The stories start with him meeting my *mamm* when she visited Pennsylvania, and how they wrote letters and fell in love and got married. It's like my *daet's* life started with her."

"That's rather beautiful."

"It's romantic, sure, but it's strange. I mean, he had a whole childhood that no one speaks of. Can I just tell you what I'm thinking without you ever telling anyone else?" Beth asked. "Because I might be wrong. But you're the only one who will give me a straight answer about anything."

"Of course." Mary leaned forward. "Go ahead and tell me. You can trust my discretion."

"All right." Beth swallowed. "Daet never told me about his childhood. Nothing. No funny stories. No sad stories. Just . . . nothing at all. And when I ask Mammi about it, Mammi won't say much. She says—" Beth hesitated, unsure if she was betraying a confidence, but then she plunged on. "She says she wasn't married, though. That's all she's confirmed for me."

Beth watched her *aent* for a reaction, but Mary just frowned, looking down at her feet.

"You were my *daet's* age, right? So you knew him growing up?" Beth pressed.

"I knew him after they moved here." Mary raised her eyes to meet Beth's. "Before your *mammi* and your *daet* moved here, they lived in Indiana somewhere. Your *daet* was about sixteen when they moved. I mean, he was starting his *rumspringa*.

But he was the most conservative teenager. He didn't care for pushing any boundaries. As soon as he could join a baptismal class, he did."

"So you didn't know my *daet* when he was little?"

"*Nee.*"

"Mammi said she never married," Beth continued. "So that means she was a single mother. But I'm curious about who my *dawdie* was."

Mary was silent for a moment, then shook her head. "Just because I don't keep big secrets doesn't mean I have big answers either. I honestly don't know. Iris didn't like to talk about the past, and no one liked to question her about it. It was considered rude to pry into someone else's pain. All I know is that your *mammi* was accepted once more as a full member of the community when she returned with your *daet* when he was about sixteen. There was no confession before the church."

"Did Mammi always live in Indiana?" Beth asked. "Before she moved here?"

"No. She's my *daet's* sister. They grew up here."

"So Mammi grew up here, left for Indiana, and came back with a child."

"*Yah.* That's all I know."

"Did my *mammi* have a man she loved at one point?" Beth asked.

"You'd have to ask her. I was the generation beneath her. There were stories the adults shared with us, and then there were the stories they didn't."

Beth sighed. "So I could have a family out there," she said. "I mean, more family. My *daet* might have brothers and sisters. I might have cousins."

"You might, depending on who fathered your *daet*." Some

women were walking toward the house, and one waved to them. "We'd best get into service."

"*Yah*. We should," Beth agreed.

As she walked toward the house, her mind spun from her conversation with her *aent*. Mammi had grown up in Shepherd's Hill, and then she'd moved to Indiana and returned with a son. . . . Even Aent Mary knew little about what had happened while she was gone.

Had Mammi left pregnant?

The church service was a comforting one. The preacher spoke about how Gott's ways were higher than their ways, and his thoughts were not their thoughts. It got Beth thinking about her own choices, and she silently prayed for Gott to guide her. She didn't want to go against Gott's will for her life, but how was a woman supposed to know what that was? Did she follow her gut feelings, trusting Gott to guide those? Or was that wrong too?

The sermon ended just after noon with the preacher calling upon the *youngie* to make their decision for baptism and to join the church, which left Beth ill at ease. Was that the right step for her?

After the service, they stayed for the community meal of soup and bread. Mammi sat with some of her friends—other elderly women who visited together in a little group, sitting on lawn chairs because of their age.

Danny found Beth as she was putting her empty bowl on the pile to be washed.

"You made it," Danny said, and his smile was as warm as the sunshine on her shoulders.

"I made it," she confirmed. "Did you like the sermon?"

"*Yah*, it was good." He eyed her uncertainly. "And you?"

"I wasn't put off by the call to baptism, if that's what

you're wondering," she said with a short laugh. "I liked the sermon. He made some very good points about Gott's way being different from ours. We always think we know what he wants from us, but we don't always."

"I guess life is complicated," Danny said.

Beth noticed that Tabitha Schrock was alone eating a bowl of soup, and she wondered how lonely it was to have come back home after all that time. One would expect that she'd find community again, but Beth could understand how all that education and a divorce could put some distance between Tabitha and the other women.

"Oh, I should tell you that my *aent* will come stay with Mammi while we go to the Singing tonight," Beth said.

"Perfect." Danny's voice was low. "I'm looking forward to it."

And Beth couldn't help but smile. She was looking forward to it too, but when she glanced in Tabitha's direction again, she noticed that another young woman had stopped to talk to her. Maybe the veterinarian wasn't completely isolated, but she did look lonesome. That was a warning right there—coming home again wasn't always easy. Every last choice came with its own consequences, good or bad or maybe a mixture of both.

That evening, Aent Mary arrived at the house as promised, and shortly after, Danny arrived in his buggy. The sun was setting, the air cooling, and the crickets chirped their evening song from the fields.

"Have fun!" Aent Mary called cheerily as Beth headed out the side door.

Danny waited in the buggy, and Beth pulled herself up

and settled in next to him. It felt nice to be getting away for an evening, she had to admit. Danny flicked the reins, and the horse started forward.

"How was your brother's visit?" she asked.

Danny shook his head. "We met Zach's *Englisch* girlfriend for the first time. Her name is Meghan."

"That's news. What's she like?"

"Nice enough. Very different. They're living together."

Beth coughed. "They're *what*?"

"Yup. You heard that right. And we've been told it isn't our business."

"Wow . . ." She remembered Zach over the years. He was older than Danny, so he hadn't spent much time with them. He'd always been a bit rebellious. She remembered when he got a battery-operated radio and would blast worldly music from his buggy. That had been a huge upset to everyone, including Mammi, who had been thoroughly disapproving of it.

"I mean, I guess there comes a point when you're grown and you've made your choices, but I think that you're always your family's business," Danny said.

"Thank Gott for that," she said. "What did his girlfriend think of all this?"

"She seemed quite upset. She went outside while we finished our conversation with him, but I don't think that went the way she'd hoped."

"That's awful."

"Zach was in his usual argumentative form too," Danny went on. "He's pointing out that Tabitha Schrock is very educated, and that it isn't a problem around here."

"The veterinarian?" Beth asked. "I mean, she got divorced and can't remarry. That's a pretty big deal."

"He's talking about her education level," Danny said.

119

"That's his newest argument about our way of life—that we don't go to school beyond eighth grade. He says that if we could go to school, we'd be able to pursue occupations that are good for the community."

"I mean, he's not wrong. . . ." Beth leaned back in the seat, watching the sun slip behind the hills, the sky smudged pink and orange.

"You don't think so?" Danny shot her a questioning look.

"I mean . . . what if we could get more education?" Beth asked. "What if we could go to school for longer and learn how to do things that *Englischers* do? Personally, I'd love to work at a bank. Wouldn't it be helpful if we understood money and banking? We just trust the *Englischers* to take care of our money in a bank account, but we don't know more. I think it would be interesting and helpful to us as a community. We'd be more self-sufficient."

"But where does it end?" Danny asked.

"Why does it have to?" she countered. "What if we had Amish doctors who used technology and science as well as natural healing? What if we had Amish dentists? That's a thought, isn't it? An Amish dentist to help us keep our teeth in good shape, who would understand our ways."

Danny pressed his lips together, and she knew she was really pushing the limits, but this was part of her frustration. He glanced over at her, and she met his gaze with an impish smile.

"Don't help his argument," Danny said with a short laugh.

"Does it bother you that Zach disagrees with the Amish ways?"

"It does, but that's not what bugs me the most," he replied. "He's trying to get Toby and Anne to consider going *Englisch*. My parents are furious."

"What does he want your little brother and sister to do?" she asked. "Just . . . leave?"

"He wants them to go to school beyond the eighth grade."

Beth was silent. Was it so terrible for the Amish to get an education, though? Was it so awful to have an Amish veterinarian instead of an *Englisch* one? Was it so terrible for an Amish woman to teach swimming so that people didn't drown? Or for Amish people to work in finance so that they could understand how money worked and help Amish businesses grow accordingly?

"What are your parents saying?" she asked.

"Daet is considering telling Zach that he can't come back until he can be respectful of our way of life."

It would be harsh and painful, but Beth could understand that line. They had to protect Danny's younger siblings from bad influences. Ironically, this was the same thing her family had tried to do—protect the younger generation from something that might influence them. But eventually, every person had to make their own choice, and a young person didn't stop thinking things through just because the older generations wished they'd just take their word for it.

"Danny, do you have a library card?"

Danny shot her a quizzical look. "That's a change of subject."

"Sorry." She smiled faintly. "It isn't really. I was thinking about family dramas and problems, and how mine has done a very good job of hiding theirs. Do you have a library card?"

"*Yah.*"

"What are the chances you could take me into town for a trip to the library?" she asked. "I want some access to their computers. I want to look up a few things on the Internet."

"Like what?" he asked.

"You've trusted me with your family problems," she said quietly. "Can I trust you with mine?"

"Beth, I'll keep your confidence," Danny said. "And I'd just assumed that you'd do the same for me."

"Of course, Danny."

Danny met her gaze for a moment. "So what's happening?"

"Well . . . honestly, I don't know what I'm looking for, but I want to do an Internet search about this lake and the area over the last fifty or sixty years—my *daet's* lifespan. I want to know who my grandfather is. Mammi admitted that she wasn't married when my *daet* was born, and my *aent* told me that Mammi left the area for a long stretch of time and only returned when Daet was a teenager. I think someone got her pregnant, and she's protecting him still."

"Who?"

"I don't know. Someone she loved? Or maybe it was something more sinister, and she was forced. Why wouldn't she say? It must be something very serious. Because if it had been an Amish boyfriend, the community would simply have made sure they married."

"I doubt an Amish pregnancy would make a newspaper," Danny said.

"I agree. That's why I'm not really looking for anything in particular, I'm just nosing around. Maybe there were other women who found themselves in the same situation. The Amish might not talk, but *Englischers* do. I want to see if I can dig up any information that might make something click in my head and make it all make sense. Who knows, right?"

"*Yah*, we could do that," he replied. "How about tomorrow afternoon? The library is open on Mondays. I could be done with my work here at three, I think."

She nodded. "I can probably do that. But I'll need to see

if my *aent* can come back or maybe someone else. I'll let you know."

And somehow she felt better already. Families meant well, but some secrets had an acidic way about them that ate away at the very foundation a family was trying to protect. If the Amish life was good and Gott-pleasing, then it should stand up to the light of day, even if some fallible human beings had made mistakes.

13

The Singing was held at the same farm as the church service had been. It only made sense for the hosting family to do both. They'd already cleaned and prepared everything for the service, and then the youth came back later on in the evening.

They arranged themselves with girls on one side and boys on the other on benches outside, the evening lit up by bonfires and kerosene lanterns. Danny sat on the boys' side. He was one of the older ones who still attended. Most of the others were younger than him now. The girls were being nice to Beth, inviting her to look at their hymn books to choose a song, and she snuck a look at him while he was watching her and he chuckled.

He'd started to wonder if he should stop attending the Singings, but it was nice to have Beth here.

"She's new," Benjie Yoder whispered, nudging Danny's arm. Benjie had just turned nineteen, so he was a little younger, but when a new girl came to a Singing, every guy there took notice unless he was already courting someone.

"That's Beth Peachy, Iris Peachy's granddaughter," Danny said. "And she came with me."

That was a hint for Benjie to look elsewhere if he was looking for a girlfriend.

"*Yah?*" Benjie looked impressed. "Are you driving her home too?"

"Sure am." Danny laughed.

Benjie grinned at him. "Just checking, because if you weren't, I'd sure try."

The warning was received. Danny didn't blame Benjie, but it did stoke up a little sense of protectiveness in him. Beth had come with him tonight, and he'd most certainly be driving her back . . . as friends, though. They weren't anything more, even though driving a girl home from a Singing was normally a date.

At least he had time with her. Maybe that would have to be enough.

When the Singing was over, they all chatted around the bonfires and toasted some marshmallows, and the boys and girls mingled.

Danny and Beth stood by one of the bonfires. The night had cooled off, and the bonfire smoke held the bugs away too. Beth rubbed her bare arms.

"Are you cold?" Danny asked.

"A bit."

Danny stepped closer and slid an arm around her, putting his hand over her other arm to help warm her up. She leaned into his side, and she felt like a breath of relief. Why did Beth Peachy have to be so troublesome and so perfect at the same time? She filled up a part of his heart that could never belong to another woman, and yet she wasn't the stable kind of woman he needed either.

"Remember when we came to that Singing one time when Zach drove us, and we snuck off on foot and got lost on the back roads?" Beth said.

Danny laughed and shook his head. "Whose idea was that? I think it was yours."

"I'm the bad influence." She chuckled. "I do think it was mine. But it was an adventure."

"Your *daet* was furious with me for that," Danny said. "And so was mine."

"We always had fun when we were hanging out together," she said. "Didn't we?"

"*Yah*, I guess we did." He looked down at her. The scent of her shampoo mingled with the bonfire smoke. "I would have followed you to the ends of the earth."

Did I say that out loud? His heart skipped a beat.

Beth looked up at him searchingly. "Really?"

"Uh . . ." He'd said it now, hadn't he? "*Yah*. I was smitten with you."

Smitten was the sweet way of saying it. He'd lain awake at night thinking about her. He'd repeated their conversations over and over in his head until he wasn't sure if they'd actually said those things or if he'd only wished it. He'd counted down the hours until he could see her again. He'd been quietly and obstinately in love with her.

Beth smiled then. "That's sweet. Would you still follow me anywhere?"

She was teasing. Danny looked back toward the fire—a safer focus right now. "Within reason."

"That's fair," she said, the laughter evaporating from her tone. "We aren't quite so young and foolhardy anymore, are we?"

"I guess not," he agreed. "But I'd still take you to a Singing and drive you around town. It's not quite the ends of the earth, but it's a nice time together, all the same."

Beth nudged his side with her arm. "It is a nice time."

The truth was, if only she'd commit to the faith, he'd do more than drive her around. He'd court her properly and build a solid Amish life with her. He'd work hard to provide for her, and he'd come home every night to her good cooking.

"Is anyone up for firelight volleyball?" one of the boys called.

Danny looked down at Beth, and she shook her head.

"Maybe I'm getting older, but I really don't want to play volleyball in the dark," she said with a laugh.

Neither did he. He was getting tired, and he'd rather have some time alone with Beth than sit with a group of younger people.

"Do you want to head home?" he asked.

"Sure." They moved away from the fire, making room for another couple to take their place, and Danny kept his arm around her as they headed back toward the buggies. It felt nice to hold her like this. As a teen, he'd dreamed of this kind of chance with Beth Peachy, and here he was.

But it wasn't the free and open chance at happiness he'd imagined would be his. Her heart wasn't quite that easy to claim, but his was still loyally hers.

I should be more careful, he thought.

When she left again, he'd rather not be heartbroken.

The next afternoon, after the majority of his work was done, Danny raked the last of the grass clippings into a pile in the middle of the back lawn. He'd been working hard to finish up by three, and he found his gaze moving toward the Peachy house as he bent down to gather up the fragrant pile of grass by handfuls and put them into the wheelbarrow.

Up the drive, he spotted an *Englischer* man. He stood halfway down the gravel lane, and he had a phone held out like he was taking pictures. He wore a pair of jeans and a cowboy hat. Was he a local? A neighbor? A tourist? Sometimes tourists would wander onto people's properties.

Danny straightened. "Hello!" he called.

The man startled, but he lowered his phone. He looked to be an older man—slim, with a mustache. For a moment, he simply met Danny's gaze, and there was defiance there. Who was this man?

"Can I help you?" Danny asked.

The man shook his head. "Nope. I'm fine. I was just looking around."

He lifted the phone again and took another photo—this one seemed to be of Danny, or at the very least had Danny in the middle of the shot. Was this an *Englischer* who didn't understand their values? Or maybe this was a neighbor and he'd come to document some complaint? That hadn't happened to the Lapps yet, though.

"This is private property," Danny called to the man.

"The sign up there says it's rental cabins." He lowered the phone.

"For paying customers, *yah*," Danny replied. "Were you interested in renting a cabin?"

The man looked like he might agree, then he shook his head. "No, not right now. Sorry to intrude."

A tourist, then. The man turned and headed back up the drive, and Danny eyed him. He didn't actually care about *Englischers* taking pictures of the lake or of Amish country. The pictures that bothered him were ones of people.

That was crossing the line. Like Zach taking pictures of their *mamm*. The Amish didn't believe in making "graven images," and photography fell under that umbrella. Some communities were more lax in those rules and said that so long as the Amish folks weren't posing and were just going about their business, it wasn't a problem. But Shepherd's Hill was more conservative in their view.

"Who was that?"

Danny turned to see Beth crossing the grass toward him. She wore a pink cape dress with a black apron and had a simple black purse over her shoulder. Her usually bare feet were now clad in black walking shoes.

"Just a guy taking pictures," Danny said. "Let me dump the grass clippings into the compost pile, and we can head out."

Danny dumped the clippings, then hitched the horse up to his buggy. His *mamm* came out with a short shopping list for him, and he pocketed it. Before too long, Danny and Beth were on their way toward town.

"Sometimes I wonder why people taking photos even matters," Beth said. "You know how the older people are so offended by it?"

Danny shot her a surprised look. "Really? You don't see the problem?"

"It isn't us taking the pictures. We aren't keeping photos. It's other people. We can't control them. They don't even believe what we do. Why does it matter?"

"Because we'd be cooperating with something we don't believe in. We'd be going along with making a graven image," he said.

"We'd simply not be making a scene about it," she replied.

Danny ran that over in his mind; while he could see her point, it still didn't sit right with him.

"The older generations made these rules for a reason," he said. "We're doing our best to abide by Gott's law, and to maintain a life that is close to him."

"My *Englisch* friend Cadence keeps telling me times change."

"Not with us."

"Oh? What about the ice house? The community used to need that ice for their iceboxes. Now we have propane-powered freezers and refrigerators. That changed."

"We still aren't using electricity, though," he countered. "And we aren't reliant on the *Englischer* system."

"Aren't we, though?" she pressed. "If you didn't have Tabitha, you'd have an *Englischer* vet. We need *Englischer* doctors, *Englischer* police when things get too big for us to handle. We need them to buy our wares. We're on our way to an *Englischer* library."

Danny remained silent. Even Zach was using Tabitha in his arguments, and he wasn't sure he liked Beth using her in the same vein.

"Tabitha came back repentant," Danny said, interrupting. "She had nothing but heartbreak out there past the fence. She came back, and she needs a way to contribute because she won't have a husband or *kinner* to support her. She has to support herself now. It's not some big victory. I heard her confess in front of the congregation."

Beth looked over at him, her cheeks pink. "I'm sorry. I don't mean to be contrary."

"You're just saying what you think." And he should take that seriously.

"I see that our way of life has some contradictions," she replied.

"I disagree."

"You don't see anything in our traditions that has . . . maybe lost its meaning over time?"

All Danny could see in his mind's eye was Zach sitting at their kitchen table and questioning the health of his favorite pie. What had Zach gained by jumping the fence? Zach was just angry now, and troublesome.

"No, I don't see how our beliefs have lost any meaning," Danny said, and he flicked the reins to get the horse to speed up to a trot. Hoofbeats rang against the asphalt in a steady rhythm. "If you look deeply enough at every single one of the rules in the *Ordnung*, there is a reason for it. We don't take photos because it stops us from vanity, and from putting more stock in an image taken of a person in a single moment than in a whole life lived, lessons learned, and a heart that is right with Gott. We don't bother with posing for a perfect picture. We aim for a Gott-pleasing life. Maybe we don't remember a face as well as we'd like once someone has been gone a long time, but we do remember the details that matter more—their heart, their character, the things they said. And when we stand for something and we ask others to respect our position, it's important that we don't cave to the pressure. One little change here, and another little change there, and before you know it, the Amish are hardly any different from anyone else. How do we stay the salt and the light in this world when we're just like everyone else? There are reasons, Beth. Good reasons. And when we spend our time picking holes in our own belief system, what do we have in the end? Just a hole-ridden bolt of cloth good for nothing, not even ourselves. And what would the *Englischers* gain by changing us? Nothing again! They wouldn't even care to visit, and we wouldn't be a good example of anything."

Danny hadn't really meant to say all that, but it had been stewing up inside of him ever since Zach's visit.

"Those are very good points, Danny."

"It's just . . . I hear this stuff a lot from Zach, and I think, if you don't believe in it, leave! And Zach did. But then he keeps coming back, trying to change our way of doing things. And why? What does he hope to gain?" Beth didn't answer, and Danny glanced over at her. He'd said way too much. "I didn't mean that you should leave, by the way."

"I'm waiting to decide until one path feels right," Beth said.

"Sometimes the right thing stays hard," he replied.

"I didn't say I needed it to feel easy," she shot back. "I need it to feel right. And that hasn't happened yet."

He focused on the road ahead. He was already battling his brother. He didn't need to battle Beth too. Beth was the sweet center of this summer, and he didn't want to ruin it.

"You were sure, when you got baptized," she added.

"*Yah*, I was," Danny said. "I still am."

Danny was the kind of man who needed those roots, and he didn't toy with the wisdom from generations past. But he also knew that he needed a woman who'd put her roots down right next to his, and who'd help keep him stable in the faith when he got buffeted too. He didn't want someone to encourage his doubt. He wanted someone to remind him of his certainty.

"I just want to be that sure," Beth said. She cast him a disarmingly vulnerable smile, and his heart skipped a beat. "I envy that."

Danny put the reins into one hand, then reached over and caught her hand in his. She squeezed his fingers in return, and he couldn't quite bring himself to let go.

When they came up to a stop sign, Danny had to release her hand to rein the horse in, and his hand felt cold where her fingers had been. After he'd looked both ways and they carried on again, she folded her hands in her lap.

Does she not want to hold my hand again?

Or maybe she wasn't even thinking about it. Maybe he could reach over and—

What was he even doing? He and Beth weren't courting. They weren't even talking about anything romantic between them, and all he could seem to think about was getting her hand back into his.

14

Beth found her gaze slipping toward Danny's broad, strong hands. He held both reins again, while just a minute ago, he'd been holding her hand . . . and it had felt so very nice. She hadn't been sure what to do with her hands when he let go, so she'd folded them in her lap—suddenly feeling rather awkward.

Why isn't he taking my hand again?

Had it just been a friendly gesture? Was she overthinking this? She probably was. She'd overthought everything with Luke back in Strasburg to the point that she'd been convinced he felt more for her than he did. Luke had held her hand once too. She didn't want to make the same mistakes again.

The Shepherd's Hill Public Library was situated away from the main street and the tourist section of town, down the road that led past the high school. School was out for the day, although it was still June, so it wasn't out for the summer yet, like the Amish *kinner* were. She eyed the big square building, wondering what it was like to join a crowd of strangers in getting an education. She'd gone to school in a one-room schoolhouse, taught by an older girl she knew already, and there were twenty-seven of them from first grade up to eighth. She couldn't imagine being surrounded by a huge crowd of teenagers every day.

But all the same, the *Englischer* kids had access to things like swim club and accounting classes, and Beth nursed a little bit of envy about that. Cadence told her that in high school they could join whatever team they qualified for. Cadence did drama, and they put on a high school musical. But if Beth had had that kind of opportunity, she would have tried out for the swim team. One of the girls from Cadence's high school had even made it to the American team for the Olympics.

But Beth was twenty-one now, and well past the age of high school. Besides, the Amish didn't compete—her *daet* had reminded her of that repeatedly. Gott gave them talents to use for his glory, and who knew how Gott would use her swimming? But trying to best another swimmer wasn't sharing Gott's love. It was prideful and accomplished nothing in the scope of eternity.

And yet . . . Beth still wondered how fast she was, how she would have done if she'd been allowed to compete. She pulled her mind away from those old longings. There was more than one way to make a fool of herself.

The library was located two blocks past the high school, and it was an old three-story brick building with an arch over the double front doors that had the library's name etched into concrete. This building had always been a library and always would be, by the looks of it.

There was plenty of buggy parking on one side of the lot, including a covered area for the horses. The other side of the lot was for cars, and this afternoon there were no other buggies there, but seven or eight *Englischer* vehicles.

Danny parked the buggy so that his horse was under the shelter.

"Look, I won't tell anyone what you find here," Danny said. "First and foremost, I'm your friend, okay? And whatever it is, my lips stay sealed."

"*Danke.*" She sucked in a stabilizing breath. "I do appreciate that, Danny."

"And maybe . . . you can extend me the same grace?"

"What are you going to be searching for?" she asked.

"My brother's social media," he replied.

"Oh . . ." She winced. "So we're both going to search for things we might not want to see."

Danny chuckled. "*Yah*, it looks that way. So, we keep each other's secrets today?"

She nodded soberly. "Agreed."

"Then let's head inside."

They made their way into the library—cool due to air conditioning, and quiet except for the sound of some children's laughter tinkling upstairs, where the kids' books were located. A sign indicated that there was a children's story hour going on right now. The main floor held the computers for public use on one end, and they headed in that direction.

There were two available computers nestled over to one side in relative privacy, and Beth and Danny headed over there. Danny pulled out his library card and typed in the number to sign in to the computer, and Beth slid into the seat.

"That's the browser. Click there," Danny said.

Beth wasn't completely comfortable with computers, but she understood the basics of using the mouse and doing Google searches. There were some scraps of paper and pencils nearby, and Danny handed her one of each.

"We can only use one computer at a time on my library card," he said. "You start."

"That hardly seems fair." She began to push her rolling chair back from the computer.

"It's fine," he said. "I'm going to take a little walk so you can search, and I'll be back in a few minutes."

This was generous of him, and she cast him a smile. He touched her shoulder, then ambled off, leaving her in solitude.

Beth wasn't exactly sure how to start, so she simply typed in her father's full name: Moses Abraham Peachy. Nothing came up. That didn't surprise her. Nothing came up for Mammi's name either. She typed in local scandals and the year her father was born. Nothing. She couldn't be specific enough.

Beth sighed.

Gott, am I doing the right thing by searching? Would it be better to wait on Mammi to tell me more?

But she couldn't trust that Mammi ever would, and knowing who you were directly related to was rather important. Besides, Gott didn't seem to be answering.

Next she typed in "Friesen Lake deaths" to see what came up. That brought a long list of articles from Canada about mineral deposits around a lake with the same name in Saskatchewan. There was a link from France . . . apparently, there was a lake with the same name there too. She sighed and refined her search to include Pennsylvania.

That brought up some hits that were more helpful.

"Fishing Excursion Almost Turns Deadly." That was a story from almost ten years ago about a young man whose boat capsized, and he had to swim to shore.

"Alcohol a Factor in Friesen Lake Death." That was from the same year. Some *Englischers* had been partying by the lake, and a teenaged girl drank too much and fell into the water. The death was ruled an accidental drowning, and the family told about the young woman's kindness, her hopes to compete in a regional soccer tournament that fall, and how everyone would miss her dearly.

A memory hovered at the edge of her mind . . . her *mammi* talking about a very sad accident in a letter she'd written to them. She'd told them about this accident, Beth was almost sure. Mammi had said that was why they must be very careful around lakes and why they should never drink alcohol. Beth had been about eleven or twelve at the time, so she didn't really recall much—just the lecture by letter. Mammi had meant well. If Beth remembered properly, her grandmother had sent a newspaper clipping of the story.

"The Deadliest Winter of 1908." That winter, there had been three Amish deaths during the ice harvest, and the article was a post on a Mennonite person's ancestry blog. Apparently, that winter three out of five brothers died in one terrible accident while harvesting ice. What exactly went wrong, they didn't know. They also noted that in 1912, a body was found in the lake that no one could account for.

That was an awfully long time ago, and Beth doubted any accidents from before Mammi's time would have impacted her very much.

The next article was "Boy's Death Ruled an Accident." It was a scan of a news story from forty-five years ago. An *Englischer* family had been in a boat on the lake when a storm whipped up, and all but one child made it to shore. A young boy drowned. It was a terrible tragedy when anyone died, but a child was worse. She could better understand her grandmother's respect for the lake.

Maybe Beth was simply being too stubborn. Maybe

Mammi's caution around this lake was simply from an accumulation of tragic deaths that had occurred over the years. Mammi would have been a young mother at that point, and she might have empathized deeply with those poor parents who had lost their son.

Who was to say what accident would have affected Mammi the most?

On the second page of the search hits, Beth spotted another story: "Amish Man Drowns." It was from a newspaper article dated fifty-six years ago—Beth had to do the mental math twice to be sure. It had been scanned on a personal blog.

Arden Bieler, aged twenty-three, drowned when swimming in the lake late one summer evening. According to the story, he'd gotten a cramp and went down. The lake, being exceptionally deep, had simply swallowed him up. Apparently, it had taken two days to recover the body that eventually came back to the surface and was discovered on shore. That thought sent a shiver down Beth's spine. The Amish community had pulled together to help the parents, and there had been a very large, very well-attended funeral that brought people from several different states to mourn the loss of this young man.

Fifty-six years ago . . . Mammi would have been a couple of years younger than Arden at age twenty-one—the same age Beth was now. The drowning happened at the end of August. Beth's father would be born late December that same year. Beth's heart hammered in her throat.

There was no proof of anything. Arden Bieler was just a young man from the Shepherd's Hill Amish community, but a little story was already patching itself together in Beth's mind that would explain her grandmother's emotional reaction to that lake. It was a heartbreaking tale about a young woman in love with a man who tragically drowned . . . whose body washed up on shore two days later.

What if Mammi hadn't known she was pregnant yet? Or maybe she did, and they'd been planning to get married that fall? Engagements were kept secret until a week or two before the actual wedding, so it was very possible for a couple to be engaged without anyone else knowing.

"Beth?" Danny slid back into the seat next to her.

Beth startled, and she looked over at Danny, her mind still spinning.

"Are you okay?" he asked.

She nodded. "We're keeping each other's secrets, right? Our lips are sealed?"

"Of course. I promise." His gaze flicked toward the screen, and she angled the monitor so that he could read the article displayed there. Danny leaned forward, his warm arm resting next to hers on the armrest of her chair. He was close enough that she could smell the scent of hay on his clothes. She could see some faint freckles on his cheek, and his eyelashes were longer than she'd realized. She'd never been quite this close to Danny before—even in the buggy or by the bonfire. When he leaned back again, she looked quickly away.

"Who is it?" he asked.

"A twenty-three-year-old Amish man who died at Friesen Lake a few months before my father's birth." She held her breath, waiting for his reaction.

Danny was silent, his brow furrowed. "Just for clarity . . . I don't want to be the one to suggest anything. This is very delicate, so who do you think Arden Bieler was?"

Danny was sweet that way—he knew the quagmire this story suggested.

"I think it's possible that he was my grandfather." She rubbed her hands over her arms, chilly now that he'd leaned back. "My *mammi* is terrified we'll drown in that lake, and she's told me that people have died there. I asked if she'd ever had her heart broken, and she avoided the question. I asked if she'd ever been married—" She swallowed.

"And?" he asked softly.

"She never was."

Maybe she'd never gotten that far with the man she loved—the father of her son. Maybe they'd had plans to be a family. Beth looked over at Danny cautiously. Would he judge her grandmother for this? He'd promised to keep her secrets, hadn't he? And she'd promised to keep his. But she was the one digging up family stories that her grandmother wanted to keep hidden.

"Oh, wow . . ." Danny nodded slowly. "So you think maybe this young man was your *daet's* father?"

She nodded. "I think it's possible. I mean, I grew up never once hearing a story about Daet's childhood. Maybe this is why. Maybe he was hiding the secret of his parentage."

"I'd understand if your *mammi* didn't want to talk about it," he said. "That would be incredibly personal."

"I would understand too," she agreed. "But don't you think it matters? If I'm a direct blood relative of the Bielers, shouldn't I know that? Shouldn't they?"

15

꩜

Generations back, young Amish people struggled with the same issues that young Amish people struggled with today. That was somewhat comforting to Danny. He knew that being pregnant out of wedlock would have been a huge problem for Iris, but she was no different than a young person today finding herself in a similar situation. Amish strictness was tempered by a streak of practicality. If a young unmarried couple found themselves in this situation, the church leadership insisted they get married. The baby would be born to married parents. Period.

Beth looked thoughtful, and she jotted down some information on a slip of paper.

"I think the truth is always better than a lie," Danny said quietly. "Your *mammi* loved your *daet* and raised him well. She did right by him. And who are we to judge our grandparents for mistakes they might have made in their youth?"

"*Yah!*" Beth's tension seemed to seep away. "I feel the same way. I think Mammi is probably afraid I'll judge her, but I won't. They raised us with very strict expectations, but maybe that was because they knew how easy it was to make those mistakes. But I still need them to trust me."

An *Englischer* woman with a little girl in tow came to a computer a few yards away from them, and Beth stood up.

"Your turn," she said.

They swapped seats. Suddenly his own little Internet search didn't seem so important anymore. Beth's was absolutely life shaking. His? He just wanted to see what his brother was up to—maybe see a picture of where his brother lived, or see him with his friends. Maybe he'd understand better then. For all of Danny's resistance to taking pictures of people, he understood that a picture could relay an awful lot. The irony was thick, and he felt a twinge of guilt about that. But as much as Beth needed to understand her family, Danny needed to understand his brother.

"It won't take me long. I just wanted to check," Danny said.

Danny typed in his brother's name, and a few hits popped up on social media. The videos that popped up caught him by surprise, though. There were several—all of which showed a frozen image of his brother's face. He clicked on a thumbnail, and the linked video popped up and started playing.

"Hi, this is Zachariah Lapp. If you enjoy this video, I hope you'll follow my channel. This is where we talk about the truth about the Amish—the stories they won't tell you . . ."

Danny pressed pause, his heart hammering. The truth about the Amish? Or the truth—as his brother saw it—about their family? He looked over at Beth, and her eyes were wide.

"It's okay," she said. "I've heard of some people doing this. He's not the only one. You're better off seeing the worst of it."

Danny put the volume down a little more and pressed play again. Zach had some videos of the family property. He didn't show the sign that said the name of their business, but he did show the cabins and the lake. Anyone local—even *Englischers*—would know exactly who they were.

"My Amish family has a lot of trouble accepting my girlfriend," Zach said. "She's not Amish, so she'll never be good enough in their eyes. I know it, and she knows it. My parents tried to be polite, but they often speak in Pennsylvania Dutch around her and treat her like an outsider."

"That isn't true," Danny said. "Our problem is with Zach, not Meghan."

"My mother cooks with lard and full fat cream every day," Zach went on. "I know that most of you would wonder about the health effects of that kind of cooking. My mother doesn't know any different, and it hurts her feelings if I want to eat more healthfully. I have a hard time digesting the food when I go home to visit."

He didn't digest Amish food well? Even Danny felt the offense of that statement. He'd never had any digestive issues, and their *mamm* was a terrific cook. Zach hadn't been gone for more than a year, and Mamm always tried to give Zach his favorites when he came by, even at short notice.

Zach described more of the traditional Amish cooking and then signed off, saying, "If you'd like to hear about the gender roles in my old Amish community, I'll post about that next. Follow me."

Danny looked at the date the video was posted. "He made this right after his visit to see us."

"I wonder how involved Meghan is with these videos," Beth said.

Danny's mind went back to Meghan standing outside, her

back to the house, waiting for Zach to come to the truck. She'd looked miserable. Would she want to be part of ruining his family's reputation? Or was there a part of her that wanted to belong?

"I don't know," Danny admitted. "There are . . . like twenty of these videos. He's been doing this for a while." He scanned the titles. "Amish Refusal of Medical Advice," "Women in Amish Romantic Relationships," "Amish Work Ethic," "Amish and Voting" . . .

"He seems to have a lot of followers," Beth said. "There are thousands. Are there that many *Englischers* who dislike us that much?"

"I don't know." Danny shrugged.

Was it dislike or just curiosity? It was hard to tell, but Zach's tone in his video hadn't been exactly positive.

"That one looks like . . . you." Beth pointed at a video at the bottom of the screen. It was the one about Amish work ethic, and the still shot showed an Amish man walking away from the camera. Danny clicked on it.

There was more description of Amish ways. "Amish believe that hard work is a way to purify their characters. You'll never find a lazy Amish person. They work from about four in the morning until after sunset. Every part of the Amish life is designed to create work. But without more than an eighth-grade education, they can't make much money." Another shot of Danny walking from a distance. "Even if a kid is really good at math, for example, and might be able to get a degree in engineering or physics, he wouldn't have those options. It's manual work for life."

"Is that you—the one who's good at math?" Beth asked quietly.

Danny shook his head, his gaze locked on the screen as

the camera panned their property again. "No, that's Toby," he replied.

Toby was so good at math that Daet got him to add up lists of numbers in his head for him when he was doing the finances. Toby's school friends called him the "Amish Calculator," and even as a boy, he'd helped in planning barn raisings, doing the math to estimate how much wood they needed to purchase.

The video ended, and Danny logged out of the computer.

"You don't want to see any more?" Beth asked.

He shook his head. "No. I think I've seen enough."

"Did you have any idea he was filming you?" Beth asked.

He shook his head again. "No." And the realization felt like more than a betrayal. "Let's head back."

Danny's mind was in a knot—like when he tried to help his *mamm* with laundry and the wringer washer ended up tangling his pants into a vicious twist. He and Beth walked back out, and it felt good to have her next to him. Normally this kind of embarrassment would be better in solitude, but Beth's nonjudgmental presence next to him was comforting.

They got back into the buggy, and he guided the horse out of the parking lot and onto the town's street again.

"I really had no idea," he said at last.

"At least my family isn't the only one with secrets." She cast him a reassuring smile. "Danny, I've heard about those kinds of videos online. There were rumors about someone in a neighboring community who was making them a few years ago. Zach isn't the only one. He isn't even the most successful one."

Danny sent back a wan smile. "*Danke*. That actually helps."

"I guess no one in the community knows about it yet?" she asked.

"I don't think so. The bishop would have come to visit if people knew. And that hasn't happened."

Would the bishop think that he'd been cooperating with his brother, since he was in the videos? Would the community recognize that Zach had acted on his own?

"I feel kind of exposed, though—complete strangers seeing me walk around our property. It's creepy."

Beth nodded. "It is. Your brother should never have done that." She was silent for a moment. "He probably thought you'd never find out."

That didn't make Danny feel better.

"Do you ever wonder what you would have done with yourself if you'd been born *Englisch* instead of Amish?" Beth asked.

Danny thought about it as he reined in at a stop sign, then flicked the reins again to keep moving.

"Nope."

"Really?"

He gave her a questioning look. "I'd be learning another business, I guess."

"What were you good at in school?" she asked.

"I don't know. I got okay grades. I liked helping out at home more."

"Hmm." She nodded.

"What about you?" he asked.

"I would have joined a swim team," she said.

Danny hadn't expected her to have a ready answer, but somehow that made sense. "Are you that good?"

"I don't know," she replied. "I might be. There was a lady who told my *daet* I should be doing competitive swimming, and of course he said we Amish don't compete. But it did make me wonder. I might be pretty good. I've kept up swimming too. As soon as the lake back home is warm enough, I swim all spring, summer, and into the fall too."

"I guess I never had anything that set me apart like that," Danny admitted.

But Toby did. Toby had a skill that was quite remarkable, even though being remarkable wasn't encouraged with the Amish. Maybe he should be thankful that he'd never been good enough at anything to make leaving tempting.

"I'm not agreeing with Zach or condoning what he did," Beth said. "But he did have a point in that if we're good at something that doesn't fall easily inside the fence, we have to give it up."

"Toby's math skills have been helpful at home, though. He adds up receipts and does the math for building plans," he said. "His skills contribute."

Beth didn't answer, and he didn't expound upon it. She knew the Amish faith as well as he did. But the closeness of their drive to the library seemed to have drifted now that they were on their way home, and Danny found himself wondering if he was the last person his age who simply loved the Amish life that had been handed down to him.

Danny dropped off Beth at her grandmother's house, and when she went back into the house, he felt a sinking feeling of disappointment. They were very different people, he and Beth. He'd had feelings for her ever since they were *kinner*, but as adults, it wasn't so simple anymore. But then, nothing seemed to be simple—not his connection to Beth, not his plan to start his own business, and not his relationship with his brother.

He continued home. He knew he'd have to fill his parents in on what he'd discovered about his brother, but he didn't want to start with his *mamm*. Her reaction would just be sadness. Daet, though, might have a solution, and that was what Danny wanted right now.

His *daet* was outside chopping wood when Danny got there. He unhitched the buggy and sent the horse out to pasture, then ambled over to where his *daet* was chopping, a log splintering as it cracked in two.

"Daet . . ."

His father stopped. "Hi, Danny. Why so sober?"

The story didn't take long. He explained as best he could what the videos were, and how many people seemed to be watching them. He told about the content—his brother's complaints and explanations about the Amish life. He told about his report on how they'd treated Meghan too. When he was done, his father dropped the ax next to the woodpile and looked out over the lake.

"Were we rude to Meghan?" his father asked after a moment. "I did tell her directly that we didn't raise Zach to live together without marriage."

"I didn't think we were rude. Shocked maybe, but not rude." But deep down, Danny felt like maybe they had been. Not intentionally, but they'd certainly not succeeded in making her feel welcome.

"We may have been," Daet said. "We did talk in Pennsylvania Dutch when we didn't want her to understand. I thought we were protecting her from getting upset, but I can understand how she might have seen it differently."

"Daet, what about the rest of it?" Danny asked. "He's denigrating everything we believe!"

"The rest is just argument and jibber-jabber," his father replied. "But Meghan is a human being, and if we've offended, we need to make it right."

"How?" Danny asked.

His father sighed and shook his head. "I don't know. I'll discuss it with your *mamm*. She's wise in these matters."

"He thinks Toby should leave here and do something more important and better paying," Danny said.

"Better paying? That's very possible," Daet replied. "But more important? What can be more important than showing outsiders what a good Christian life looks like? We are a good example, an influence. We don't know how many seeds we've planted in the hearts of *Englischers* who were drawn to our rentals out of curiosity alone. I've dedicated my whole life to this, and I've never regretted that choice."

Daet made it all seem so logical and simple. And yet . . . it wasn't always simple, was it? Beth's family had complications they'd have to work through, and so did Danny's. Behind the scenes in every good family, there were hardships no one imagined.

16

⚬⚬⚬

Tabitha tied the back of her black apron and scooped up her medical bag off the Peachy family's gravel drive. She followed Jonas past the house. A kerosene light shone from the kitchen, this time of day being light enough outdoors but downright dim inside. The sun was low, casting rose-gold light over the rolling fields. Cattle were settling in for the night—some lying down and chewing their cud, and others still peacefully grazing. It was the time of evening when people sat on their porches, and when an Amish family started to unwind from a busy day and enjoy each other's company.

"*Danke* for coming, Tabitha," Jonas said, breathing hard as they hurried down the well-beaten path that led to the Peachy family's cow barn. Jonas always walked briskly, and Tabitha had to break into a jog half the time to keep up. But she could appreciate the rush right now. Calves waited on no one.

Behind them, Mary Peachy was unhitching the buggy for them. There was no time to waste. Tabitha did note that the grass around the front of the barn had been recently mowed,

151

and the chicken coop had what looked like a new shingled roof. The Peachys were a well-off family, and they took good care of their animals.

Tabitha had been cleaning up after dinner when Jonas had pounded on their door, breathless and anxious. A cow was having trouble delivering a breach calf, which meant the baby was coming out tail first, and the hooves and head were all pointed the other direction.

"I tried pushing the calf back up and finding the hooves, but I couldn't get it," he said for the seventh or eighth time already. As a rancher, he knew how to deal with most calving complications.

"Don't feel bad," she said. "Sometimes it's harder to fix."

Sometimes they lost a good cow in delivery too. Or the calf. Or both. But Tabitha was already running scenarios in her mind, trying to plan ahead.

Gott, give me wisdom.

It was the prayer she always sent up whenever she went on a veterinarian call. His eye was on the sparrow, and on the cattle too.

The barn door flung open, and Nathaniel Peachy waved them in. Nathaniel was a slim man in rubber boots and a dirt-smeared white shirt with the sleeves rolled up to his elbows. He hadn't been exactly thrilled to welcome an Amish woman veterinarian, but it looked like he was willing to overlook that in the face of an emergency.

"Where is the cow?" Tabitha asked.

"In the last stall."

"I need her in the head gate," Tabitha said briskly. "Otherwise, I'll get trampled."

The cow bellowed, and Tabitha picked up her pace, heading in her direction. Every second counted at a time like this.

"Jonas, open the door to the corral." She knew this property well, having come for several veterinarian calls already. "And, Nathaniel, we need her up on her feet. If she stays lying down like that, I can't get any leverage to get that calf out."

At this point in a delivery, it was going to take muscle to get the calf's body aligned for delivery and then to pull the animal out of the birth canal. Contractions alone weren't going to do the job.

Nathaniel shot her a surprised look. *Nee*, he wasn't used to a woman giving orders in his own barn, and Tabitha knew that.

"We don't have time for me to quietly and respectfully explain the next few steps," Tabitha said. "I apologize for my tone, Nathaniel, but please, every second counts if we're going to save your cow."

The older man muttered something, but he and Jonas did get to work hauling open the rolling door and prodding the cow up to her feet.

"Come on, girl," Tabitha said, clapping her hands sharply. "Let's move!"

The cow lumbered forward, and Tabitha could see the calf's tail peeking out the back of the cow. That was a dangerous sign. Normally, feet were visible—either front or hind.

"We had her in the head gate before," Jonas said as he pushed the cow back toward the restraint. "She wasn't doing well, so we put her in the stall."

"*Yah*, that was a good plan until I could get here," Tabitha said. "I'll work as fast as I can."

She pulled a plastic sleeve out of her bag and pushed her hand into it. This would protect her clothes—mostly. This was still going to be a messy job. She let the men get the cow into the chute that ended in a head gate, and when the restraint clanged shut, she took a moment for a deep, calming breath, moved the cow's tail aside, and plunged her plastic-sleeved arm into the cow's birth canal.

The cow mooed in irritation and stamped her feet, but Tabitha stayed focused, moving her hand along the rump of the calf and forward until she felt a leg. The calf had come too far down the birth canal, and if it stayed like this, the cow and calf would die.

"All right," Tabitha said. "Now I'm going to push this calf forward, but I might need you to finish it, Jonas. Your arms are longer than mine. There's another sleeve in my bag."

Jonas pulled out the plastic sleeve and put it on. Then Tabitha put her hand against the calf's rump and started to push steadily forward. The tail disappeared. This would hurt—there was no doubt—but anything else and the cow would die an excruciating death trying to calve in breach. So the cow bellowed, and Tabitha continued pushing that baby back into the mama.

"I'm sorry, I'm sorry, I'm sorry . . ." she murmured between her gritted teeth. She had the baby as far as she could push on her own. "Jonas, I'm going to pull my arm out, and I want you to do what I was doing and push that baby another few inches, okay?"

Jonas stood next to her, and when she pulled her hand free, he pushed his into the birth canal. Nathaniel stood to the side, watching closely. The cow looked exhausted. There was no saying how long she'd been laboring with no progress because of the breach position, and that would drain the animal's strength.

"Okay," he said. "I think it's done."

"My turn." She took over then. The calf was in a better position, and she grabbed a back leg and pulled the hoof toward her into the birth canal. She had to do the same thing on the other side, getting the other hoof. This was going to be a backward delivery, but the baby would come out.

Tabitha got a good grip on one leg and pulled, throwing her weight back. The calf came forward. She paused, waiting on another contraction, and when it came, she pulled again. Tabitha stopped to breathe as the contraction ceased, and she looked up to see Mary Peachy leaning against the rail of the corral, watching.

"Good evening!" Tabitha called.

"Evening," Mary replied.

As another contraction began, Tabitha grabbed hold of the calf by the shanks and heaved forward. This time, she didn't stop with the contraction. They were too close to getting this calf out.

"Jonas, help pull!" she said, and Jonas took over, grabbing the calf's legs and tugging hard.

"Steady . . . steady . . ." Tabitha could see the umbilical cord now, and the fact that this was a bull calf. And with another pull, the calf slipped free and hit the ground.

That always seemed like such a cruel welcome to the world—a four-foot drop to the hard ground—but it was helpful to get the calf startled enough to take a first breath.

Tabitha grabbed a handful of hay and started to rub down the calf, clearing away mucus. She felt the face, pulling mucus away from the mouth and nose, and he moved. She sent up a silent prayer of thanks.

"You're alive, little guy," she said with a grin. "That's a good first step!"

She'd been half afraid the birth would have been too much and the calf would be stillborn, but this was wonderful news.

"A bull calf?" Mary asked, sliding through the rails and coming over to get a closer look.

"*Yah*. He looks like he's okay too," Tabitha replied.

Mary squatted down with a handful of hay, and she helped to clean the calf off. That freed up Tabitha to circle around and check on the cow. She was looking more alert already, now that the birth was over.

"Hey there, big girl," Tabitha said softly. "You did good. You've got a baby."

"It's her first," Jonas said.

Tabitha looked up to see Jonas peeling that sleeve off. She did the same, although both of her hands were messy now.

"She looks like she's doing fine," Tabitha said. "We'll need to get them into a stall together so they can bond, though. And she needs fresh water. She'll be thirsty."

If they didn't isolate the two together, the cow might not realize she had a baby to take care of. Once bonded, cows were excellent mothers. Until that bonding happened, though, it could be hit or miss.

"Let's just get that stall opened up for them," Jonas suggested.

They carried the calf into a corner of the stall where he'd be safe to start out. Tabitha gave him a dose of calf paste, which was a colostrum supplement to help the calf get some antibodies started. Then they released the cow from the chute and herded her into the stall with her calf. For a couple of minutes, the cow just stared at the calf, then back at them in mild confusion.

They lit three kerosene lanterns to get some light now that the sky outside had turned dusky, and the added light seemed to help give the cow some extra energy.

"You have a baby," Tabitha said. "Go on, now. You've got a job to do."

The cow sniffed at the calf then, and the calf lifted his damp head up to sniff back. He struggled to stand, then collapsed back down to the straw-covered floor.

"*Danke* for your help, Tabitha," Nathaniel said. "It was much appreciated. I feared I'd lose my cow."

And he might have if she'd arrived just ten minutes later.

"I'm glad I could help," Tabitha replied. "Nathaniel, I want to apologize for any offense I may have given. I know that it's a difficult balance to have me as the veterinarian, but I want you to know I meant no disrespect."

"*Nee*, it's fine." Nathaniel gave her a faint smile. "You might be half the size of a snow pea, but you make up for it with brain. Jonas and I couldn't get that calf back up the birth canal on our own."

"It has to do with the angle." She tried to demonstrate with her hands, then let them drop. "*Danke*. I'm truly glad I could help."

When Tabitha had finished cleaning up, she said good-bye to Nathaniel and Mary, and she and Jonas headed back out into the darkening evening. Jonas would take her home now, and then everyone could rest.

"You're quite impressive, you know," Jonas said as he led the horse from the stable and out to be hitched up.

The sun had dipped below the horizon, and the sky glowed red in the west, a handful of stars pricking through the warm gray expanse. Tabitha waited, her leather medical bag at her feet. Jonas worked quickly. In their friendship, she'd learned that Jonas preferred to just hitch up on his own, and Tabitha wasn't about to complain.

"I thought your *daet* would be mad I ordered everyone around," she said.

"It's your job, Tabby."

"I know that, and you know that, but sometimes it can be delicate," she replied, but then they exchanged a smile. He understood.

Jonas finished with the horse, and Tabitha put her bag into the buggy first, then hoisted herself up. He hopped up on the other side and took the reins. From across the farmyard, Tabitha could see lanterns bobbing around through the barn windows as Nathaniel and Mary finished up with the cows.

Jonas flicked the reins, and the horse pulled them around and up the drive.

"You know, the funny thing is, I'm finding some acceptance with the farmers now," Tabitha said. "Your *daet* respects me as a veterinarian. The other farmers are learning that I'm good at my job, and they aren't acting uncomfortable when I work now. But I'm still struggling to find my footing with the women."

"I have no advice there," Jonas said.

She smiled. "That's okay. I guess I can prove myself as a veterinarian. I have skills that the men can see, and that they need. But proving yourself to women—not as a veterinarian, just as a fellow Amish woman—is harder."

"Are they mean to you?" he asked, casting her a sidelong look.

"*Nee*, not mean. They're just distanced. I'm different. There's no getting around it."

Crickets chirped from the fields, and Tabitha leaned back in the seat.

"Are you still brushing up on your quilting skills?" he asked.

"*Yah*, I am." She laughed softly. "And before you tease me, I'm getting better at it. Rose has been teaching me. Amanda's busy up there on the hog farm, though. She says I should have paid closer attention when we were *kinner* and Mamm was teaching us."

"She isn't wrong," Jonas teased.

"Oh, hush." She laughed. "*Yah*, I should have paid closer attention. But ten years of no quilting, no sewing, or knitting, or anything . . . your fingers forget."

"You're good at other things," Jonas replied. "It's forgivable."

"Not to the women, it's not," she replied, and she nudged Jonas's arm. "I'm glad our friendship isn't based on my quilting abilities."

"You'll find your place, Tabby," he said, the joking dropping from his tone. "You will."

Jonas reached over and gave her hand a quick squeeze, then he released her fingers just as quickly. It was a warm, friendly gesture, and she felt a wave of longing for simpler times.

But there were consequences to having left the community for so long. Things changed. People changed. And while Tabitha hadn't realized how much she'd changed in those years away, she was finding that out now.

"*Danke*, Jonas," she said quietly, and when she looked over at him, he glanced over at the same time and their eyes met. For two heartbeats, they just looked at each other. Jonas was a handsome man—that was easy enough to see—but when he looked at her like that, she saw something deeper. She saw the man inside of him—the Jonas most people didn't get to see. He not only understood her, but he liked her. And she felt the same way about him. With his warm gaze locked on her like that, her pulse sped. Tabitha looked away first.

She turned toward the window and watched the moon hanging low in the sky. "I'll find my place," she said, trying to sound casual again. "But the women's respect will come when I prove I can quilt. You'll see."

But a small part of her heart closed around the fact that Jonas didn't need her to fill any traditional place in the community for him to like her. And that meant more to her than he'd ever know, or that she'd ever tell him.

17

The next evening, Goldie lay in a pool of sunlight on the floor near Mammi's feet. The old dog had been considerably more limber lately, and she dozed.

But Beth had been thinking about the news stories she'd dug up at the library ever since she'd returned. She hadn't wanted to say anything right away because she didn't want to upset her grandmother unduly, and sitting here in the cross breeze, she decided it was time to ask her questions.

"Mammi, I went to the library with Danny yesterday," Beth began.

"Hmm . . ." Mammi's knitting needles clicked as she worked, a worn piece of paper sitting next to her with the pattern written out in that shorthand that made perfect sense to advanced knitters. *Click, click, click . . .*

"I was looking up the history of Friesen Lake," Beth went on. "And there were quite a few accidents here. I can see why you're careful."

"It's a dangerous lake," Mammi agreed quietly. "We must respect forces that are stronger than we are." She stopped and put a finger on the pattern page, pursing her lips. Then she went back to count her stitches, her lips moving silently.

Beth's gaze went out the window. From here, they could see the drive that led up to the road, and the vegetable garden with its leafy rows. The lake wasn't within sight, and somehow, it made the questions easier to ask.

"Mammi, did you know a boy named Arden Bieler?" she asked.

Mammi's fingers stilled. "Why?"

"I just wondered. A newspaper article said he drowned in the lake."

Mammi lowered her knitting. "That happens sometimes. It's why I told you to be careful and not to swim there. It's incredibly deep."

"*Yah*, I can see that," Beth said. "But did you know him? Personally? He would have been your age, wouldn't he?"

"He was older."

"But not by much." Beth had done the math.

"Two years." Mammi met her gaze.

"Did you . . . Were you . . . Was he more than a friend?" Beth felt her own cheeks warm at the question.

"He took me driving," Mammi said, and she smiled faintly. "I liked him a lot. He'd drive me home after Singing, and he'd come visit me with my parents and we'd all eat popcorn together. My *mamm* and *daet* liked him too."

"So he was your boyfriend, Mammi!"

"Oh, we didn't call it that when I was young," Mammi said. "We had friends, and we had fiancés. Nothing in between. He was a friend."

"Did you love him?" Beth asked.

Mammi was silent, and she picked up her knitting again, counting those stitches.

"I told you how I felt about Luke," Beth said. "Was this something similar?"

"Luke wasn't the right one for you, dear," Mammi said. "The right one will choose you without any hesitation."

"Did Arden choose you?" Beth pressed.

"He never mentioned marriage. But he took me driving, and he held my hand, and he called me the most beautiful girl he'd ever met." Mammi shrugged weakly. "Once upon a time, back before my wrinkles and my white hair, I was a pretty girl."

"Mammi, I didn't know about that!" Beth said.

"It might be hard to believe now."

"No, Mammi, I have no problem believing you were pretty! I meant about a boyfriend. Because that's what we'd call it today in a more liberal community. He'd have been your boyfriend."

"Well, he died. So it hardly matters."

"You must have been crushed."

"We all were. His parents most of all. His mother just . . . withered."

"Did anyone know you'd been special to him?"

"A few of my friends knew." Mammi's knitting needles started to work again. "But it's in the past now. It was a very long time ago, and while I cared for him, we never did get married. I got to grow old, and his life ended in his youth. Sometimes that's how things work out."

Her words were matter-of-fact, but Mammi's eyes misted, and she had to stop knitting.

"Did you find it hard to get to know another man after Arden died?" Beth asked hesitantly.

"Well, there wasn't really anyone else my age who was showing interest, dear. I was a pretty enough girl, but the other boys already had fiancées. I settled in to help my *aent* here at the lake house. Back then, she sold vegetables at a roadside stall, and she did a lot of quilting and baking for the Amish Market. So I helped. The quilts could fetch quite a lot of money, even back then. That's why my *aent* left this place to me when she passed away. I suppose she thought I could use a roof over my head."

A knock on the door drew both of their attention, and Mammi set her knitting aside and pushed herself to her feet.

"Mammi . . ." The story had gone off the rails, or at least off the track that Beth had been hoping to follow.

Mammi looked back, her eyebrows raised questioningly.

"It's okay," Beth said with a smile. "I wonder who's at the door."

The conversation was over, it seemed, but Beth knew a little bit more about her grandmother's heart. Once, a long time ago, Mammi had been in love with a young man named Arden Bieler. And he'd died. That's all Beth knew for certain right now. But she had to wonder if this Arden Bieler—who had never mentioned marriage, but who had obviously cared a great deal about Mammi—was the man who'd fathered her *daet*.

This wasn't easy for Mammi to talk about, and Beth knew that because she'd never breathed a word about this before. But she was sharing more now, and Beth felt the honor of hearing Mammi's story. It felt like a growing trust. They'd get there. She could feel it.

Beth followed Mammi to the door, and when Mammi pulled it open, Danny stood there with a basket of muffins held out in front of him like a shield.

"Good evening, Iris," Danny said. "These were left over

from the Sunday church meal, and my *mamm* wanted to share some with you, if you'd like some."

"Oh? What do we have?" Mammi said, ushering Danny into the house. "Are those blueberry?"

"*Yah*, there are blueberry and some cranberry orange, my *mamm* says."

"This is very kind. Tell your *mamm danke* from me," Mammi said.

Danny's gaze flicked over Mammi's shoulder, and he met Beth's with a faint smile. He was here for her, and she couldn't help but smile back. They'd been finding ways to spend time together—just as old friends, she'd been telling herself—but she found her pulse speeding up when he found an excuse to come by.

"Do you have time for a walk?" Danny asked, addressing Beth.

Outside, Beth could see that clouds were rolling in, but the cool air was welcome as it whisked past Danny and into the overwarm kitchen. Would it be all right to leave Mammi alone for just a few minutes?

"Do you mind if I walk a little bit, Mammi?" Beth asked her grandmother. "I could use some fresh air. I won't be too long. I'll stay within earshot if you need to call me."

Mammi was setting the muffins out onto a platter, and she cast Beth a smile. "Of course not, dear. Be careful by the water."

"Always, Mammi."

And she now understood a little better why Mammi worried about that lake. She'd lost so very much to those watery depths. Could she even swim? That thought had only occurred to Beth now as she and Danny headed outside together and the screen door clapped shut behind them.

Beth had never seen her grandmother so much as touch her feet to lake water.

"Today, my *mamm* got a visit from one of her friends. The fact that I had my arm around you at the Singing is already a big piece of gossip," he said. "I'm sorry."

Beth chuckled. "Is that going to cause trouble for you?"

"For me?" Danny grinned. "I was worried about you."

Beth rolled her eyes. "The worst part would be my mother getting her hopes up if someone wrote some gossip back to her in a letter."

"Is your *mamm* hoping you find someone while you're here?" Danny asked, his tone turning more cautious.

"My *mamm* is hoping I find a husband every time I leave the house." She laughed.

"*Yah*, mine wants me married too."

"They mean well," Beth said. "They want us to be happy and settled."

"Mine wants to make sure I don't end up like Zach," Danny said.

They headed around the house and back down toward the lake. Danny's sleeve brushed against her arm as they came to a narrow part of the path.

"Go ahead." He put a hand on the small of her back and nudged her forward, and she couldn't help but feel a little flutter at his touch.

She stepped onto the beach first, and Danny joined her. Gray clouds tumbled in from the west, blotting out the evening sun and whipping her dress around her calves. The lake went from glittering in the light to a dull gray as a cloud slipped over the sun. Beth stepped closer to Danny, his warm arm pressed against hers.

"My grandmother knew that young Amish man who drowned here fifty-odd years ago," Beth said.

"She knew him?" He was silent for a moment. "I suppose that stands to reason."

"They were special friends."

Danny's gaze flicked toward her, and for some reason, she felt some heat in her cheeks. That was private information —or at least it was now. Once upon a time, people had known.

"Was she there when he drowned?"

"She didn't say." Beth sucked in a deep breath.

"And this man who drowned . . ." Danny lowered his voice. "Was he . . . ?"

Was Arden Bieler her grandfather? That was the question, wasn't it?

"I'm not sure," she replied. "The timing would be right, but she hasn't said he was anything more than a special friend. She did say that he'd never once mentioned marriage. So that doesn't sound like it, does it? But she's been trusting me with more of the story, and I think we'll get there eventually."

"Imagine how hard it would be to tell something so personal to one of your nieces or nephews," Danny said. "Let's say you had to sit down with a judgmental twelve-year-old and tell her something mean you'd done."

"Am I the judgmental twelve-year-old in this scenario?" She chuckled.

"*Yah*, compared to your grandmother, you are." He nudged her arm teasingly. "But you know what I mean, right? We haven't lived a fraction of the time she has, and yet you need to hear her most private stories."

"I know," she agreed. "It would be embarrassing, and

humbling, and I'd avoid it. So it might take a bit more time, but I do think Mammi will tell me what I need to know."

"I think so too," he replied.

The wind gusted around them, the sky steadily darkening.

"Would you always love this life, even if something big changed?" Beth asked. "What if someone betrayed you deeply? What if this community fell apart? What if you didn't have your family around you anymore?"

"Do you mean, what if I found out that I'd been lied to about my parents or about my family history?" he asked, and his compassionate gaze met hers.

"*Yah*, something like that."

"Isn't our faith something different though?" he asked. "It's about Gott, not about people."

"Faith in Gott, *yah*," she agreed. "But our baptism is a lifelong vow to the church. Can we break it later? I suppose. But it's probably better not to swear an oath like that at all than to swear it knowing that you may break it later."

"I like to think that the church would be my comfort in hard times like that," he said.

He ran a hand over her arm just as a fat raindrop fell next to his fingers, followed by another one on her cheek. The wind rushed through the trees overhead. The rain was starting, and Danny had farther to get home than she did.

"You want your family stories to reassure you," Danny said, planting a hand on his head to keep his straw hat in place. "Right?"

"Maybe I do," she admitted.

She wanted them to sit her down and tell her that the Amish way of life was good and right. She wanted them to tell her a family story that proved it. Instead, there were regrets and secrets.

"Maybe it's what you do with these family secrets that matters most," he said. "Not every story in the Bible was for us to emulate. Some were meant to teach us what to avoid. Our parents and grandparents weren't perfect. Sometimes they've earned their wisdom the hard way."

Danny took a step away from her, but his warm gaze held hers. "I have to get back."

And she wished he'd stay—even with the wind snapping her skirt and the sky growing ever darker with the clouds rolling in. But she had to get back to Mammi too.

"*Yah*, me too," she said as rain came in those big, fat drops.

"I'll see you later," he called, turning to run down the path toward home.

Thunder boomed overhead as the rain began to fall harder, pattering against the rocky shore. Beth ducked her head against the rain as she headed toward the kitchen door.

Beth startled as Tabitha came around the house at the same time.

"Hi, Beth!" Tabitha called.

"Hi!" Beth jogged up and pushed open the door for Tabitha. "Come in, come in, before you get drenched!"

Tabitha pressed inside after Beth, and they banged the door shut just as a bolt of lightning lit up the sky. Goldie woofed a greeting, but when a boom of thunder rattled the windows, she whined and crept closer to Mammi, who sat at the kitchen table with a mug of hot tea in front of her.

"Hello, Tabitha," Mammi said with a smile. "So nice to see you. Are you here for Goldie?"

"*Nee*, Iris, I'm here to visit you," Tabitha said. "I didn't get to chat with you after service the other day, so I wanted to come by and say hi. I didn't expect this deluge, though."

Tabitha was coming by to show Mammi some care, and Beth was grateful. They all turned and looked out the window then. The rain was coming down in sheets now, whipped by the wind. All Beth could think was that she hoped Danny had gotten inside by now.

This looked like a storm that meant business.

18

Tabitha got her horse into the Peachy stable—a much safer place for her than outside under the buggy shelter. She was thankful now that she'd left Fritz at home with his proper feed for his sensitive belly. The milk cow stood as close to the stable as she could, and Tabitha led her inside, too, and gave her hay and water to wait out the storm.

When she got back into the house again, Beth had stoked up a fire in the wood stove, and Iris had a platter of muffins and a pot of hot tea waiting.

"I had no idea we were expecting a storm," Tabitha said, and she shook her damp skirt as she stood in front of the stove. Had she known a storm was coming, she would have stayed home. These roads were treacherous enough in rain, let alone a blowing storm like this one. "I put your milk cow into the stable too. I hope you don't mind."

"*Danke*," Beth said earnestly, joining her at the stove. She wasn't as wet as Tabitha was, but she'd made a dash through the rain too.

"Here," Iris said, handing each of them a muffin. "No reason you have to go hungry while you dry off."

The visit was a pleasant one. Iris seemed happy to just sit and listen to Tabitha and Beth chat. Beth was curious about Tabitha's story—how she left the Amish for Michael, went to school, listened to the lavish encouragement she got from the *Englischer* teachers who told her how special her scholastic abilities were . . . She'd told the story many times now, explaining how it all happened and how she'd been excited to see how far she could go. She didn't tell people that she wasn't completely sorry that she'd left, though. That was a small, conflicted knot inside of her, because if she'd never gone to school, she'd never have the opportunity to work with animals in this way, to save their lives and to enjoy the challenge and the satisfaction that veterinarian work brought her. Without her schooling, she wouldn't have the same intellectual challenge.

The *Englischer* teachers had been wrong that she was special for her scholastic abilities, though. That didn't make her special. There were plenty of brilliant Amish people who applied their smarts to the work at hand. But they were right about the fact that she'd never be fully happy unless she was following her passion, and hers was to work with animals in the medical field. Tabitha carried around a small amount of guilt over the fact that her rebellion when she jumped the fence had resulted in such a satisfying career that she'd been able to keep.

But she couldn't tell people that—they wouldn't know how to take it. So instead, she told them other truths, such as how she wished she hadn't married Michael. He had been a complete mistake, and he'd broken her heart. That was normally enough information for most people.

When their dresses had dried from standing close to the fire, Tabitha and Beth sat and drank the hot, sweet tea. Iris excused herself to go to the sitting room to knit again, and she waved off their offers to join them.

"*Nee*, I'm fine. Keep chatting," Iris said. She was working on a warm, dark gray shawl that was taking shape. Dark gray was the accepted color for winter shawls in this community, and the only difference one might see between one woman's shawl and another's was in the quality of the knitting or crochet, or in the quality of the yarn itself.

When Mammi had settled in the sitting room, Beth and Tabitha chatted for a while more, refilled their cups, and listened to the downpour outside.

"Did you know the other woman?" Beth asked tentatively. "The one who cheated with your husband."

"*Nee*," Tabitha said. "And I didn't want to meet her either. It was so painful that I couldn't trust myself to behave like a Christian if I was put in her presence."

"And he wouldn't give her up?"

"*Nee*." Tabitha's mind went back to that painful time when she'd been praying for Gott to save her marriage and her husband had been flagrantly cheating with another woman. "She knew he was married too, and she didn't care. Or it didn't stop her. He refused to give her up, and I don't know what he expected. He probably knew I'd leave him, but it took the responsibility off his shoulders to end our marriage. He was just some poor man with his heart torn between two women . . ." She made a face. "I'm not as bitter as I sound. I've made my peace with that. I left Michael, and he didn't contest anything in the divorce. The week after we signed the papers, he married her."

"It's horrible," Beth murmured. "I don't know what I

would have done. If you'd stayed *Englisch*, you could have married again, though."

Tabitha slowly shook her head. "It's possible to be the loneliest you've ever been while married. No, I couldn't do that. I could feel Gott telling me to go home, and when Gott tells you to do something, you've got a choice—ignore his voice until you don't hear it anymore, or obey and have the comfort of his peace. I came home, and I'm glad I did. I made mistakes, and there are consequences for them, but I'm where Gott wants me."

Beth was quiet as she sipped her tea.

"Do you ever think that holding us Amish back from getting more of an education is wrong?" Beth asked after a moment.

"That isn't my decision to make," Tabitha said carefully.

"You're our veterinarian, and I can only see a benefit to that. You're Amish, so you understand our ways," Beth said. "And you're good at your job. If more of us could pursue those jobs that are beneficial to our community—"

"How many of them are really needed?" Tabitha asked.

"A veterinarian, for one. Nurses. Midwives. Maybe even engineers."

"Engineers to make new, more convenient tools?" Tabitha asked gently, and Beth blushed.

"All right, but nurses, and maybe dentists too. Midwives for sure. Maybe even people in finance."

"The education is expensive," Tabitha said. "It would cost the community more than we could pool. Then there would be the competition to be chosen for that education. We'd be pitted against each other. There would be hard feelings. There would also end up being two different classes of Amish—the educated and the uneducated. Our unity and humble connection to each other would be forever altered. No, I see why we do things the way we do. We can hire out those services. It's best to see the reasons why instead of trying to find new ways."

Beth rubbed her hands over her arms. "You have a point there. It's a sacrifice to stay Amish in some ways."

"Anything worthwhile requires sacrifice," Tabitha replied.

And yet, Tabitha knew that she was different and outside of the Amish social circles because of this education and her job. There was a barrier, and it wasn't the way things were supposed to be.

A gust of chilly, wet air swept through the kitchen, and they both looked up as they realized that wasn't quite right. There was a bang from the other room, and Tabitha jumped up a heartbeat after Beth did. They both ran toward the sound.

The bang was the sound of the wind whipping the outside door back against the wall. The door stood open, waving on its hinges. Iris was gone, and so was Goldie. A flash of lightning lit up the room, illuminating Iris's knitting lying in a heap on the floor.

Tabitha's heart hammered to a stop, and she and Beth both ran to the door and looked out into the darkness.

"Mammi!" Beth shouted, but the wind turned her words back on her.

"We need a lantern," Tabitha said.

Beth dashed back into the kitchen, and Tabitha shaded her eyes, looking down the yard. The light from the window illuminated just past the garden. Rain flattened the plants, but she couldn't see beyond that. There was no sign of any movement by the stable either.

When Beth returned with a lit kerosene lantern, they

plunged out into the night. With only one lantern, they'd have to stay together, but that might be for the best in this storm, Tabitha thought. The last thing they needed was to have two women lost out here in the darkness.

"Mammi!" Beth shouted.

They circled around the house, scanning for any sign of Iris, but there was none. Beth called for her grandmother over and over again, and Tabitha kept silent. Where would Iris have gone? But then she realized something—Iris wasn't alone.

"Goldie!" Tabitha bellowed. "Goldie, come!"

Tabitha looked up toward the drive that led to the road, then across the front grass. Then she spotted the dog. Past the back garden, past the Adirondack chairs, the dog appeared, just visible down by the beach.

"Goldie!" Tabitha said. "Over there! Lift the lantern!"

Goldie stood by the beach, her eyes glowing green, reflected in the lantern light, and then she vanished again, but Tabitha was glad that her ploy had worked. If Goldie was on the beach, then Iris probably was too. Goldie was well trained and would have a hard time not obeying a direct order to come, but she wouldn't leave her mistress in a dangerous place either.

Tabitha's clothes were drenched through already, and a rivulet of cold water cascaded down the center of her back. She shivered as a gust of wind slammed against her, but they hurried in the direction Goldie had disappeared.

"I can't believe Mammi would go to the lake!" Beth said. "She's terrified of that water!"

Tabitha stumbled over a tree root as they emerged onto the rocky shore.

The lake was veiled in mist from the steady downpour,

reflecting the lantern's flickering light back at them. Goldie paced along the shore, limping slightly, but her canine attention was on the water. Then Tabitha spotted the old woman, waist deep as she waded out.

"Mammi!" Beth gasped, and she put down the lantern on the rocks, kicked off her shoes, and plunged into the water, lifting her skirt high. The water rose up to Iris's chest, and Beth kicked her legs up and started to swim, finally reaching her grandmother. She reached for the old woman's shoulder.

"No!" Iris shouted, twisting to free herself. "No! Let go of me!"

Tabitha picked up the lantern and raised it high, a prayer in her heart. She couldn't swim, but Beth could.

"Mammi! Come back!" Tabitha could tell by Beth's voice that she was on the verge of panic. "Come out of the water, Mammi—"

Iris lunged forward, and then she vanished. One moment she was there in Beth's grip, and the next she was gone. Tabitha's breath seeped out of her. That lake was deep, and it had some spots where the bottom suddenly just dropped out. Her heart thudded to a stop, her breath bated, and then Beth hauled her grandmother up above the water again, the old woman's white face shining like a ghost as she gasped for air.

Beth pulled Iris backward and hauled her closer to shore. Tabitha waded out and helped get a grip on the old woman.

"Let go of me!" Iris wailed, flailing at Tabitha. "I saw him! I saw him! He was here! Help me!"

Saw who? Tabitha looked over the water—there was nothing to see. Just the mist from rain pummeling the water's surface.

They pulled Iris back to shore, and Goldie shoved her nose

between them, trying to help her mistress and not seeming sure what to do.

"Good girl, Goldie," Tabitha said, putting a hand on the dog's warm head. "You did good, didn't you? Good girl."

Iris sank to the ground, sobbing. She looked back and forth along the waterline and then simply collapsed into a little heap. She'd lost her *kapp* somewhere, because her head was bare and some of her white hair had come loose from her bun and streaked down her face. Her blue dress clung to her skin, her arms looked thin, and a red scratch on her forearm bled in a blurry trail down her arm and dripped off her elbow.

Tabitha and Beth helped Iris to her feet.

"Who did you see?" Beth asked, dipping her head down to her grandmother's level. "Is someone out here?"

Iris looked around again, and she shook her head but didn't answer.

Tabitha lifted the lantern and looked along the shoreline and toward the bushes that crowded the water farther up where the beach ended. She couldn't see anything—or anyone. All was still. A flash of lightning lit up the beach in one brilliant burst, and Tabitha squeezed her eyes shut against the glare.

Was this just a confused old woman who thought she saw someone? Or was there something more to it? Tabitha blinked her eyes back open, and it took a moment to adjust to the darkness once more. But Beth still had a good hold on her grandmother.

"Come, Goldie!" Tabitha called, and they each took a side of the trembling old woman and helped her over the rocky beach and toward the grass. They made their way toward the warm, beckoning glow from the back kitchen window.

The rain continued to come down in sheets, and the wind buffeted them. Twice, Iris stumbled and they caught her.

They got to the back door, and Tabitha pushed it open. Beth and her grandmother went inside first, then Goldie slipped in after them. When Tabitha got into the warm kitchen, she slammed the door shut behind her and stood there dripping onto the floor. Beth led her grandmother to a kitchen chair, and the old woman shivered. Beth started to stoke up the fire in the stove, and Tabitha went into the sitting room to grab a lap blanket she'd seen there earlier. She draped the blanket around Iris's shoulders.

"What happened?" Beth asked her grandmother gently. "Why did you go out there?"

Iris pulled the blanket closer around her. "I don't know. I'm sorry, dear. I didn't mean to cause trouble."

"You said you saw someone out there," Beth pressed. "Who did you see?"

For a moment, Tabitha thought she saw some knowing flicker through the old woman's eyes, but then it was gone.

"I don't know," Iris said, and she looked down at her cut arm. "I think I'm bleeding."

Beth looked up at Tabitha, and the old woman's words echoed in her memory. *"I saw him! I saw him! He was here! Help me!"*

"Can I see?" Tabitha asked, looking down at the cut on Iris's arm. It was only a scratch, but with the old woman's thin skin, it was bleeding quite a lot. "I'll get you bandaged up, Iris. It's not too bad."

But who had Iris seen in her mind's eye?

19

⚶

The storm rattled the house like a tin pot, and Danny stood by the window, watching the rain pour down the glass. He'd changed his clothes already, and his wet pants and shirt were hanging downstairs on a drying rack.

Anne and Mamm sat at the kitchen table, sorting through some fabric remnants together for a lap quilt project Anne wanted to start. Daet sat across from them, his financial ledger in front of him and a pile of receipts in one hand. He liked to keep everything in order for tax time.

Tobias stood at the stove, making some coffee soup for the family to enjoy while the storm raged outside. Coffee soup was hot milk with a small amount of instant coffee added to it and a large amount of sugar. Simple enough, but it was tasty with some bread to dip in it, and Danny and his siblings would take turns making it when Mamm said they were allowed. Today was Tobias's turn.

But Danny's mind wasn't on the business's finances or even on the coffee soup that was starting to smell good. He was thinking about those videos his brother had posted—his thoughtful refuting of Amish customs and beliefs. Even Beth seemed to have her doubts about the Amish ways, thinking they should be able to get more education. Danny didn't want more schooling himself. What he wanted was to open his shop, and he was getting antsy. But more schooling? That didn't interest him beyond the general classes Amish men took so they could learn the bookkeeping for their own businesses or other skills they might need to acquire.

How far did Beth's doubts go? He'd assumed that she'd get baptized and join the church once she worked out her personal issues with her family, but he wasn't so sure now. Her doubts weren't bringing her around to certainty the way his had. Her questions kept spiraling outward. And it wasn't just her questions that left him feeling unsettled . . . it was her support of his brother's ideas.

This wasn't a choice between him and Zach, and he knew that. But maybe he'd wanted her to side with him a little more fervently anyway. Zach was causing untold heartache for their family, and he was publicly humiliating both their family and their community. And maybe Danny wanted her to believe in their way of life a little more strongly, too, because he was getting tired of being the strong one all the time. Beth had always been special to him, but seeing her this visit back to Shepherd's Hill was different. He knew the risks, but he couldn't seem to pull his heart back.

Out the window, the lights from a large vehicle turned down the drive. In the dusky, rainy light, Danny couldn't see much, but as the truck got closer, he thought he recognized it. It was the same one driven by the *Englischer* man who'd been taking pictures earlier.

"Daet, come look at this truck. Do you recognize it?" Danny said.

181

Daet got up and came to the window. The man in the truck stopped a few yards from the house, and the cab light came on. The man looked down at something in his lap, then up again, toward the lake.

"I've seen him taking pictures," Daet said.

"Me too," Danny said. "And Zach had video of me working. I'm wondering if he doesn't have someone coming by and taking pictures or something."

"Why would he do that?" Daet asked.

"I don't know." Now it felt stupid. "It's just, why is that man coming here repeatedly, taking photos?"

Daet shook his head. "I don't know."

"It seems weird to me," Danny said. "Not safe."

And ever since Danny had seen those videos of him working around the property, he'd started to feel a little less safe too. Someone had been videoing him, and his brother had been using that footage for his own social media content, disparaging the things that Danny held dear.

Toby and Anne both came to look out the window. The man turned off the light in the cab, turned the truck around, and headed back up the drive. He hadn't done anything wrong, exactly. People turned around in a stranger's drive sometimes, but did they come back repeatedly, taking pictures and seeming a little too preoccupied with the property?

"Do you think he's connected to Zach?" Toby asked.

"I don't know," Danny admitted. "Maybe not. This whole thing just has me on edge."

"Can I see the videos he posts?" Toby asked.

"No," Daet said firmly.

"Why is he doing that?" Anne asked. "Why is he so angry about our family?"

"I don't think it's about our family, exactly," Danny said,

but it did feel that way sometimes. When he posted his videos, he talked about his own upbringing, his own family, his own experiences. He talked about them.

"Zachariah always was a mouth-first kind of boy," Mamm said. "It was his personality. If something felt off to him, instead of quietly thinking it over, he'd talk loud and long about it until he could figure out what it was he didn't like about it. That's what he's doing now."

"Except he's talking to a much bigger audience," Danny said. "Using video of me without my permission, and publicly bashing everything we believe in."

"It's not the world at large that worries me," his father replied, and Danny looked over his shoulder to where his younger siblings stood. Zach and Meghan's opinions could still impact Toby and Anne. Danny knew that young people had to face other ideas sooner or later, but it was more complicated when it was their own big brother who was trying to change their minds about things.

"Your mother and I have been talking about it," Daet said, and he exchanged a look with Mamm. "And we think that it might be time for us to get tougher on Zach."

"Tougher how?" Danny asked.

"He might need to stop coming by here," Daet said quietly. "He's not respecting our ways or our rules. He's causing a ruckus every time he visits. And it's not good for our home."

"You mean, shun him?" Anne asked, her voice shaking.

"*Nee*, not shunning," Mamm interjected. "He never did get baptized, so he can't be shunned. So you can empty that fear out of your head. But in our home, there are rules to be followed, and if Zach cannot at least respect them, then he will have to stay away until he is willing to do so."

Toby and Anne were silent, and Danny glanced between

his parents. They looked united on this, and Danny didn't blame them. Zach was causing problems, and it was their responsibility to stop it.

Besides, there were Toby and Anne to consider. If even Beth was finding his arguments compelling, what about younger *kinner*?

"There is a lesson to learn by watching your brother's mistakes," Mamm said, turning her attention back to sorting the cloth remnants. "He has support in these new ideas of his."

"Meghan," Anne said.

"*Yah*. But she isn't a bad girl," Mamm said. "I think from her point of view, she's helping. She cares for Zach, and she wants to support him, and she doesn't understand us."

"Then maybe she should try," Anne muttered.

"*Yah*, I agree. We aren't bad people either," Mamm said. "But it seems Zach is telling her we are."

"That isn't fair!" Toby burst out. "If I ever left, I'd never tell people my own *mamm* and *daet* were bad people! I'd come back to visit all the time, and I'd bring you money to make things easier too. I wouldn't treat my own family like that!"

Danny eyed his younger brother. Toby's face was flushed, and he scrubbed a hand through his blond hair. Was Toby thinking about leaving already? Was that much damage done?

"The lesson is in who you choose to spend your life with," Mamm went on, her tone low and calming. "The partner you choose is a very important decision. Zach chose an *Englischer*. She encourages his doubts and tells him that he's right when he isn't. She doesn't bring him peace and harmony in his life, and it isn't even her fault. She just doesn't understand, and likely never will. But Zach's choice in a romantic partner will affect his entire future. When you choose someone, you have to look at it in a mature way. You need to choose someone who will love you and be faithful to you for life. You need to choose someone who will be a good parent to your *kinner* together, and someone who will be able to buoy you up in your faith when you hit valleys. That partner in faith is incredibly important—more so than you think when you're young and experiencing some powerful feelings toward someone."

"You need to be equally yoked," Daet added.

Was Zach equally yoked right now? It could be argued that he was—he didn't seem to believe in the Amish faith anymore, and Meghan didn't either. And Danny could see how his brother might feel very supported by a woman who would back him up in all of his complaints and doubts.

But was that what Danny wanted? Did he want a woman to help shake a loose joint, or a woman who would help him firm up the faith he had? Because Danny wanted to live an honest Amish life. He wanted to band together with his community, worship in the same spot he had sat in since he was a boy, seated in order of his birth with the men he'd grown up with. He wanted his own *kinner* to have the same sunny, faith-filled childhood he'd had, a childhood close to the earth and populated with cousins and friends . . . and the girl who came to visit most summers and stayed with her *mammi* across the lake. Beth had been a part of his sweetest memories.

But Beth was struggling with her own doubts right now, and he wasn't sure that she wanted that same rock-solid support in bringing her back to the Amish ways. Sometimes people voiced doubts because they wanted help in resolving them. But not always. Sometimes, like with Zach, it was just how they saw the world.

Mamm and his younger siblings continued talking about how a marriage partner might change a person's direction in life. They discussed how it might affect child rearing, and even relationships with family. It all flowed over Danny in a familiar wave. He'd been told all of these things over and over the last few years, but this afternoon, he felt the implications for his own life.

He'd been spending a lot of time with Beth. He held her hand when she let him, and he held her secrets too. His feelings for her were tumbling forward. But if they ultimately didn't want the same things, it would be safer to take a step back now before they said too much, before they shared too much, and before his heart tipped over the edge and landed squarely in her hands.

20

Up in Mammi's room, Beth helped her grandmother change out of her wet clothes and into a warm, dry nightgown. The storm continued to rage, and Beth could just barely see a tree thrashing outside the window. The wind moaned around the house like some wounded beast.

Downstairs, they had stoked up the stove to warm the kitchen. Tabitha lent a hand too, running up and down the stairs, carrying towels to heat on the stove. Mammi shivered, her thin shoulders shaking as Beth unwound her wet hair and pulled a comb through it.

"Once we have your hair in a warm towel, you'll feel better," Beth said. "I remember when you used to do this for me when I was little. You'd comb out my hair, and you always told me that a wet head caused colds."

Mammi reached up and touched her wet hair gingerly.

"It's okay," Beth said. "We'll get it dry. In fact, I think we'll do better by the stove downstairs, don't you think?"

"By the stove?" Mammi whispered.

"*Yah*. Much warmer. Come on, let's go down."

Mammi complied and stood up when Beth took her arms. She shuffled around the bed and followed Beth toward the stairs. She seemed less confused now and was willing to do what Beth asked of her, but something of her grandmother was missing tonight. It was like a piece of her had slipped away.

Beth took the stairs slowly, waiting as Mammi navigated each step. At the bottom of the stairs, Tabitha was standing with a folded towel in her arms, watching them with her lips parted and her gaze locked on Mammi's trembling feet, nodding silently as she stepped down each time. Beth was glad that Tabitha was here. If she'd been alone, she never would have thought to call Goldie to find Mammi. She would probably still be poking through bushes . . . and only Gott knew what would have happened to her poor grandmother.

As they reached the bottom of the stairs, Beth exhaled a shaky breath, and Tabitha visibly relaxed.

"I've got a warm towel for you," Tabitha said. "Let's get a chair closer to the stove."

Tabitha moved the chair, then slid the towel over Mammi's shoulders. Mammi smiled up at Tabitha then.

"*Danke*, dear," Mammi murmured. "That feels very nice."

"I'm just going to comb your hair out so it can dry, okay, Mammi?" Beth said.

Mammi nodded, and Beth continued combing out her grandmother's long, thin white hair, letting the warm air from the stove dry it into little wisps. Then she put another towel over Mammi's shoulders.

"I'm going to start some tea," Beth said. "That will help us all feel a little more settled, I think."

Beth filled the kettle at the sink and put it onto the stove with a hiss. Then she prepared the big ceramic teapot and opened the tea bag tin.

"Only two bags," Mammi said. "Or it gets too bitter."

Beth shot her grandmother a smile. "Two bags."

That sounded more like Mammi, and she put the two bags into the pot and returned the tin to the cupboard. Mammi leaned forward now and reached back to pull her hair over one shoulder. She was coming back to herself again, and that was a relief. This time, it had taken longer than others when she got lost in the past.

But what had Mammi been remembering in that water?

"Does this happen often?" Tabitha asked softly.

"This? I mean . . . not this bad. She's gotten a bit confused and lost in the past, but she's never run away or seen something that wasn't there before. Not like this. This scared me."

"Me too," Tabitha breathed. "I'm not sure when the storm is going to let up tonight."

Beth had a sudden dread of being alone in this house with Mammi tonight.

"Stay the night," Beth pleaded. "It's too stormy to drive safely anyway. We have extra rooms, and—" Beth smiled hesitantly—"and I'd feel better if you were here."

"I can stay if you want me to," Tabitha said. "It is a bad storm."

Up until tonight, Beth had felt very grown up, but right now she didn't feel ready to be the adult in charge of everything. Not just yet. She'd known her grandmother needed help, but somehow she hadn't connected that to the idea that Mammi would need her to take over as the decision-maker and be the one responsible for everything.

Things had taken a turn for the worse tonight, and they were not going to get better, Beth realized.

Beth and Tabitha made a comforting dinner of brown buttered noodles, sliced sausage, and green beans from the garden. Beth even opened up a jar of applesauce on the side since she thought Mammi might eat a little bit of it, and the more food she could get into her grandmother tonight, the better Beth would feel.

After dinner, Tabitha went upstairs to make up a spare bedroom for herself. Beth had offered to do it, but Tabitha waved her off.

"Sit with your *mammi*. I'm perfectly capable of making a bed," Tabitha called as she jogged up the stairs.

Beth could hear her footsteps creaking from the other side of the house, and it did feel nice knowing there was someone else here. She wasn't completely on her own just yet.

Mammi had finished some noodles, a couple pieces of sausage, and all of her applesauce. The green beans remained untouched, though.

"Can I get you more noodles?" Beth asked.

"No, *danke*, dear," Mammi said.

Beth refilled her grandmother's tea cup without asking and nudged it closer. Mammi gave her a smile of thanks.

"Mammi, can you explain what happened outside tonight?" Beth asked softly.

"I don't know, dear," Mammi said. "I don't know . . ."

"You hate the water," Beth said, her own anxiety rousing again. "Why did you go out there?"

"I do hate it," Mammi agreed. "That lake is dangerous and deep."

An image rose in Beth's mind of her grandmother vanishing under the surface of that dark water, and a terrible shiver slid down her spine. What would send her grandmother out to a lake that terrified her?

"You thought you saw someone, Mammi," she pressed gently. "Who did you see?"

"I don't know."

Mammi looked down at her hands, then at the dog, but wouldn't look at Beth. She wasn't going to say, it seemed, but Beth had a feeling that Mammi did remember. It was painful, and maybe she was so used to guarding her secret that it was hard to say it out loud.

"You told me about Arden Bieler," Beth prompted. "Were you there the day he died?"

Mammi startled, and tears welled up in her eyes. "What?"

"Were you there that day?" Beth repeated.

"I—I was. It all happened so fast. I thought he'd pop up to the surface and swim back like always. He didn't. He just . . . didn't come back up. And the longer it took, the more everyone panicked."

"Oh, Mammi . . ." Beth put an arm around her grandmother's shoulders.

"Do you understand why you have to be so careful?" Mammi turned toward her then, fire in her eyes. "Do you understand, Elizabeth? I know you can swim well. I know you love the water. But it can happen so fast! And it took two days for his body to come back up! Two days!"

Mammi shuddered and turned back toward the stove again.

"It's that deep," Beth whispered.

"It is *that deep*. When I tell you to be careful with that lake, there is good reason. I am not a foolish old woman. I might be forgetful sometimes, and I might get confused, but I am not being silly when I warn you about that lake."

"I know, Mammi," Beth said.

"Good. When you get old, people stop listening to you.

But we aren't suddenly old and foolish. We know a thing or two still."

Beth sucked in a deep breath. "Mammi, I'm going to ask you something, and I know it's going to be hard to answer, but it's important that I know."

Mammi looked up with an uncertain frown.

"Is Arden Bieler my grandfather?" Beth asked quietly.

"What?" Mammi didn't turn away this time. She met Beth's gaze with her own confused look. "Why would you ask that?"

"You can tell me, Mammi. The year makes sense. Arden died a few months before my *daet* was born. And I just wanted to know . . . was Arden Bieler my *daet's daet*?"

"No, Elizabeth," Mammi said, her voice rising in irritation. "Arden Bieler was a boy I was sweet on, sure enough. And he was sweet on me too. But we didn't cross those lines, Arden and me. He didn't get me pregnant. I adopted your *daet*."

"You adopted him?"

"*Yah*. I wasn't married. How else did you think I got a child?"

The old-fashioned way, obviously. But she'd been wrong. Her father hadn't been the child from an illicit relationship. He'd been adopted!

Beth heard Tabitha's footsteps on the bottom stairs, and a flood of embarrassment hit her face. How much had Tabitha heard? This was a private discussion, and it would be Beth's own fault if Tabitha overheard.

"Oh, good," Beth said a little more brightly than necessary. "You're back downstairs. Mammi, Tabitha is staying the night. It's blowing too hard for her to go home."

"You're staying?" Mammi asked. "Well, that's nice."

Beth let out a shaky breath as her grandmother ran her hands down her thin hair, now almost dry. Family secrets could get out so easily, and while Beth needed her answers, she didn't want to spread them far and wide either. But Tabitha looked cheery enough, and Beth could only pray that she hadn't overheard.

21

Tabitha stood in the guest bedroom, listening to the patter of rain against the glass. Wind moaned around the house like someone crying. It was only a storm. Storms came and they passed, and it was ridiculous that Tabitha found herself feeling homesick. She missed her bedroom back home, and even her father's grumbles and complaints.

He'd worry, and there was no way to change that. She couldn't get home, and Daet didn't have a phone, not even in the barn. Times like this, she missed the *Englisch* conveniences she'd left in the past. Cell phones, text messages, immediate communication, instant relief. Instead, Daet would likely stay up. He'd watch for her buggy. He'd pray for her safety. He wouldn't sleep.

A good father worried—it was part of his job. How many times had he told her that growing up? And she'd never really appreciated how much worry she'd caused her father when she left the faith and married Michael either. She'd thought she was so grown up and that he had no right to worry

194

anymore. How many nights had he stayed awake praying for her back then?

"I brought you a nightgown you can borrow, and a game of Uno if you're interested."

Tabitha startled out of her own thoughts and looked over her shoulder. Beth was at the door, holding up a kerosene lamp. Iris was already in bed in the room next to Tabitha's, and the lamp had been blown out.

"*Yah*, that sounds fun," Tabitha said, and she went to the door to take the cotton nightgown from Beth's hands.

The wind outside gave another heartbroken wail, and Tabitha shivered. What was with the wind tonight?

Beth stepped inside the room. "*Danke*. It's been a tough day."

"It really has."

Tabitha exchanged a sympathetic smile with the younger woman. Beth went over to the chair by the window and started to shuffle the deck of cards.

"How are you holding up, Beth? You have a lot to handle here," Tabitha said.

Beth shuffled like a pro, cards fanning out and zippering together.

"I don't even know right now. I'm scared for my *mammi*. I'm afraid I won't be able to take care of her on my own. I'm overwhelmed."

"That's fair," Tabitha said. "Caregiving isn't easy. I daresay your *mamm* didn't know how bad it was when she sent you."

"I'm an adult," Beth said. "I should be able to do this."

She started to deal, the cards flicking into neat piles on the windowsill as a gust of wind rattled the glass. At twenty-one, Beth was a legal adult, but she seemed very young to

Tabitha, who had just turned thirty. Besides, her years away had grown Tabitha in different ways.

"You still need breaks," Tabitha said. "And you need other people pitching in." Tabitha picked up her cards and looked at what she had to work with. Beth flipped over the first card.

"*Yah.* I'm realizing that. You go first."

Tabitha put down a card. "You might need some medical advice too."

"Oh, my *aent* said she brought Mammi to the Amish doctor already."

The Amish doctor was knowledgeable in herbal remedies and had doubtlessly seen a lot, but he wouldn't be an expert in dementia. But Amish communities were very devoted to their local doctors.

"What about Danny Lapp?" Tabitha asked, hoping to draw Beth into cheerier territory. "I heard that you seem to be spending a lot of time with him lately."

Beth's cheeks pinked as she played another card. "I heard that rumors had started."

"People talk. But, Beth, there is absolutely nothing wrong with having friendships and taking time for yourself."

Beth nodded. "Your turn."

"Right." Tabitha couldn't put down a card, so she picked up one from the deck. "He's nice, is he?"

"*Yah*, he's really nice." Beth smiled at last, and she seemed to relax a little bit. "I've known him for years, actually. Whenever I came to visit my *mammi*, I would see him, and we used to play together. Then we'd sit and talk when we got older. And for a little while we wrote letters, but he was a terrible letter writer, and I gave up."

Tabitha played her turn, and Beth put down a card in quick succession.

"It wasn't his strength, huh?" Tabitha chuckled.

"I daresay it's not the strength for most teenage boys."

"True." Tabitha smiled. "I've only ever heard good things about Danny Lapp, if that helps."

Beth shrugged bashfully. "I know. He's a good, solid Amish man." Her smile slipped.

"But?"

"He's very serious about the faith," she said quietly. "And I'm . . . questioning things."

"Ah." Tabitha knew that feeling very well. "What are you questioning?"

Tabitha put down two cards, and Beth picked one up.

"If all of this is necessary," she said.

"Like what?"

"Like . . . stopping school at eighth grade. Why can't we go on? Or why we have to wear dresses in winter, and why we can't drive cars or have phones. Those things. I'm sure it sounds silly to you."

"No, I questioned all of that too."

"I wish I could drive," Beth said. "I wish I could get in a car and go see my *mamm* whenever I want to, or go to town faster. I wish I could have a phone and just call my *mamm* instead of writing a letter. I wish things were easier for us, like they are for *Englischers*."

"Your *mamm* wouldn't have a phone, to start," Tabitha said. "And if you drove up in a car, you wouldn't have the same free, easy, supportive relationship with her that you have now."

"I know."

They both played a few more rounds, putting down cards and picking from the deck when they didn't have anything they could play.

"Still, I understand," Tabitha said. "My *daet* is worrying right now. If we had phones, he wouldn't have to worry."

"Right?" Beth brightened. "Things don't have to be this hard!" She put down a card, leaving one in her hand. "Uno."

"But that said," Tabitha went on, "if I had a car, I'd have left already. A storm wouldn't have kept me here. You'd be on your own tonight."

"*Yah*, I guess. . . ."

"We slow down, and it makes us rely on each other," Tabitha said and put down one more card. She still had a handful left. She wasn't going to win this game. "What would I have done if you didn't welcome me in tonight? I needed your help. And it turned out that you needed mine too. We're here for each other."

"Of course."

And Tabitha could see that Beth couldn't see past the basic Amish ways. There were a lot of things she was taking for granted—a strong community being one of them.

Beth put her last card down, a little smile on her lips. "Good game."

"Good game," Tabitha replied and tossed her cards on top of the pile.

Beth picked them up and started to shuffle again, her nimble fingers working quickly.

"I've lived that convenient life," Tabitha said, "and the truth is, it's lonely. You'd think all that ability to contact people would make connections easier, but it doesn't. Texting is weird. You can't tell a person's tone or see their eyes. It can be hard to tell exactly what someone means. They can be lying too."

Like Michael had been, countless times.

"I hadn't thought of that."

"*Nee*, you wouldn't," Tabitha said. "It's the sort of thing you figure out later."

Beth tapped the cards together into a neat pile.

"The way I see it," Tabitha continued, "we choose the Amish life, and that comes as a package. Gott was leading our ancestors just as he leads us, and he gave them wisdom for how to live a good life. That hasn't changed. We trust in Gott, and in our ancestors' relationship with him. There are rules we might not fully appreciate right now, but in time we end up seeing the value in them, just as they did. But we don't get to pick and choose from the *Ordnung*."

"Danny believes in all of it, though," Beth said. "I mean, he sees the value in every rule. He doesn't question things."

"He's stable and content," Tabitha said.

"*Yah*, but it makes me feel downright wicked for questioning our beliefs." Beth dropped the deck of cards into her lap. "I'm the wild, unstable one, right?"

"I didn't say that."

"I know. But Danny's brother Zach jumped the fence, and that has been incredibly hard on their family. I think that I might be too much for Danny."

Tabitha wished she had advice for that, but she was in much the same position. She was too much for some other women in the community too. Too educated. Too opinionated. Too dangerous. Tabitha didn't know how to be less.

"Okay, but just because you're too much for one man doesn't mean that you are too much as a woman or as a person," Tabitha said. "Remember that. You don't have to be every man's perfect match. That's not your job on this earth."

Beth was still for a moment, her expression thoughtful. Then she smiled. "*Danke*, Tabitha. I like that."

"It's hard-won wisdom." Tabitha returned her smile, and Beth smothered a yawn.

"Do you want to play another hand?"

The room felt warmer now, somehow, and outside, the moaning wind sounded less ominous.

"Sure," Tabitha said.

They played another round—this one Tabitha won—and then Beth gathered the cards back up.

"I'd better turn in," Beth said. "Good night. *Danke* for the talk."

"Good night, Beth," Tabitha said. "Sleep well."

"You too."

Beth closed the door behind her with a click. For a moment, Tabitha sat on the edge of the bed, then she got up and went to the window. The rain was still coming down, but not quite so hard as earlier, and she sank into the chair and looked out into the night. It was difficult to make out much detail, except she could see the soft glow of a light coming from the Lapp house around the lake.

Tabitha remembered that old ice house from when it was a favorite spot for teenagers to hold parties. That was back when it had just been shut down and before the Lapp family bought the property. *Kinner* in their *rumspringas* would find places to drink beer and have parties, and the old ice house had been a popular gathering place. Somehow, they'd assumed it was quite private, but looking at the ice house from Iris's guest room window, she saw just how observable they had been all that time.

Tabitha had only gone to one or two parties before she'd gotten uncomfortable and didn't go to any more. There were other teenagers who had gone to plenty. Katherine had been one of Tabitha's close friends before Tabitha married Michael and left, but back in her teenaged years, she had loved those wild parties. Now Katherine was a properly married mother of seven, a member of the church in good standing, and a respected woman. And Tabitha, who had found the parties to be too raucous and uncomfortable, was now considered the dangerous one.

She remembered a time when Katherine had been drinking and she'd gotten sick to her stomach. Tabitha had taken her home, and on the way, they'd had to stop and let her be sick on the side of the road.

"Don't tell my parents!" Katherine had pleaded. "They'll be so mad if they know I was drinking!"

And of course, her parents had taken one look at her and known exactly what she'd been doing. They'd solemnly thanked Tabitha for bringing her home, and Katherine had been sent to help her older sister at a more distant farm the very next week. Tabitha had felt embarrassed after that—Katherine's parents had known that Tabitha had been at that party too. There was no hiding it. It was then that Tabitha had made her own decision that she would not do anything she'd be ashamed to have the whole world know about.

So when she'd left the faith, she'd had no shame in her choice. And when she'd come back to visit in blue jeans, it was with the knowledge that she would not hide her actions as if she was guilty, because she wasn't.

But not everyone had the luxury of living their life shamelessly in full view of everyone. She'd overheard Beth's questions to her grandmother earlier today. Some people had secrets, and in order to stay in good standing with the church, they had much to hide. Iris had adopted her son, but that meant someone had given him up. There was likely an Amish teenager who had had a baby and couldn't keep him.

But none of this was Tabitha's business. She'd only overheard because she was sheltering here through the storm, and it wasn't right for her to snoop into other people's private lives.

Tabitha changed out of her clothes and into the borrowed nightgown. She needed to use the washroom before she slept, so she picked up her lamp and opened her door with a soft creak.

The hallway was dark, illumined slightly by the pool of kerosene light, and the floorboards creaked under her bare feet. At the washroom door, she paused. She could hear a voice from the next room reciting a passage from the Bible that Tabitha knew well. It was the twenty-third Psalm.

"*Der Herr ist mein Hirte; mir wird nichts mangeln. Er weidet mich auf grüner Aue und führet mich zum frischen Wasser . . .*"

Tabitha translated in her head. *The* LORD *is my shepherd; I shall not want. He maketh me to lie down in green pastures. He leadeth me beside the still waters . . .*

Then Iris's recitation stopped, and for a moment there was silence. That was one of Tabitha's favorite passages too. Her mother had embroidered the German Luther Bible translation of that Psalm and hung it in their kitchen.

Then Tabitha heard the sounds of quiet sobs.

Tabitha froze. Was Iris all right? Should she knock on her door and check?

"Oh, Gott forgive me." Iris's muffled voice broke the silence. "Forgive me, forgive me, forgive me . . ."

No, she would not knock. She would leave Iris alone.

She slipped into the washroom and shut the door as quietly as she could. Standing there at the counter, her kerosene lamp brightening the room with a cheery glow, Tabitha exhaled a shaky breath. She hadn't meant to overhear such a personal moment between a woman and her Gott. She felt a wriggle of guilt at having heard words that were meant for Gott alone.

But she couldn't help but wonder . . .

Forgive her for what? What horrible burden was weighing this old woman down?

22

After the storm shook and rattled past, the community of Shepherd's Hill was left dripping with rainwater and glistening in early morning sunlight. The birds twittered with renewed energy and hopped along the grass, pulling up worms in a post-storm feast. The horses were relaxed again now that there was no more thunder or lightning to spook them, and Danny sent them back out into the small pasture.

Then Danny guided the wheelbarrow outside the stable and looked toward the Peachy house. All seemed still except for a single tendril of smoke coming up from the chimney. Someone was cooking.

How had they fared through the storm, though? How was Beth?

All night long while the wind moaned and howled and the lake churned and waves lapped the shore, Danny had slept fitfully. When he woke up, he was thinking about Beth and wondering if he could hold his feelings back for her if he tried. His mother's discussion of what was important in a romantic partner had struck a nerve for him. The problem was, he wasn't spending time with Beth because she was a solid and logical choice. He was drawn to her in spite of all the very rational reasons against it.

"All finished, Danny?"

Danny turned to see his father standing with a thumb stuck in one suspender.

"*Yah*, all done." Danny carried on over to the muck pile and dumped the wheelbarrow full of soiled hay.

"We've got a couple coming to stay in the ice house cottage. They're arriving this afternoon," Daet said. "Is the cottage ready?"

"*Yah*, Mamm and I finished everything. We've got the cottage cleaned, the sheets and towels are all changed. I cleaned out the wood stove and brought in more wood. And I fixed that tile in the bathroom. It's guest-ready," Danny replied.

"Good." His father eyed him. "Are you all right, *sohn*?"

His quagmire with Beth wasn't going to be easily resolved, but he did have one other problem that needed his attention too.

"I was thinking of calling Zach," Danny said. "I wanted to sit down with him and see if I can't smooth things over with him."

"I'm not sure it'll do any good," Daet said.

"It might, though," Danny said. "And if he brings Meghan along, I can tell her how sorry we are if we gave the wrong impression by speaking in Pennsylvania Dutch while she was here."

His father frowned in thought, then nodded. "That has been on my mind these last few days. I don't want our rudeness to impact that young woman, or Zach, for that matter. We must right our wrongs."

"I'll go down to the phone hut, then, and call him," Danny said.

His father nodded. "*Yah*, go ahead." The sound of a horse and wagon drew their attention. It was the dairy wagon making the weekly delivery. "I'll get the milk."

Danny walked up to the phone hut, which took him past the Peachy drive. The phone hut was another half mile beyond. He looked down Iris's drive on his way, and he spotted the stable door open, so someone was doing chores. Probably Beth. She had a big job on her hands, staying with her *mammi*. Was that an extra buggy under the shelter? He thought it was, and he strained to look but didn't slow his steps.

The gravel road was tamped down from the rain, so there was no more dust, and a couple of potholes were filled with muddy water. The grass in the fields had sprung up in fresh exuberance from the rain so that everything was greener, lusher, and fresher from the downpour the night before. Birds now sang their songs from the treetops, and Danny slapped at a mosquito on the back of his neck. Rain brought growth, and bugs too.

The phone hut was a little building at the side of the road, with enough space for a couple of buggies to park. It was small and snug, and it housed a single telephone that sat on a small desk with a stool. A calendar hung on the wall, and there were a couple of pencils and a pad of paper. That was all.

Danny went inside and shut the door behind him. He pulled out a slip of paper with his brother's cell phone number on it.

"Hello, this is Danny . . ." he whispered to himself. "Hi, this is Danny. No. Hi, it's me. No."

He wasn't used to phone conversations, and for a moment he just looked at the telephone, then picked up the receiver and dialed the number.

"Hello?" He knew his brother's voice.

"Hi, it's Danny."

"Danny! Hey. Hi." Then his voice lowered. "It's my brother." It came back at full strength again. "How's it going over there? Everything okay?"

"*Yah*. I mean. *Yah*. There was a good storm last night, but no damage. How are you?"

"Just rain here. No big deal."

"Good. Good . . ." Danny hated this. Phone calls meant you couldn't look a man in the face or read his expressions. It was awkward. "Look, I was hoping you and I could sit down together and talk."

"*Yah*, okay. We could do that. I thought Mamm and Daet would be pretty mad at me right now."

"*Nee*, not mad. A bit confused."

"Right. Well, I think it's good we talk about these things," Zach said. "We never did growing up. There was one way to see things, and that was it. So I know it's uncomfortable for them, but they need to open their eyes to how things really are."

"I wanted to sit down and talk without them," Danny said. "Just you and me."

"Sure. I'm happy to," Zach replied. "When?"

"What works for you?" Danny asked. "I mean, when aren't you working?"

"Tomorrow evening?" Zach asked. "Let's say about seven, at Romeo's Pizza here in town?"

"I can do that," Danny said. "I'll see you then."

"*Yah*, you bet," his brother replied. "See you then."

Danny wrote a little note on the pad, noting the time and place, and then tore the page off and shoved it into his pocket. At least he and his brother could talk alone—no performances for other people. Just two brothers.

They'd have to find some common ground that way, wouldn't they? But he had to wonder what Zach would say about those videos. Would he take them down?

Danny shut the phone hut door behind him and headed back down the road again. A truck rumbled past, and Danny carried on, his pulse still beating faster than usual, the way he felt when a bull spotted him across a field and he knew he had to keep an eye on that animal.

He carried on down the road, just slightly downhill to make the walk easier. As he approached the Peachy drive, a buggy was leaving, and he spotted Tabitha Schrock.

"Good morning, Danny!" Tabitha called.

"Good morning," he called back, and she continued onto the road, the horse trotting briskly.

Beth stood outside, her hands on her hips, and he waved. She waved back. He'd just stop in and see how they were. He started down the drive, and Beth glanced over her shoulder toward the house, then walked in his direction. He felt like his feet lightened, and soon they met in the center of the drive.

"How was the storm?" he asked.

"Eventful." She sobered. "Tabitha got stranded with us, and then Mammi got lost out there by the lake."

"What?" Danny stepped closer, and without thinking, he caught her hand. "Iris was lost?"

"*Yah*. She got confused and thought she saw someone in the water. I had to drag her out. She went under, and—" She sucked in a quavery breath. "It was scary. I'm so glad Tabitha was here."

"So . . . no more walks leaving her alone?" he asked.

"I don't dare leave her unless she has someone else with her," Beth answered. "It was really scary. I couldn't convince her that there was no one there, and she went off the edge where it gets deep. If I hadn't been right there, she might have drowned."

Danny tightened his grip on her hand. "Are *you* okay?"

"I'm a bit rattled."

"Where is Iris now?"

"Doing dishes. Now, she's back to normal. Everything seems fine. But last night she was different." She swallowed. "She was completely confused. And . . ."

"Come on." Danny tugged her hand and led the way around the house. Along the side of the house beside the woodpile, there was a spot where they could see both the front and the back doors of the house—at least the steps leading up to them. Iris wouldn't be able to leave without them seeing her.

An ax was stuck into a big block of wood, and Danny worked it free and picked up a piece of wood to split. Might as well be useful.

"Was it connected to Arden Bieler?" he asked quietly.

"I thought so at first," she replied, then slowly shook her head. "But when I asked about him, she told the story that he'd drowned, and she'd been there. But it wasn't during a storm. He just went under and didn't come back up. And when I asked if he was my grandfather, she kept saying my *daet* was adopted."

Danny split a piece of wood with a satisfying crack. "And you believed her?"

"*Yah.* I did. I think my *daet* was adopted. And I think my *mammi* lost her sweetheart that summer. But I don't think he was my grandfather."

Danny set up one of the pieces and brought the ax down. It split. Then he did it all over again. He'd make some kindling for the women to use in the stove.

"So the person she thought she saw in the water . . ." He looked over at her. "Who was that?"

"She didn't say. She just thought she saw someone."

A shudder went down his back. How frightening for an old lady to be enduring these kinds of confusing episodes. Poor Iris. She really couldn't be left alone anymore. He'd have to keep an eye on this place—more so than he normally did. Beth picked up the newly split kindling and held it in a bundle between her hands.

"Is that enough for you?" Danny asked. "Knowing she adopted your *daet*?"

"Not really. Who was the family? What happened to them? Why did he need to be adopted?"

"Maybe she'll tell you yet," Danny said. "If she's able to. She's obviously not worried about you marrying a cousin."

Beth rolled her eyes. "That did occur to me, Danny."

He laughed softly. "Maybe it was an *Englisch* family?"

"Maybe." She nodded slowly. "I'm starting to think it might be."

He liked the way she stood there, watching him chop, and he swung the ax and planted it back into the big block of wood. Beth set the little pile of kindling beside the ax.

"It's actually a good thing to have an outside family bringing in new blood," she said. "And more than that, Mammi was in Indiana for several years, so the family could be from there."

He could tell not knowing still bothered her. She shifted her weight from foot to foot.

"I get it," he said. "If I found out all of this new information at once, I'd be reeling too."

She nodded. "It's a weird feeling. I feel like I might be a different person than I thought."

"On a DNA level, maybe," he replied. "But you're still the same girl I've been thinking about for the last fifteen years."

"You thought about me that much?" She looked up again.

Did she really not know how he felt about her? Maybe he'd been better at hiding his feelings than he thought. She'd been on his mind constantly.

"I saw you every summer. I remember when I was too young to be allowed to go around the lake, and so we'd wave at each other."

"I remember that. I called you the Lake Boy."

He chuckled. "I called you Iris's Girl. And then when we were old enough to be allowed out of the yard, I sat with you on that dock, and we used to walk around the whole lake—remember? And you'd get your legs all scratched up, so I'd give you a piggyback across the worst of it."

Beth laughed softly and shook her head. "We were silly."

"You were special," he countered. "And we might not have seen each other more than three months a year, but I knew you. You were earnest and smart and always so ready to be a grownup when we were *kinner*. And then when you were a teenager, you thought I was boring and dorky."

"I did not!"

"You did too." He caught her hand and looked down at her slim fingers. "And maybe I was a bit dorky, but that hurt, because I thought you were like an angel. Beautiful and completely out of my reach."

He didn't dare look up. He'd never breathed a word of this to anyone before. He'd simply stored it all up in his heart. Her fingers were soft in his hand, and he stood there, starting to feel foolish now for having said anything to her.

"I didn't think you were dorky," she whispered. "I was just awkward and didn't know how to talk to boys, and you weren't just a kid anymore. That was the summer after we tried writing letters and it didn't work, remember?"

"*Yah.*"

"Are you any better at letter writing now?"

"Not really." A smile tipped up one side of his lips. "I'm better at this."

He gave her fingers a gentle squeeze. He was better at standing with her next to a woodpile, listening to her talk about whatever was running through her head. He was better at helping with a chore and watching emotions flicker past those deep blue eyes. He wasn't a poetic kind of guy, even if his emotions plunged as deep and mysterious as Friesen Lake. They didn't come out of him that way.

"So, who am I if my *daet* was adopted?" she asked.

"You're Beth," he whispered, and he met her gaze, wishing he had more words and longing for her to understand what he meant. "I still know you, even if you're questioning everything."

Her gaze softened then, and they both took a step closer at the same time, bringing her so close that he could feel her warm breath against his chin. She was the girl who'd tangled him around her finger years ago and had never really let go. She was the girl he thought about all year until she'd appear one day on her grandmother's beach. She was the woman now who'd grown more mysterious with those few years of absence, and yet she was still the Beth he'd always known. And he did know her! She'd been more open with him than anyone else, he was sure of it. Even if it was just because she'd had nothing to prove to him.

He touched her cheek, and looking down into her clear

blue eyes, his heart stuttered in his chest. She was so close, and it wouldn't take much to just dip his head down and catch those lips—

Danny heard the back screen door open. She stepped back, slipping her fingers free of his grip. He shut his eyes for a second, his own heartbeat thundering in his ears.

Iris came onto the back stoop, and Goldie followed her. She carried an ice cream bucket in one hand, and she held the screen door until her dog was out, then let it go.

Beth cast him one last longing look, then headed across the grass toward her grandmother.

"What are you doing, Mammi?" Beth asked, and she sounded just a little too bright and eager. She was off-balance too.

"What's that?" Iris looked over, and her gaze seemed sharp and keen.

"What are you doing?" Beth repeated.

"I'm getting some peas. I think there are a few that are ready. I like them early."

"Oh, okay."

"Daniel?" Iris said. "Oh, was that you chopping wood?"

"*Yah*, that was me," Danny said, and he lifted the bundle of kindling as proof. "How are you doing?"

"I'm just fine," Iris said. "How was the storm at your place?"

"Oh, we got by." He looked out toward the lake.

She'd gone out into the water. The thought chilled him. But looking at Iris Peachy now, she didn't seem capable of that kind of confusion. She was just the same sharp old lady they'd always known.

"Good, good," Iris said, and she stepped into her garden and bent down by the pea vines. "Thank your *mamm* for

213

those muffins. They were very handy when Tabitha Schrock came by yesterday afternoon. She stayed the night—the storm was too bad to drive home. So I was glad to have the extra baking. Gott works in mysterious ways, am I right?"

"*Yah*, he does," Danny agreed.

Beth looked back over at him, and he gave her a weak shrug. A smile sparkled in her eyes.

If Iris didn't come out when she did, I would have kissed Beth.

He would have tried, at least. Maybe she would have smacked him. That moment hadn't been planned, though, and it might have been downright foolish, but he'd do just about anything right now to get another moment like that with her . . .

But Iris glanced between them, her bright gaze seeming to take in his intentions.

"I'd better get back," Danny said. "I'll give my *mamm* your thanks."

"*Danke*, Daniel," Iris called cheerily.

"See you later, Beth," he added.

"Bye, Danny." Beth met his gaze again, and that sparkle in her eye made his feet feel lighter as he headed down to the beach and around to the path that led home.

Maybe he wasn't any good at letter writing, but one of these days before she left again, he was going to find the words to explain how he felt about her. It might not mean anything if she wasn't going to join the church, but he still wanted her to know what she'd meant to him all the same. Just as soon as he found the words to explain it to himself.

23

Two big quilting frames were set up in the middle of Rose and Aaron's farmhouse. They lived on a dairy farm not far from Tabitha and her *daet*. The partition between the kitchen and the sitting room had been rolled back, opening up a big space to let the women work. Several local women sat around the frames, hunched over the fabric, their own bags of supplies at their sides. The kitchen table had a few plates of snacks on it, and Tabitha's two sisters, Rose and Amanda, were at the counter preparing more.

Stepping into Rose's home and seeing her sisters together at the counter sent a rush of warm nostalgia through Tabitha's heart. Once upon a time, before any of them had married, there had just been the three Schrock sisters, and in a moment like this one, Tabitha longed for those days again, before life got complicated.

"You made it," Rose said as Tabitha shut the door behind her. Rose was putting together a plate of cookies and pastries, and Amanda stood next to her, filling glasses with juice.

"I made it," Tabitha said, and she went over to give them hugs. She gave Amanda an extra-tight squeeze. She hadn't

215

seen Amanda since Service Sunday, but it was expected that a newly married woman would be busy. Amanda and Menno had been married only a few months, and on Visiting Sundays, Amanda and Menno didn't materialize at any family gatherings—again, expected of newlyweds. They'd want that time alone together.

"How's Menno?" Tabitha asked.

"Good." Amanda squeezed her back. "How's work?"

That always stung just a little. She could ask her sister about her husband, and the biggest thing in Tabitha's life was her job. Not that it wasn't a hugely important part of her daily life, but she noted the differences all the same.

They chatted for a couple of minutes, talking about two new sire hogs that Amanda and Menno had acquired, about a new feed system that Menno had heard about but would want Tabitha's opinion on . . . Amanda talked about cooking for her husband, and how she needed to find more recipes for pork, because he had an abundance of pork in the freezer in town. Amish people would sometimes rent small, locked freezers set up in the back of supermarkets, and they'd keep their extra meat there.

"You've been eating more," Rose said, teasingly patting Amanda's hip.

"Oh, stop!" Amanda said. "Of course I have been. I do nothing but cook."

"And you're loving it," Tabitha commented.

"*Yah.*" Amanda blushed, and Tabitha and Rose exchanged a grin. Their sister was happy, and it was good to see. Amanda deserved this happy new marriage and the kitchen of her own to fill with her good cooking.

Tabitha glanced over at the quilting frames. The women were bent over their work, chatting as they sewed. Katherine

Blank was at the double wedding ring pattern circle of quilters, and she was laughing as she listened to another woman telling a story. She looked up then and spotted Tabitha. She smiled a hello.

This was it—Tabitha's chance to grow some friendships. She looked over the two quilting frames, and she knew the skills needed to do the double wedding ring pattern were beyond her right now. But the nearest frame held a log cabin pattern, and she could handle those straight lines and simpler blocks. The women working on the log cabin quilt were older, though. These were the widows. Tabitha took a deep breath.

She might have hands as steady as a well-built barn when it came to veterinarian work, but joining these women at a quilting frame had her fingers shaking.

"I was thinking you might want to join Aent Dina, Mary, Sarah Mae, and the others at the log cabin frame," Rose said, seeming to read Tabitha's mind.

"That's more my skill level," Tabitha murmured.

Rose nodded. "Besides, they'll be happy to teach you a few tricks, I'm sure."

"*Danke*, Rose. I'll do my best."

"You'll be fine," her sister reassured her.

Tabitha took her place at a free chair in front of the log cabin quilt next to her maiden *aent*, Dina. There was a pile of completed blocks, and Mary Bieler was working on another, her needle flashing as she stitched the pieces of cotton together. Her fingers obviously knew the work because she looked up with a friendly smile, her needle still moving at the same speed. Then her gaze dropped again as she pulled the thread through.

"Hello," Tabitha greeted them all. "Hi, Aent Dina."

"You made it," Aent Dina said with a smile. "I'm so glad, Tabitha."

Some of Tabitha's nervousness started to seep away, and she cast a big smile around the quilting circle. She'd known these women all her life—most were grandmothers of her friends from school. Miriam Lapp was Danny Lapp's grandmother—so not exactly one of her school contemporaries, but certainly a young man she'd seen around lately with Beth Peachy. And these women had known her in her youth.

Aent Dina had never married, but she was a favorite among her great-nieces and great-nephews. She would knit little green frogs for the *kinner* to play with, and she always had some hard candies in her purse.

"We just need you to connect blocks with a quarter-inch seam," Mary said.

"I can do that." Tabitha heaved a sigh of relief. She could do a little more than that with some confidence since her sister had been teaching her, but she was glad to have an easier job ahead of her tonight.

Tabitha worked in relative quiet, listening to the older women chat. They talked about their *grosskinner*, about friends who had moved away, about news from circle letters, and about gossip from other communities.

And Tabitha sewed carefully, watching the seam and using small, even stitches. The quality of these quilts reflected back on them, and a good-quality quilt could gain a good amount of money for their medical fund. This was important. When a community was known for high-quality sewing, the quilts could fetch far more at auction, and a community's quilting reputation was only as strong as their last auctioned quilt.

The conversation had turned toward one of Mary's grandsons, who was incredibly tall at six foot seven.

"My husband always said that our grandson was going to be very tall. Abram died when he was only two, but Abram said it. He said that boy will be knocking his head on a door frame, and he was right," Mary said.

"He knew it," Sarah Mae murmured. "My Bernard thought our grandson would be tall, but Jonah is only average height. But he thought he would be."

"It can be hard to tell," Dina said.

"Sometimes I wonder what Eli would have thought of how our *grosskinner* turned out," Miriam Lapp said. "He would have been so very proud of Danny, but he'd have been heartbroken about Zach. Just heartbroken."

"Sometimes it's a mercy they didn't see the painful things," Aent Dina agreed. "The Good Book says the righteous are taken away from the evil to come. They are at peace with Gott."

Tabitha finished a seam and clipped her thread.

"I suppose my grandparents would have been heartbroken about me too," Tabitha said quietly.

The women fell silent, and all eyes turned to her. She shouldn't have said anything. Just being here was a gift, and she knew better than to bring up difficult things.

"But you returned, dear," Aent Dina pointed out. "Mistakes were made, but you came back."

"That's true," Miriam said firmly. "My dear girl, I daresay you have more in common with us than you think."

"Do I?" Tabitha looked up, and instead of irritation, she saw sympathy in the eyes of these older women.

"You lost a husband," Miriam said.

"Well . . . he didn't die. He simply chose another woman," Tabitha said. "I lost a marriage, I suppose—"

"Oh, you lost him, all right," Miriam interjected. "You have had to grieve that loss, too, but you have it worse than we do. We have memories of loving husbands who were faithful until the last. That carries a woman along after she loses her husband. You don't have that."

"We don't all have that," Sarah Mae said, her voice low. The women nodded solemnly.

"What do you mean?" Tabitha asked, leaning forward.

"I mean that not every woman has a marriage that leaves her with pleasant memories once her husband passes," Sarah Mae replied. "I didn't. My husband had a terrible temper. He was cruel, hard, and the *kinner* were terrified of him. I endured that man, and when he died, I mourned for him, *yah*, but it wasn't the same as other women who lost a loving husband. Life would be hard without a man to provide, but it was much, much easier in other ways."

Tabitha stared at the old woman, stunned at her candid confession.

"You're shocked she said it," Miriam pointed out with a small smile. "Welcome back home, dear girl. You're one of us now. You've experienced a loss those lovely young wives will never understand. And that pain brings wisdom."

"I suppose it does," Tabitha said, and she blinked back a mist in her eyes. "I tried giving my sisters advice, but—"

Her advice hadn't been helpful to her sisters at all.

"Ah, that's a mistake to offer advice," Miriam said with a chuckle. "You can't do that."

"I learned that the hard way," Tabitha admitted.

"Some painful experiences are too unique," Aent Dina said. "They aren't useful as warnings. They're better as commiseration."

"Unless they ask," Sarah Mae said. "If they ask, then

they'll listen and they'll take your words into consideration at the very least. If they don't ask, they'll only be resentful when you try to help."

"Aent Dina," Tabitha said, "did you have advice for me when I was with Michael?"

"I was never married, dear," Aent Dina said softly.

"True, but you had a brain and eyes in your head," Tabitha replied. "Did you have advice that I wouldn't have wanted to hear?"

"Of course, dear." Aent Dina smiled sadly. "I thought Michael was a little too high on himself. He valued his own comfort more than your happiness. And he was rather cocky. I thought he was a mistake from the start, but you wouldn't have seen that. You were blinded by love."

She was right, of course. Tabitha wouldn't have listened.

"Do you have advice for me now?" Tabitha asked. "I'd listen now, you know."

"I'm proud of you, dear girl," Aent Dina said. "You are home again, and you're contributing, and you're here with us. My advice would have been to come to a quilting circle, but here you are."

Tabitha shot her *aent* a fond smile. "That's nice to hear. If you do have advice"—she gazed around the circle—"I'm not too prideful to hear it now."

"Well, then . . ." Miriam started.

The others cleared their throats, and Miriam went silent.

"*Nee*, I want to hear it," Tabitha said. "I won't be truly part of the community again until I can humbly hear the advice of women who know more than me."

"I would say to be careful with Jonas Peachy," Miriam said. "I'm sorry, dear. That will be hard to hear because we can see that you two are close, and I'm sure your heart is

221

involved. But you can't marry him, and this friendship of yours can't ever be more."

Tabitha blinked. Her friendship with Jonas was that obvious? Of course people had been watching. It was what a community did—they kept an eye on each other.

"We aren't courting," Tabitha said. "He isn't my boyfriend."

"I've said it, and I'll leave it alone." Miriam raised her hands, palms outward.

"We aren't dating," Tabitha repeated. "Really, this is only friendship."

"It starts that way," Sarah Mae said. "Mutual respect. A shared sense of humor. Conversations that leave you both wanting to talk for longer. And you never need to even touch your finger to his for your heart to get entangled. We were all young once. We've been there too. Just a thought. That's all."

And they were right—Tabitha did not want to take their advice. She'd asked for it, and every part of her was balking at what they had to say. She and Jonas knew the boundaries of their friendship. But when she looked around the circle, she saw knowing looks on those weathered faces. She was proving them right.

"It is hard to hear because he is a good friend," Tabitha admitted. "But I will think on it. *Danke* for your honesty with me."

Perhaps she had finally found her place to belong now that she was back. Her place was no longer with the young single women and wives. It was with the women who had known painful loss, women who would no longer be looking for another husband to fill that hole in their hearts. That was exactly where Tabitha was in her life's journey too. Perhaps she'd arrived here earlier than most, but life could be hard that way sometimes.

Besides, she'd been spending time with Iris lately, and she felt a calling to be a support to these older women too. She could give back.

Strange—the women she'd overlooked most easily in her carefree youth could very well be the circle where she would be at home now that she'd returned.

Danke, Gott, she prayed in her heart. *I think I see my place.*

24

In Romeo's Pizza, nestled in the heart of downtown Shepherd's Hill, Danny sat in a back booth with a glass of ice water in front of him. Outside the window, the sky was still bright, the sun low in the west and casting long golden rays across the parking lot. The restaurant wasn't very busy tonight, which was a relief. A few tables were filled with *Englischer* families enjoying pizza, but two servers stood by the *Please Wait to be Seated* sign, chatting. He was glad that there weren't any Amish folk here besides himself. He didn't need the added pressure of people he knew watching him try to talk to Zach, because Danny honestly had no idea how this was going to go.

Except for one Amish server—a girl wearing the Romeo's Pizza apron on top of her cape dress. She was a few years younger than Danny, and besides giving him a friendly look, she was occupied with a full table of *Englischers* who were celebrating a middle-aged man's birthday. "Uncle Doug," they were calling him.

Danny spotted Zach when he came inside, but he didn't come alone. Meghan was right behind him, and Danny sighed. Great. So this wasn't going to be an honest talk between brothers. It would be something different—something a little less honest.

Gott, please help us make peace, he prayed.

Meghan said something to Zach, he nodded, and she headed in the direction of the washrooms. Then Zach came over to the booth and slid in opposite Danny.

"How come you brought Meghan along?" Danny asked, keeping his voice low.

"She's my girlfriend." Zach gave him a flat look.

"*Yah*, I know, but I was hoping to talk as brothers."

"We're still brothers," Zach replied. "I know Mamm and Daet don't like her, but I won't have anyone putting themselves in the middle of my relationship."

"Mamm and Daet like her fine," Danny said.

"*Yah*? She's *Englisch*. I know how they think."

"You haven't had an honest conversation with them in the better part of a year," Danny said. "How do you know what they think? Mamm and Daet like her. She's a perfectly nice person. She just doesn't understand our ways."

"That's not her fault," Zach said.

"*Nee*, you're right. It's yours," he shot back.

Meghan emerged from the washroom hallway then and headed in their direction. Danny clamped his mouth shut. How much could he even say in front of Meghan? He wasn't sure. Zach beckoned her over and slid over to give her space.

"Hi, Meghan," Danny said. "It's nice to see you again."

Meghan slid into the spot and cast Zach a nervous smile. Their waiter, an *Englischer* young man, came over and took their order—a pepperoni pizza to share and Cokes all around.

"I wanted to talk about your videos," Danny blurted out.

Zach froze, and Meghan's face suddenly blazed red. So she knew about them, all right. Of course she would. But Zach looked taken by surprise.

"Who told you about them?" Zach asked after a beat of silence.

"No one. I found them myself."

His brother shrugged. "Maybe I shouldn't have used my real name. When it started, it hardly seemed like it mattered. But then it took off, and I got all these followers. You can't change the name you use then. I would have had to start over and delete everything that was working." He smiled wanly. "I don't know if that means anything to you or not."

"I get the gist," Danny replied. "How come you were taking video of me working?"

"I wanted to show an Amish man working."

"Why me?"

"Better my brother than someone else in the community," he replied. "You might not believe me, but I don't want to be shunned."

And shunning was possible for someone who hadn't been baptized if he did something bad enough that affected the community.

"I'm as Amish as anyone else here," Danny said. "I don't want you using those videos of me."

Zach sighed. "Okay. *Yah.* I get it. I can take those down."

"*Danke.*" Danny was silent for a moment. "Why did you start posting videos about our culture? Is it just for attention?"

Pride was what the Amish would call it, but stating that outright would put his brother's back up.

"*Nee.* It's not about getting likes and follows. It's about telling people the truth."

"What truth?" Danny demanded. "You make us look like heartless, uneducated louts!"

"I'm sorry if it offends you, but—"

"Offends me?" Danny shook his head. "You make our parents sound abusive and stupid. They are neither of those things. You make us sound like we enjoy staying uninformed, and that isn't true at all. You know as well as I do that we keep learning for our whole lives. Maybe we learn more about farming and animal husbandry, or about building or water management, but we're learning about things that matter to us."

"That's the thing—learning about things that matter to the Amish," his brother said. "But there is a whole country out there, you know. A whole world."

The food arrived, and they all stayed silent while the waiter deposited the pizza in the center of the table, passed out plates, and then brought their drinks. Danny thanked the man, and when he retreated again, Danny bowed his head.

When he raised his head after grace, he found Zach and Meghan both staring at him. Zach's gaze was irritated, but Meghan looked nervous still.

"You don't say grace anymore?" Danny asked.

"*Nee*," Zach said.

"Oh. Well . . . dig in. It's blessed anyway," Danny said dryly.

They each took a slice of pizza, but Danny didn't feel hungry anymore. His slice lay untouched on his plate.

"How is your sister Anne?" Meghan asked.

"Fine," Danny replied.

"I'm curious," Meghan said. "Don't you want more for her?"

"More than what?" Danny asked.

227

"More than a life of serving a husband and being relegated to her home?" Meghan's words were more aggressive than her tone. She looked honestly worried. "She listens to you. I can tell she believes everything—"

"She's fine," Danny said, more firmly this time. "What does my brother tell you, exactly?"

Meghan looked over at Zach, eyes wide.

"I tell her the truth," Zach said. "I don't sugarcoat anything."

"So you tell her that our sister is being repressed?" Danny asked, then he turned to Meghan. "Here's the thing. Women have the exact same education level as men in the Amish community. They run the home—they have absolute power over that domain. The men provide the money, but the women spend it. When a man gets married, he knows that it is his Gott-given duty to provide for his wife and their *kinner* for the rest of his life. That's his job—providing for them. And the happier and more joyful his wife is, the more successful he is. A woman can run a small business on the side, if she wants to. Plenty of women do. You see them in the Amish Market all the time."

"What if she doesn't want children?" Meghan pressed.

"What if she does?" he shot back.

"What if she wants more in her life? What if she wants more schooling? A career outside the home?"

"Anne doesn't."

"Anne doesn't know there are other options," Zach said quietly.

"So Anne is your goal now. Free her from the family who loves her and from the faith community she was raised with?" Danny demanded. Because if they were going to be targeting Anne with their harmful ideas and trying to lure her away from her family and her faith, then Danny was more than willing to stand against them.

"I remember being her age!" Meghan said. "I remember being told I was stupid and I'd never amount to anything. I wasn't raised Amish, but I was raised without the support I craved."

That took Danny by surprise, and he looked at the young woman. Her face was pale, and she looked ready to argue.

"Meghan, that's awful," Danny said earnestly. "I promise you, no one speaks to my sister that way. No one. Look, you don't seem to understand what our culture is really like. My brother has filled your head with a lot of garbage that isn't true. Sure, he might pull out a true detail here or there, but he's stringing them together to make our life look different than it really is."

"I don't lie to her!" Zach snapped.

"It amounts to the same thing," Danny retorted. "Meghan, you should spend more time at our place. You should get to know my parents and my grandmother and our neighbors. You'd see something very different than my brother has been portraying in those videos."

"You think she'd be welcome?" Zach barked out a laugh. "She's not Amish, and she never will be! Do you think our parents want her influence around Anne and Toby? Because I can guarantee you that they don't."

"*Yah*, she would be welcome!" Danny was sick of this. "Do you have to abide by Daet's rules when in our home? Sure. So do I, for that matter. Zach, we like Meghan, but she hasn't been given a chance to get to know us. You make us look like a bunch of backward beasts, and we are nothing of the kind. Anne doesn't need rescuing, but you'd make Meghan believe that she does. That's not Meghan's fault—

it's yours. We all think Meghan has a really good heart, and we like her."

"So you say now—"

"Oh, cut it out," Danny said, annoyed. "Meghan, we're sorry we spoke in our language when you were over last time. It was rude of us. We were trying to hide the awkward discussion we were having with Zach, and we were embarrassed. But my parents want me to tell you that they are very sorry for offending you. We ask your forgiveness."

Meghan blinked at him, and for a moment, he thought she wouldn't say anything, but then she nodded. "Of course. It's forgotten."

"*Danke.*" He shot her a smile. "We'll teach you a few words too. Before you know it, you'll understand what people are saying when they forget to keep it to English."

She smiled then, and it transformed her whole face. "What is *danke*?"

"It means 'thank you,'" he replied. "See? You're learning the language already. Sometimes I accidentally include Pennsylvania Dutch words when I talk. If you ever come across one you don't know, just ask. Our brains are always working in two languages."

"Zach said that—" Meghan's gaze flicked toward Zach momentarily. "He said your parents wouldn't approve of us living together."

"No, they don't," Danny said. "I don't either, not that it's my business. But the reason is that we believe in getting married and making the commitment. We believe a woman is worth a vow. A man, too, for that matter. We believe in choosing to be together as man and wife and committing to each other for a lifetime, not just ending up together long-term. I've always been taught that there was a difference between the two."

"It *isn't* your business," Zach said firmly.

And Danny could feel that he'd slid over the line there. Zach and Meghan were both adults, and they were not baptized Amish. Danny couldn't expect them to live like Amish when they weren't.

"I know," Danny said quickly. "But if Meghan is going to spend more time with the family, then she should at least know where our ideas come from."

Meghan looked away, and Danny had a feeling he'd offended her anyway.

"I'm sorry if I overstepped," he added.

He picked up his slice of pizza then. Maybe it was a good thing that Meghan had come along this evening. Zach seemed to have given her a very different view of the Amish culture and beliefs than was even fair. And maybe Danny could see why she'd be defensive around them considering all of that. Meghan excused herself and slipped out of the booth. She didn't head toward the bathroom, though. She headed for the door. Danny's breath caught.

"Now you've done it!" Zach said. "I told you that us living together is none of your business. If Meghan and I are happy, what do you care?"

"I don't, really," Danny said. "I mean—" He sighed. "Look, Zach, you can't come into Mamm and Daet's house and tell Anne and Toby that all the stuff Mamm and Daet taught them is wrong. If you try that, Daet will ban you, and we'll never get a chance to figure out these differences and make our peace."

"*Yah*? Well, you don't get to tell my girlfriend that we aren't supposed to be living together either," Zach snapped.

"Deal!" Danny said. "It's not my business. I agree. So let's just agree to be respectful of each other. You respect the house rules and don't tell our younger siblings that flouting the rules is okay. And we'll respect that you and Meghan have your own relationship that isn't our business. But we've got to have a way to see each other and stay civil. I don't want to lose my brother."

Zach's gaze moved toward the door, where Meghan had disappeared. He pulled a few bills out of his pocket and dropped them on the table.

"I don't know," Zach replied. "I'm not asking Meghan to act like our life is shameful. We're not going to pretend we don't live together when we do. It's been an important step in our relationship."

Were they at an impasse already?

"I'm sure we can figure out a balance," Danny said. "And maybe you could reconsider making those videos—"

"Those videos pay my rent!" Zach stood up, but he didn't look angry now. He looked tired. "I have an eighth-grade education when everything requires a high school diploma at the very least. Do you know how hard it is to make enough money to live?"

Danny shook his head.

"It's really hard. I'm always stressed. I can't *afford* to marry her! I can't afford to support a wife and kids! So when I tell you, Anne, and Toby that you'd be wise to get more education, I know from experience. Okay? And you might not understand this, but I love you guys, and I want you to have more chances than I have. I actually care."

Zach marched out of the restaurant, leaving Danny with most of a pepperoni pizza and a couple of crumpled bills that Danny was pretty sure his brother needed more than he did.

What had just happened here tonight?

Gott, was this a step forward, or did I mess it up?

He wasn't sure, but he suddenly had an irrepressible longing to go find Beth and talk it out with her. He had a feeling she'd have some insights that he couldn't see right now, although it might not encourage her to make her commitment for the faith at all.

Somehow, Danny was pretty certain those happy family gatherings he was hoping for that would include Zach and Meghan together at the table weren't going to take place.

No matter what he tried, Danny seemed to be stepping wrong.

25

Tabitha was peeling potatoes into a pot when she heard a buggy arrive through the open window. She didn't stop peeling, watching as her father ambled over to the window to look outside.

"Huh," he said.

"Who is it?" Tabitha asked.

"The Peachy boy."

Tabitha rolled her eyes. "You can call him Jonas, Daet." She dried her hands on a towel. "I wonder if he needs me."

Her father gave her a wry look, which she ignored. There had been a lot of comments lately about her friendship with Jonas, but he knew what she meant. Normally when Jonas swung by, it was because someone needed her veterinarian services.

Daet opened the side door before Jonas had a chance to knock, and Tabitha headed over to the mudroom, drying her hands as she went.

"Hi, Abram," Jonas said. "How are you?"

"Can't complain," Daet replied. "You?"

"I'm fine. My *aent's* milk cow, though, is another story."

His gaze moved past Daet and met Tabitha's, pleasantries discarded. "Aent Iris's milk cow has some sort of inflammation. She looks uncomfortable. She's either pacing or leaning against the fence. She won't drink," Jonas explained. He clamped his hand on his head as a gust of wind attempted to dislodge his hat.

"Right," Tabitha said, pulling off her kitchen apron. "If she's leaning, that's a very bad sign. Give me a minute to gather my things."

Tabitha grabbed her medical bag and opened it, tossing some extra supplies inside. Before starting dinner, she'd returned from a rather emotionally draining call about a dog that had been hit by a car. The poor thing had been in terrible shape, so she'd had to help the family choose a merciful good-bye. It had been the right thing to do, but the *kinner* had sobbed. Not every veterinarian call had a happy ending, and not every animal patient could be helped. She hated that part of the job.

"Daet, I'll be back when I can," Tabitha said, giving her father an apologetic look. "Take the roast out of the oven in half an hour."

"I'll figure it out," Daet muttered, and he waved her off. "Go do your job. I'll feed myself."

Tabitha sincerely hoped that roast wouldn't be ruined because she was hungry already and would be hungrier still by the time she got home later tonight, but she didn't have time to worry over it. She might be the woman of her father's home now, but she wasn't able to put her time into housekeeping like another single daughter might.

Within minutes, she had settled herself in Jonas's buggy, and they were headed up the drive.

"I was dropping my *mamm* off to visit with Aent Iris when

I noticed the cow," Jonas said. "If Aent Iris can't afford to pay you, my *daet* will cover the bill."

"Did Iris mention anything about the milk?" Tabitha asked.

"There wasn't much milk the last few days. They were afraid she was drying up."

Tabitha peppered him with a few more questions. Some things Jonas knew, others he didn't, but it gave her a clearer picture of what she was walking into. Mastitis was a common ailment in milk cows, and it could be deadly if left untreated. And after her last call with the poor wounded dog, she needed a win.

Gott, let me be in time . . .

But a weakened cow leaning against the fence wasn't a good sign.

"You okay?" Jonas asked.

"I lost a dog. He was hit by a car," she said. "There was nothing I could do."

"I'm sorry, Tabby." He reached over and gave her hand a brief squeeze. She wished she could hold on to his hand a little longer, but she wouldn't. Instead, Miriam's warning about being careful with this relationship was ringing through her mind.

When they turned into the Peachy drive, Mary and Iris were standing outside, leaning against the fence that enclosed the small pasture. Beth didn't seem to be around. The cow was a few yards from the fence, lying on her side. She mooed miserably—there were variations to a cow's tone of voice, and Tabitha knew them well.

Tabitha bent down and squeezed through the rails of the fence, then pulled her bag through after her. She lifted her skirt so she could take longer strides and stepped over a cow pat. The cow's udder was noticeably swollen and reddened around the teats. She had some foam around her lips too. She was dehydrated.

"You're sore, aren't you?" Tabitha murmured. "We'll get you sorted out, sweet girl."

Tabitha worked quickly.

"Mary, would you start a kettle on the stove inside?" she called over to Jonas's mother.

"*Yah*, right away," Mary said, and she and Iris headed back toward the house. Jonas passed them, heading in her direction.

"Jonas, would you fill a clean five-gallon pail about three-quarters full with water from the pump?"

"Sure thing," he replied. "What are you doing?"

"She's dehydrated. We're going to push water with some additives to help her get the liquid she needs in her system. I'll give her some antibiotics at the same time."

When Jonas had the fresh water, Iris came out with the kettle, and Tabitha had Jonas add the piping-hot water to the cold to warm it up. It was important to have warm water for this so as not to shock the poor cow's system any more than it already was. Tabitha started with a dose of antibiotics using a drenching gun, which basically pushed the liquid medication to the back of the cow's throat so she'd swallow it down. But that wouldn't be enough for the water. Cattle didn't like tubes pushed down their throats any better than people did, but this cow was weakened and she didn't have the strength to fight too much as Tabitha slid the tube from her little hand pump down her esophagus and into her rumen. Then she started to steadily pump warm water down the cow's throat and into her belly.

The additives to the water worked like a sports drink for

cattle, helping the animal to absorb the water and use it in her system as efficiently as possible. When she'd finished pushing the water, she carefully removed the tube, and the cow shook her head to free herself from it. She was already looking a little perkier. Dehydration could do terrible things. But add in the antibiotics and, if Tabitha was correct, this cow would be right as rain soon enough. She went back to her bag and pulled out some ointment for the cow's teats. It would reduce inflammation and aid in some quicker healing. She squatted down next to the cow and worked the soothing salve over the afflicted area.

"Let her rest," Tabitha said. "I'll just keep an eye on her for a few minutes here and see how she's doing."

"*Danke*, dear," Iris said. "I was going to start some baking—"

"Go on inside," Tabitha urged. "I'll just stick around for a few minutes."

The women headed back into the house, and Tabitha leaned against the fence. Jonas joined her. The cow was resting, her head up and her tail flicking—that was a good sign.

From where Tabitha stood, she could see across the pasture to the road that ran in front of the house, and she spotted two people walking—a young man and a woman. She squinted, trying to get a better look. All she could properly make out was that they were walking close together with that slow, meandering way of a young couple with nowhere really to go.

"That's Beth and Danny," Jonas supplied.

"Oh . . ." She laughed softly. "Those two are falling in love with each other, aren't they?"

"You think?" he asked.

"You don't?" She shot him a surprised look. "Come on, Jonas. Has it been that long since you were in love that you

238

don't see the signs anymore? Look at how she's leaning into his arm like that."

"And he's not moving away," he said.

She and Jonas leaned on the fence, their attention trained on the walking couple. It wasn't so long ago that Tabitha had been finding any excuse possible to see Michael. He would come by and take her for walks. He'd give her rides to school, and she'd walk around in a dreamy fog thinking about him. She'd thought she was hiding her feelings, but looking at this young couple, she doubted she'd hid anything.

"They're walking slowly too," Tabitha said. "The point of that walk isn't to get somewhere."

"They're going slower now," Jonas agreed. "Is he walking her back?"

The couple stopped, and Beth dropped her head, then looked up at Danny. They seemed undecided about something, then turned around and started back up the way they'd come.

"They're making their walk longer," Tabitha said. "Didn't you ever do that?"

"*Yah*, I may have." Jonas sounded amused. "But you see, the trick is, you have to get the girl to suggest it, or else she'll say no, she has to go home."

"Is that how you do it?"

"It's how I did."

"I'm not sure I like this sly, conniving side to you." She laughed.

"What? I'm not conniving. I just . . . know when I want more time with a woman."

"Fine," she said. "That's fair, I guess. We women like to think that these things are more accidental than they are, I guess."

"Not accidental." Jonas nudged her shoulder. "Sorry to ruin it for you."

Tabitha looked toward the cow again. Her udder still looked engorged and swollen, but she seemed more alert now, and she heaved herself up to her feet.

"She's up!" Tabitha said.

"Good. Right?"

"Very good," she agreed.

Beth and Danny disappeared behind some trees that lined the road, then emerged out the other side a few moments later. She could leave now. The cow was doing better already, but something held her back. It was nice to stand out here on a warm June evening with Jonas.

"Do you think there's a courtship in the works there?" Jonas asked.

"There's something," she replied. "There's definitely some feelings between them."

Tabitha looked up at him, and Jonas glanced down at her at the same time. His dark brown eyes caught hers, and she found herself unable to look away.

"Don't you remember feeling that way?" she asked, and she felt a little breathless.

"Admiring a woman and thinking about her all the time?" he asked, his voice low. "I suppose so."

"It happens to the best of us." She tore her gaze away from his. There, that was better. That silly man didn't know what a direct look like that could do to a woman.

Tabitha leaned over so she could see past a copse of trees, and she collided with his arm. And when she looked up at him in surprise, she found herself trapped in those warm eyes again. She swallowed.

She knew exactly what it felt like to fall for a man, and she was getting dangerously close to that edge . . .

The sound of the house's screen door clapping startled

them both, and Jonas turned around. Tabitha rubbed her hands over her arms and bent down to collect her bag.

"Iris has some pie if you two are interested!" Mary called.

"What do you say?" Jonas asked.

Nee, she'd stayed too long already, and her heart was longing for something it couldn't have.

"I'd better get back home," Tabitha said. "I'm sorry, Jonas. I've already made supper, and my *daet* is probably waiting on me."

"*Yah*, sure, I'll give you a ride back," Jonas said.

That was much safer. A ride in a buggy with Jonas might not be exactly safe territory, but the longer they stayed here, the closer to sunset they'd be. And the thought of riding with him through the velvet twilight made her heart tumble. Tabitha did remember those old feelings of romance and excitement. It was intoxicating, even addictive.

And in this case, it was wrong. She was divorced. This couldn't go anywhere.

"*Danke*," she said, forcing a bright smile, and she turned back toward Mary. "It'll probably take twenty-four hours for the swelling and redness to go down on her udder, so let me know if it doesn't. You should notice improvement by tomorrow, though."

"*Danke*, Tabitha!" Mary called back. "I'll let Beth know when she gets back!"

The widows had been right—Tabitha was getting too close to Jonas. She needed to stop spending so much time with him. There was no future together.

26

Over the next few days, Beth saw quite a bit of Danny. He seemed to be there whenever she needed a break. Sometimes she'd walk down to his family's home while someone visited with Mammi, and other times when Mammi was puttering around inside the house by herself, Beth would meet him on the beach, and they'd sit on that pebbled shore and toss flat stones out over the water to see if they would skip.

Tabitha had come back to give the milk cow more antibiotics. While the cow was improving, it wasn't happening quickly enough for Tabitha to feel satisfied that they'd found the root of the problem. That was how she explained it, and Tabitha was good at her job.

So they kept milking the cow twice a day and tossing the milk. It couldn't be safely consumed.

Visiting Sunday came and went. Beth had gone along with Mammi to see some family and friends. Mammi needed the support—she couldn't just take the buggy and go visiting like in years past. So Beth hadn't seen Danny on Sunday, but today when Sarah Mae came by to visit with Mammi,

Danny took Beth out to the Bontrager egg farm to pick up Mammi's egg order. It wasn't a long buggy ride—about ten minutes—and when they pulled into the Bontrager drive, there were a few *Englischer* vehicles parked by the little sales shanty set up next to the stable. They'd need to stand in line.

"Who did you visit with on Sunday?" Beth asked Danny as they got out of the buggy. She carried the empty cardboard egg flats to return.

"My grandmother and a couple of great-uncles and great-aunts came to our place," he replied.

"Did you have a good time?"

He tied the horse to a hitching post, and they headed in the direction of the lineup.

"*Yah*. It was a good time to hear the old stories—" He winced and leaned over and nudged her shoulder with his. "I'm sorry. I'm getting family stories when you aren't. I didn't think before I spoke."

"It's okay. That's normal to hear stories from the older generation," she said. "What kinds of stories do they tell?"

"Oh, the time my *daet* fell out of an apple tree and broke his arm. The time my great-uncle went fishing and caught a catfish as big as my grandmother from the bottom of our lake. How my grandfather died of a heart attack in the middle of harvest."

They settled a few feet behind an *Englischer* couple, who turned and gave them a cordial nod. Beth and Danny nodded back. Their conversation would stay private enough since they were talking quietly in *Deutsch*. Danny got to hear stories from his family. And Beth had now heard some, but none of the stories she wanted to hear most.

"I tell stories about you, you know," he added.

"What?" She looked over at him. "Like what?"

"Like that time when we were about ten or twelve, and we walked all the way to the railroad tracks to put a penny down and have it squashed, and that rainstorm caught up with us, so we had to sit in Old Man Gordon's barn until it passed. Or that time we were weeding your *mammi's* flowerbed, and that mouse came out and ran up your arm. You screamed and ran and jumped in the lake."

Beth laughed. "I really am part of your childhood stories, huh?"

"*Yah*, some of the best parts."

She felt her face warm, and she dropped her gaze.

"Maybe I'm the only one who remembers those old times when we were young so fondly," he said.

"*Nee*, I remember those times too, but I didn't tell my *mamm* the stories for fear she wouldn't let me go visit Mammi on my own anymore."

"Ah!" He chuckled. "Smart."

She watched as the person at the front of the line carried a stack of thirty-count flats of eggs to a waiting van. The Bontrager *kinner* were setting aside more for the man. He must be a local baker or something to need so many.

"I had to be careful. I loved coming to see Mammi, and I didn't want her to change her mind about sending me." She glanced at him. "I loved coming to see you too."

"I used to watch for when you'd arrive," he said. "You always came out to your *mammi's* backyard, and you'd stand there for a little while."

"*Yah*, I was trying to see if you were outside," she said. She'd looked forward to seeing Danny just as much.

"Were you really?"

"Of course. You might be a terrible letter writer, but I missed you."

Danny chuckled. "Maybe I'll try my hand at letter writing again."

"For me?" She shot him a grin, and the first customer got the last of his eggs and they all moved forward.

"*Yah*. You're the only one who's ever asked me for a letter. I'll . . . think of more interesting things to include."

It wasn't his news and gossip that were the problem with his letters. It was that they read like a weather report, and she'd wanted his letters to tell her what he was thinking about, not what the neighbors planted. She'd wanted him to put into words the way he felt when his brown eyes shone warm just for her.

The couple ahead of them paid for a single flat of eggs, and then it was Beth's turn.

"Hi," Beth said. "I'm here to pick up my grandmother's egg order—Iris Peachy. I think it's three flats."

"Of course." Ellen Bontrager was a portly woman in her forties, and she gave Beth a smile. "Danny, I have your *mamm's* order too. I think she ordered two flats. Let me check my book."

They got their eggs and paid, then brought them to the buggy and arranged them carefully in the back so the eggs wouldn't break.

As they headed back toward home, Danny reached over and took her hand. She scooted closer, enjoying the momentary privacy.

"So what happens when your *mammi* moves in with you?" he asked. "Is that it for your visits to Shepherd's Hill?"

"It would have ended eventually anyway," she said. "I'd end up with a job where I couldn't just take a summer off."

"So . . . this is your last summer here?" he asked.

Her heart gave a squeeze. "It doesn't have to be the end

of us, though. You could come see us. It's a two-hour bus ride. It isn't too bad."

"And you could come here. We'd book the ice house cottage for you."

"You'd lose money."

"It's only money, Beth."

But that assumed that she'd stay Amish, didn't it?

"Have you ever thought of joining a more liberal community?" she asked. Danny was silent for a few beats, and she looked up at him. "I mean, it would free things up for me. Maybe they'd be okay with me getting my high school diploma and working at a bank. Maybe they'd let me get a little more schooling after that, or let me teach kids how to swim. You never know."

"I don't want to hold you back, Beth," Danny said, "but I do believe in our conservative ways. I know it's restrictive, but it also protects the things that make us so different. I think you should go as far as you want to go, though. You'd never be happy otherwise, but . . ."

"But?" she pressed. She'd make him say it out loud—maybe it would be easier for her that way.

"But I want to stay here. I want to keep to this way of life." He squeezed her hand. "If you wanted this life too, I'd be a really happy guy."

The lake glittered through the trees as they came up to Mammi's drive, and Danny let go of her hand to turn the horse. As they approached the house, Mammi came outside with her purse over one arm, her friend Sarah Mae behind her.

"Where are you going, Mammi?" Beth called.

"I have to get a few things in town," Mammi called back. "I won't be long!"

Beth cast Danny an apologetic look.

"Go with her," he said softly. He understood. "I'll put your eggs inside on the kitchen table."

"*Danke*. I'll see you later."

She couldn't let Mammi just go off in the buggy alone lest she find herself lost or one of her episodes happen. But she also didn't like to make Mammi feel like she was in need of babysitting either. She and Danny both got out of the buggy, but Danny went around to the back and Beth headed toward the older woman. She gave Sarah Mae a quick wave.

"Maybe I could come with you?" Beth asked.

"If you'd like to, dear," Mammi said. "But hurry. We don't have much time to waste."

Sarah Mae looked relieved that Beth had arrived to take over, and she held the door open for Danny as he brought the eggs inside.

Danny came back out of the house and cast Beth a private, warm look. But he was no longer the boy she used to play with, or who wrote such terrible letters. He was now a devoted Amish man with broad shoulders and a sweet gaze that could make her forget what she was going to say.

Beth said good-bye to Sarah Mae, who'd left her own buggy hitched up, and went to hitch up their horse. A few minutes later, Beth and Mammi were trotting down the road toward town.

They passed the Lapps' drive, where Danny had driven back home and was unhitching his own horse. He looked up as they went by and gave her a little wave.

"He's a nice boy," Mammi said.

Mammi noticed me staring. Beth felt her face warm.

"*Yah*, I know."

Danny was very nice, but he was also Amish to the core.

He wanted a quiet, calm, reassuring Amish life, and Beth wasn't sure she could ever provide that. Could she commit to a proper Amish life? Could she be the kind of woman Danny needed? She didn't want this summer to be the end between them, but they were old enough now to make some serious choices.

A wave of sadness washed over her at the thought. She was getting attached to Danny again, but this was no longer a childhood friendship, was it? This was two adults who could very well move things forward if they so chose. Did she want more with Danny? Did she want him to court her properly and take her driving the way Amish men did when they were serious?

"He's always been a little sweet on you," Mammi said.

"He told me that." She smiled.

"Love doesn't always come around when you feel ready for it," Mammi said quietly. "It doesn't always come around twice. I lost Arden, and while he wasn't talking about marriage with me, there was a connection there that I didn't find again. I think when you're young and pretty, you take things for granted that you shouldn't."

"Are you saying that Danny might be my last chance at marriage?" Beth asked.

"Not really . . ." Mammi sighed. "I'm saying that you shouldn't take a man's heart for granted when he lays it at your feet. That's precious."

"His heart isn't at my feet, Mammi," she said.

"Are you sure?"

I'm at a greater risk of losing my heart to him than he is of falling helplessly in love with me.

"I won't go breaking his heart, Mammi," Beth said, giving her grandmother a reassuring smile. "I promise."

248

Once they were in town, Mammi had a list of things she wanted to do. First was the bank, where she withdrew some money, and Beth watched the tellers work, wondering what it might be like to work there too. Then they headed over to the dry goods store. The dry goods store carried bulk food, flour and sugar, even a few canned goods. They also had a squeaky rack that held patterns for Amish clothing, postcards, and a few greeting cards for birthdays and anniversaries. Mammi took one of the small grocery carts and started down the aisles.

The store wasn't busy. There were a couple of other families shopping at the same time. Some Amish boys stood by the rack of postcards, looking over the pictures of Shepherd's Hill scenery—no people included in those photos.

"Could you grab me that big bag of sugar, dear?" Mammi said.

Beth did as her grandmother asked and lugged the big bag off the shelf and dropped it into the cart.

"And the flour. Two more bags, please," Mammi said.

"Mammi, we have plenty of flour," Beth responded. "What's next on your list?"

"No, we're out," Mammi said, shaking her head.

"There are two full bags in the bottom cupboard," Beth said. "I saw them myself."

"No, dear. I need flour." Mammi's voice trembled. "I have to be able to bake."

"But we already have two bags, Mammi."

"I need flour!" Mammi's voice started to rise.

"Okay, okay . . . I'll get it for you."

This hardly seemed like something to argue over, so Beth hoisted two bags of flour into the cart. Mammi would have all sorts of flour now. She'd have to bring flour with her when she moved.

There was an *Englischer* family in the shop today—a farming family by the looks of them. The mother wore her hair back in a ponytail, and she wore jeans and a T-shirt. She had a little girl on one hip—the child looked to be about two or three—and she was tired and fussy, tipping her head onto her mother's shoulder and whining.

A young boy followed along behind. He wore shorts and flip-flops and a bored look on his face. The dry goods store wasn't going to be entertaining for a boy his age. He looked over at them, and Beth shot him a smile. He smiled faintly back.

"Mose!" Mammi suddenly said.

"What, Mammi?" Beth asked, but her grandmother slipped past, her shopping forgotten.

"Mose, what are you doing?" Mammi hurried up to the boy and bent down. "Let's go. Come. We're leaving now."

"Mammi?" Beth said. The boy looked equally surprised to have an old Amish woman ordering him around.

Mammi ignored her and caught the boy by the wrist. "Let's go, Mose! Don't dillydally!"

"Mammi!" Beth said, hurrying up to her grandmother's side at the same time that the *Englischer* woman turned back, her eyes wide with alarm.

"Gavin!" the woman said, and the boy tugged back, trying to pull his hand free from Mammi's grip, but she wasn't letting go. He pulled harder, jerking at her grasp to get himself free. He might hurt Mammi doing that, but Beth understood the instinct.

"Mammi!" Beth put a hand over her grandmother's wrist and tapped her hand. "Mammi, this isn't Mose."

Mammi blinked at her. Her eyes were wide, and she had that look about her again—the one where her mind had slipped off to another time and place.

"He's not Mose!" Beth repeated. "He's this lady's child."

"I'm not Mose!" the boy said loudly. "Let go of me!"

Mammi released the boy, blinking in confusion. She drew her hand against her body, and the boy took a huge step backward toward his mother, who grabbed her son and pulled him away. The toddler had stopped whining now and stared in wide-eyed shock.

"I'm sorry!" Beth said quickly. "I'm really sorry. My grandmother has dementia, and she thought that your son was someone else. I'm really sorry."

The woman relaxed slightly and nodded. "It's okay."

But she put a protective hand in front of her son's chest all the same.

"Mammi, let's pay for our things and go," Beth said, and she mouthed another *sorry* to the *Englischer* woman.

Beth led her grandmother back to their cart, then headed over toward the cash register. The cashier was an Amish woman, and she gave Beth a wary look.

"Is Iris okay?" she whispered.

"She's struggling these days," Beth replied. "I just need to get her home."

"Let me ring you up quickly," she said in Pennsylvania Dutch. "I'll just put this on your grandmother's tab."

"*Danke*." Beth exhaled.

Mammi turned around, looking at the *Englischer* boy with a perplexed frown, but she didn't try to approach him again.

"Let's go, Mammi," Beth said, and she nudged her grandmother along while she pushed the cart one-handed toward the exit.

Beth lifted the flour and sugar into the back of the buggy by herself, returned the cart, then helped Mammi up. Mammi kept looking back at the store with that same frown on her face, but Beth didn't mention it again until they were back on the road and headed in the direction of home. Whatever other errands Mammi might have had in mind could wait until another day. Beth's heart was still pattering at an anxious rhythm.

"Mammi, what happened in there?" Beth asked.

"I . . . thought that was Mose," Mammi said. "I really thought it was him."

"But he was an *Englischer* boy, Mammi," Beth said. "Did he look like my father?"

Mammi glanced over at her mutely, and she looked like she was choosing her words carefully. She twisted her apron between her fingers.

"Mammi, do you know who I am?"

"Of course I know who you are, Elizabeth," Mammi said irritably, and her lips wobbled.

So Mammi was back in the present. Good. But Beth needed to get at the information she wanted.

"Mammi, I was hoping you could tell me a story," Beth said, trying to put some cheer into her voice. "It's one I've never heard before."

"What story?"

"Of how you adopted my father," she said. "I'd love to hear it. And I think it's important."

"I don't talk about that."

But why?

"I'm not just anyone, Mammi. I'm Elizabeth, your granddaughter. Mose was my father. I need to know about how he came to you. That's part of my story too. Please tell me, Mammi."

For a moment or two, Beth thought her grandmother

would refuse, but when she looked over at her, she found Mammi staring at her thoughtfully.

"Maybe you should know." Mammi sighed.

"Can you tell me now?"

"When we get home." And Mammi looked away, out the side window.

Beth would just have to wait, but her pulse sped up all the same. Mammi was ready to talk.

What story could be so scandalous as to cause this much caution in one old woman?

27

Mammi was silent and sober the rest of the ride. Whatever peace she normally exuded was gone, and Beth felt like she could see waves of anxiety flooding her grandmother's frame. She sat straight, hands clasped in her lap, lips pinched together. Beth had never seen her like this. Even at Daet's funeral, Mammi had been heartbroken, an absolute wreck and also determined to be a comfort to Mamm, Beth, and her siblings. But she'd let go then—she'd cried. She'd mourned. She'd let people comfort her.

This tense, tight version of her grandmother made Beth nervous.

Would Mammi really tell her what had happened, or would she change her mind before they got home?

They headed out of town and down the side road that led toward Friesen Lake. There was a sign for *Lapp Short-Term Rentals* at the corner—that looked new—and the lake glistened through gaps in the trees.

Beth didn't try to break the silence between them again, half afraid that any attempt to ease the tension with small talk would put them on to a new path away from the story Mammi had promised to tell.

What had happened surrounding her father's adoption? Whose baby was Daet? Was he the son of *Englischers*?

Unless Mammi was going to confess that all of it was a lie and Daet was her child, after all? Beth's mind spun with possible scenarios as they drove the rest of the way home, and when they got back, Mammi headed into the house. Beth unhitched the gelding and put him in the pasture with Bessie. Some of the swelling had gone down in her udder, and she looked more comfortable, but she wasn't completely better. Bessie was like so much else around here—improved, but not completely healed.

Beth headed into the house, half expecting Mammi to have escaped to her bedroom, but Mammi sat at the kitchen table, just as erect as she'd been sitting in the buggy, waiting for her.

Beth pulled out a chair and sat down, her breath bated. "Mammi?"

Mammi's gaze moved over to Beth, and she sucked in a wavering breath.

"It starts with Arden Bieler," Mammi said softly.

And Beth exhaled that slow breath. She'd guessed this much.

"And not in the way you think," Mammi added with a small smile. "No, Arden was not your *daet's daet*. But he was a boy I cared for very much. I was smitten with him. I'm not sure that he felt the same way in return—at least not to the same extent. He cared for me, but had he lived, would he have proposed? I don't know. Maybe not. But he didn't live. He died out there in the lake."

Mammi's chin trembled. "I didn't marry. I told myself I

had loved Arden too much. And then I told myself that no one could compare to him. But the truth of the matter was that no one else came calling, and I was too scared to go find another community."

"But you did leave . . ." Beth said with a frown.

"Eventually, I did. But that came later." Mammi licked her lips. "I was single, and everyone had given up on me marrying. My *daet* had died in a farming accident when I was young, and my *mamm* died when I was twenty-three. So I was staying in this house with my maiden *aent*. We would let out some rooms and make money that way. The years slipped by, and then one year this family came to stay at the lake. They were staying in those old cabins that the Lapps fixed up, and I'd watch them from the lakeshore."

Beth frowned. "How old were you then?"

"About twenty-eight."

"And my *daet*?"

"Just wait, dear." Mammi smiled gently. "It's important that you understand why I did what I did. Now, this family had a son of their own, and they also had taken in a foster child. I knew that because I chatted with the mother once when I saw her in town shopping. But they treated that foster child like a slave when they thought no one could see. I could see a whole lot from here, though. He was sent to get things from the car, made to clean up after everyone, shouted at, demeaned . . . And more than once I saw them hitting him. Not a spanking. A fist to the face. They shoved him, kicked him. The birth child was nicer to the foster child, but there was still a big divide between them. I was stunned. I wanted to help the boy, but I didn't know how! So I would go down there with some baked goods and I'd try to spend some time with them, but they didn't like that. They said I was being weird and intruding. But I made sure that little boy got something sweet to eat, and I prayed for him. Oh, how I prayed for him."

"Did you become a foster mother?"

Mammi pressed her lips together and was silent for a moment. "No. I didn't."

Beth was getting ahead of Mammi again, and she fluttered one hand. "I'm sorry. Go on."

"There was a terrible storm one afternoon while the family was there. It sprang up out of nowhere, and the two boys were still on the lake in a boat. They were fishing without any life jackets or anything. Somehow, the boat tipped, and they both ended up in the water. One managed to get back into the boat, and the foster boy started to swim. It was dim, and the rain was coming down in sheets, and no one had noticed the boy who was swimming. The one boy paddled the boat toward shore, and his family pulled him to safety. I couldn't swim, so there wasn't much I could do, but I did wait for the boy who was swimming, and when he got close enough, I waded out and pulled him onto the shore. I was going to wave down his family when he stopped me. He begged me not to. He pleaded with me to let him run away and not tell anyone I'd found him."

"What did you do?"

"I knew how they treated him. I'd seen it with my own two eyes. So I took him inside. No one noticed. In fact, it took another twenty minutes for them to start calling his name."

"What was his name?" Beth breathed.

"Nelson."

"Oh . . ." Not Mose.

"They shouted for him, but by that time, he'd told me more of the abuse he'd suffered at their hands, and I wasn't

257

sending him back into that. To think there were parents who could mistreat a child like that! He was about eight at the time. Not very old at all. And there I was, a woman who longed for *kinner* of her own but had never married. He just kept begging me not to send him back, and I asked if he'd like to stay with me."

Beth could see in her mind's eye that frail little boy, drenched from the lake, wide eyes, pale skin, terrified of being sent back . . . Her heart squeezed at the thought. She would have done the same—she wouldn't have sent him back.

"That was my father?"

"*Yah*. He was your father."

And now it was all clicking into place. There had been a drowning when Beth's father would have been a young boy, and Beth had assumed that Mammi would have felt the drowning more deeply because her own son was the same age. But that child . . . he hadn't died!

"So the news story of the boy who drowned . . ."

"His body was never recovered, remember? That was how they reported on it. That happens sometimes with those deep currents. It held Arden down for two days, after all."

An icy shiver slid down Beth's neck.

"My *aent* sent me that newspaper clipping in the mail. I was gone by then. My *aent* said she'd keep my secret," Mammi went on, "and Nelson said he'd love to live with me. But I couldn't keep him at the very lake where he disappeared. Someone would recognize him for sure and for certain. So that very night, I bundled him into our buggy, and I took him to Indiana."

A missing child, whisked away to another state. That sounded very illegal.

"You . . . abducted him?" Beth stared at her grandmother in shock.

"Technically." Mammi's cheeks pinked. "I like to think I rescued him, but what I did was very much against the law. I couldn't give him back to them, Elizabeth. I couldn't! And he was convinced the police wouldn't believe him. He was just a boy, and they got money for taking care of him, you see. So they had good reason to hold on to him. But on that buggy ride, we drew up a new identity for him. He was my son, and I was a widow. We called him Moses. I gave him a few names to choose from, and he liked that one best. He stayed quiet until he learned Pennsylvania Dutch, but he was a quick learner. I gave him lessons, and he listened really closely when people talked. I taught him how to be Amish, and he was grateful. He loved our way of life—the peacefulness, the Christian charity, the food. He loved the quiet and working with his hands. He was so grateful to me for taking him in, and he was such an obedient son! He didn't rebel. He'd seen the worst of what was past the fence, and at night when he prayed before going to sleep, he would thank Gott for this Amish life with me."

"But you did come back here . . ." Beth prompted.

"*Yah*, we did. When my *aent* died and left the lake house to me, we came back, but he was old enough then that no one recognized him. He was just another Amish teenager."

"People must have known you didn't have a teenaged son," Beth said.

"They did."

"Did they guess who he was?"

Mammi shrugged. "If they did, they didn't breathe a word. The younger generation didn't know me, or remember much about me. They didn't ask questions. It was the people my

259

own age I had to trust with discretion. But they understood. My *aent* had taken care of the rumors herself while I was away. She told people the truth who needed to know it, and everyone else was simply given silence. Those who knew understood why I'd done it, and they knew I didn't have anyone else to turn to. I was on my own with Mose, and it just became an unspoken rule—no one talked about where Mose came from."

"So they lied for you," Beth whispered.

"*Yah*. Gott forgive me, but they did. But I kept him safe, you see. I never let anyone hurt him again. He was in foster care because his single mother died of a drug overdose. He had no one else. All the same, he could have left at any point. He could have gone back to the city, or tried to find his people. He didn't want to. I didn't hold him here against his will, if that makes it any better. I told him I'd return him at any time if he wanted to go back, but he didn't want that. I didn't even need to spank him once. I could sit him down and explain right and wrong, and he'd do his best to choose right. He had such a good heart, and when it came time for his *rumspringa*, he skipped it! He went to the bishop himself, and he asked to be in the next baptismal class."

Her father had escaped horrific abuse to an Amish community, and he'd fully embraced it. That was the part that left Beth stunned. Her *daet* had embraced his new life so fully that no one had guessed he wasn't born Amish, even his own *kinner*! No wonder he'd been so insistent that his *kinner* learn how to swim . . . His own ability to swim had saved his life that night.

Mammi must have been looking for Mose in the water that night. A stormy night, very much like when she'd found Mose the first time . . .

"Did he tell my *mamm* about any of this?" Beth asked.

Had her mother been holding this information back too?

But Mammi shook her head. "I don't believe so. I told him that there should be no secrets between a husband and wife, but he told me that I was his mother in every way that mattered and there was no reason to talk about it."

So that was why she'd mistaken the *Englischer* boy as her son in the shop today. Because Mose had been an *Englischer* boy too. And maybe Beth understood now why this secret had needed to be kept.

Mammi had sacrificed everything for her son—including her own clear conscience!

"*Danke* for telling me, Mammi. This helps things make sense for me." She caught her grandmother's hand and gave it a tender squeeze.

Mammi squeezed her fingers in return. "I cannot die with this on my conscience. I abducted my son, and I would do it all over again if I had the chance, because I don't know any other way I could have kept him safe."

Beth's mind went back to her *daet* coming in from work, a smile on his face as he hugged them all one by one . . . to his stories about his *Englischer* pals who worked at the sawmill with him. Whenever Beth complained about the difficulties of a cold winter morning or that she couldn't compete in swimming, he'd say the same thing: "*We are so very blessed, Elizabeth. This life protects us from so much. Be thankful for all you have. I couldn't be happy anywhere else.*"

"You did make him happy, Mammi," Beth said, tears welling in her eyes. "He truly believed in our Amish faith, and you gave that to him."

Mammi nodded, "*Yah*, I did. But I also broke some laws

in the process. And I can't face Gott until I somehow make restitution for it."

Restitution . . . What was she referring to? Because the only thing that Beth could think of was her elderly grandmother turning herself in to the police. Would they put her in prison? How would they handle a crime that happened so long ago?

"No, Mammi!" Beth shook her head. "I'm glad you told me, but you can't tell anyone else!"

"I don't know how to make this better, though," Mammi said, her voice trembling. "You don't understand the weight of my guilt. I've been carrying it for years. Your *daet* is dead, and everyone in his *Englischer* life believed he died in that lake. I've been praying for some time now, asking Gott what I should do to make this right, but I haven't gotten an answer yet, and I'd rather not meet my Maker without fixing this somehow. I might need to just go to the police department and tell them my story."

"No," Beth said earnestly. "Not yet. We'll both pray on it, Mammi, okay? We'll both pray."

"Well . . ." Mammi smiled. "I do feel a little better having told you all that. I know you were concerned about where your blood ties might fall, but no need to worry. Your biological family is out there with the *Englischers* somewhere. Heaven knows where! Marry any Amish man you choose."

And maybe it did explain a lot—her *daet's* refusal to talk about his childhood, her grandmother's refusal to tell stories, and Beth's own longing for a different kind of freedom. This might explain why Beth was drawn to the outside world. Maybe it wasn't rebelliousness. Maybe it was simply in her blood. Her father had been the opposite, though. It was in his blood to be *Englisch*, but he'd chosen an Amish life with all his heart.

28

Jonas kicked the dirt off his boots, then headed up the steps for supper. His father had come in earlier, and he found both of his parents in the kitchen, talking quietly. When he came in, they silenced.

"It smells good," Jonas said.

He had caught a whiff of his mother's delicious meat-filled cabbage rolls, and he looked around the kitchen, wondering what his parents had been discussing so quietly.

"You're back from chores," his *mamm* said with a smile. "Good. The food is ready, and your *daet* and I wanted to talk to you about something."

His father took his seat at the head of the table, and his mother put down two cork hot pads and brought a pan of cabbage rolls to set before him. There were potatoes on the side, some coleslaw, and brown buttered noodles. His stomach rumbled.

"What's this about?" Jonas asked.

"About your sheep," Mamm replied.

"Oh!" Jonas perked up. "Daet, have you reconsidered? We'd be the first ones to bring sheep cheese to market, or sell wool," Jonas said. "I know there's a learning curve, but we can do this."

Daet didn't answer, and he bowed his head for grace. Jonas did too, and for a moment all was silent as they privately thanked Gott for the food. Jonas added in a quiet thanks for his *daet's* apparent change of heart.

Daet cleared his throat to indicate the prayer was over, and they dished up the food. It smelled amazing, but Jonas didn't take a bite yet, waiting on his father to say something.

"You need a wife, son," Daet said, taking his first bite.

"I thought we were talking about sheep," he replied, confused.

"We'll get there," Daet said. "But first things first—you're lonely."

There was something about his father's tone that put his guard back up. He was fine. Being accused of loneliness felt like a personal affront. Lonely people were doing something wrong in an Amish community.

"My life is actually pretty full right now," Jonas countered.

"Full, yes," Daet said, "but not filled with the right things."

"What am I doing wrong?" Jonas demanded.

"Now, now," Mamm interjected. "This is getting heated right away, and that's not the goal here. At your age, we already had two *kinner*. In our generation, people got married young. And I don't know what's gotten into you *youngie*, but you're putting off the most important part of your life."

"Mamm—"

"No, you need to listen to me," Mamm went on. "Now, Miriam Yoder broke your heart. She broke ours too, you know. We thought she'd be our daughter-in-law. But you can't just give up."

"I haven't given up."

"You have."

"Mamm, I'm not courting anyone right now because I haven't found the right woman. I've been praying on it, and I told Gott that I don't want to waste my time and emotions again. I want to wait until it's the woman Gott has for me to marry. And with that prayer, nothing has worked out. And I'm okay with that. The right woman will come along."

"She can't," Mamm said softly. "You have a woman in your life already."

Jonas looked over at his father. Daet shrugged and nodded.

"I'm not involved with Tabitha," Jonas said earnestly.

"We know you can't marry her, but from the outside it certainly looks like something is developing," Mamm replied. "And I have to tell you, as a woman, if a man has another woman that close in his life, I wouldn't try to compete."

"Tabitha is a friend, and that's all," he replied. How many times did he have to tell people this?

"If she is such a good friend, then she'll understand and back off," Daet said, his voice low.

"I'm your mother. I love you more than anything, son, and you deserve more out of your life. You deserve a woman who loves you, and who is free to commit the rest of her life to you. You deserve a family of your own."

There was nothing more frustrating than well-meaning family putting the pressure on a man to do what only Gott could do. His mother reached into her dress pocket and pulled out an envelope. She handed it across the table.

"What's this?" Jonas asked. The return address was from Sugarcreek, Ohio. Why did that sound familiar?

"It's from Nellie Stoltzfus," Mamm said. "She's the matchmaker who has had so much success lately."

"Mamm . . ."

"Now, before you get upset with me," Mamm said, holding up a hand, "I did contact her, but I didn't make any promises. I only asked if she knew of any women who might be interested in a man of your age and description."

Jonas opened the envelope, which had already been torn open, and pulled out the single sheet of paper. The matchmaker said she would need references from their community—from the bishop, from elders, and from family. And she did have three particular women who would make a nice match. She included first names only, and a brief description of each.

Sarah—twenty-eight years old, never married, working in a flour mill, cheerful, hardworking, lovely singing voice.

Vannetta—thirty-two years old, widowed, two young children, petite, slim, excellent cook, some health issues.

Christina—twenty-nine years old, never married, middling cook, very skilled quilter, bright and happy personality.

He looked up at his parents. "What do you expect me to do with this?"

"Pick one," his father said gruffly.

Jonas stared at them in silence.

"Abram . . ." Mamm said in gentle remonstration. "Son, obviously it's not so simple as that, but it would be a start. These are young women who come well recommended, and meeting one of them—or all three, if you wanted to just say hello—would be an excellent first step."

Jonas's chest felt like it was constricting. He understood the logic of being set up, but something inside of him balked at the idea. He didn't know any of them. A good cook or a good quilter—what did that even mean when it came to connecting with a woman on a level deep enough to marry her? What did he care if she could quilt or sing? Tabitha was a middling cook, and she'd never been a good singer, but their connection was natural and easy.

He froze. He could see the problem. He was thinking about Tabitha now.

"I just don't feel it, Mamm," Jonas said. "Not right now. I'll give it some thought for the future."

"All right," Mamm said, and she took the letter back. "I wish you'd think seriously now, though. Time passes. These women will marry. You might not have as many options later."

Daet cleared his throat. "I'm going to put it for you this way, *sohn*. You're wasting your time on Tabitha Schrock, and you have to know it. She can't marry, and you can't move anything forward with her."

It seemed futile to remind them yet again that they were only friends.

"But you're stuck, *sohn*," his *daet* said, softening his tone. "You're hopelessly stuck, and if I don't help you, you'll stay that way until it's too late."

"Daet, I'm fine."

"You are not fine," he replied. "So I'm going to sweeten the deal for you. When you choose a woman and get married, I will give you a section of land to build on and buy you your first twenty sheep to start your herd."

"That's kind," Jonas said. "But I'd rather work up to it slowly. We can start with a few sheep and—"

"No, *sohn*," his father said quietly. "You don't understand. If you don't choose one of these women to get to know, or find some other single woman who is looking for marriage, then I will not help you toward any of these goals. This is my ranch, these are my cattle, and I'll run things my way. If you want to start branching out, you can do it

267

on your own land, if you can find some available land and purchase it yourself."

Jonas stared at his father, stunned. Daet was using his ambitions toward sheep farming to try to strong-arm him into a marriage he didn't want?

"But I highly recommend one of these young women in the letter," Daet went on. "And not only because your mother went to the trouble of reaching out to this matchmaker and the matchmaker went to the trouble of looking into matches for you already. Your *mamm* wrote a very lengthy letter, describing your nature, your strengths, your personality, your sense of humor, and even your ambitions for sheep farming. And this woman has had some great success in matching couples up. She has a good insight into human nature and what makes a relationship work. The clients she chooses to work with are good people—moral, decent. And she's good at this, Jonas. You don't have any women here in Shepherd's Hill who have caught your eye. So I think the wisest course of action would be to write back to her honestly and tell her more about yourself. Then you can meet with her and some of these young women and see if you feel any connection."

Cooperate, and there would be the career of his dreams with a herd of sheep and building up his own niche in the local market.

Go his own way, and either work under his *daet* the same old way he always had or try to save up the money for a down payment on his own land.

"You deserve to be loved, Jonas, and we want you to have a partner in life," his mother said, holding the letter out to him again. "You deserve all the happiness of a loving wife and *kinner* who call you *daet*."

Jonas accepted the letter and tucked it into his pocket.

He felt cornered, even though he knew they were only trying to help.

"Now eat up," Mamm said with a nod toward his plate. "You must be starving after a long day of work, and I made the cabbage rolls for you especially."

His favorite meal. Mamm knew him well, and knew how to soften him up again. His parents loved him, and while his *daet* could be ornery, he had Jonas's best interests at heart. He knew all of that.

But something was holding him back—an image in his mind of the smiling veterinarian, her hands dirty and her eyes shining. When he decided to find another woman to marry, that friendship would have to be over.

A nice woman wouldn't compete for his attention, and shouldn't have to.

If he turned his energy toward finding a wife, it would be a good-bye to Tabitha Schrock. And that severing would hurt. Was he ready for that?

29

Beth awoke the next morning to silence. There was no sound of Mammi's slippers shuffling down the hallway or dog toenails tapping along while Goldie followed her mistress around the big old house. No clatter from the kitchen. Just the soft twitter of birds from outside her window.

Beth pushed herself up. She'd overslept—really overslept! The sun was up and climbing the sky. Far off she heard the *thud-crack* of someone chopping wood. Danny, maybe?

She swung her legs over the side of her bed and stood. Then she quickly dressed, stabbing herself twice with the straight pins she used to hold her dress together. While she looked out the window, trying to see if Mammi was outside in the garden, she swiped the brush through her long hair, then twisted it up into a bun at the back of her head and secured it with bobby pins. She snatched a *kapp* from the shelf on her way out of her bedroom.

"Mammi?" she called.

Silence. Then she remembered Tabitha's trick with Goldie, and she called out, "Goldie! Come!"

From outside she heard a woof of response, and Beth's heartbeat started to settle down. Goldie would be wherever Mammi was, and Goldie was outside. It was a beautiful July morning—what better place to be?

Beth quickly brushed her teeth, then jogged downstairs and headed out the back door. She knew Mammi wasn't in the garden, but she was outside somewhere.

"Mammi?" she called.

Goldie woofed again, and she came out of the bushes by the beach, tail wagging.

"Hi, Goldie," Beth said, walking across the sun-warmed grass in her bare feet. "Where's Mammi, huh?"

The lake shone like glass this morning, sunlight glittering off tiny ripples in the surface of the water. A trail of geese paddled along near the shore, where grass and bushes stumbled tipsily into the water. Mammi stood on the shore, her back to Beth, her hands clasped behind her back.

"Mammi?" Beth walked up to her grandmother, and the old woman looked up at Beth, tears shining in her eyes. "Mammi, what's wrong?"

"Just thinking, dear girl. Just thinking."

Beth looked out over the water. Some *Englischers* from the cabins were on the Lapps' dock. A man, a woman, and two older *kinner*. They had some inner tubes and floating mattresses out on the water. The *kinner's* laughter drifted over the water toward them. Shouts. Playful splashing. She felt a pang of envy at their carefree ability to swim today. The rhythmic cracking sound of chopping wood was coming from the Lapps' woodpile, and she could just make out Danny's back as he worked.

"Have you had breakfast yet?" Beth asked.

"No . . ." Mammi sighed. "I'm not hungry."

"I'll cook something for you."

Mammi looked over at Beth again and smiled faintly. "You want me to stop thinking about it, don't you? Just douse it like water on a fire. But even when my mind betrays me and slips into the past, it's still on my mind. I know what I did wrong, and I know I have to do something about it."

"You don't," Beth said earnestly. "Mammi, what kind of life would my *daet* have had if you'd sent him back to those people? It would have been misery. You rescued him!"

"If it's so simple, then why can't I shout that from the rooftops?" Mammi asked, raising her eyebrows. "No, I've learned over the last seventy-odd years of life that when you feel like you have to hide something, it's wrong. It's a pretty simple recipe."

A woman stood on the dock, dripping wet, and then dove off into the water. The boy climbed up to take his turn, and the *Englischers'* playful shouts suddenly stopped short. Then there was a frightened shriek. Beth's blood chilled, and she looked for the source of the problem. She couldn't make out much.

"Mammi, wait here." Beth reached out and squeezed her grandmother's arm, then started off around the lake at a run. She pulled up her dress to her knees and sped along the path, and she could feel the sting of the blade-like grasses and twigs from bushes scratching her legs, but she didn't slow.

Danny had started in the direction of the dock too, and Beth ran past him. Time was everything in a moment like this.

"Where is she?" a girl's voice wailed. "Mom! Mom!"

"Did she go under?" Beth called as her bare feet hit the wooden surface.

"Yes! She went down!" A pale, tear-stained face turned toward her.

A man was splashing around in a panic, looking around himself.

Beth grabbed a T-shirt lying on the dock and tore at the pins in her dress. She'd be dragged down too if her legs were tangled in the long fabric. She jumped down into the water, out of sight of the people nearby, and tore her dress off the rest of the way. She had on an undershirt and underwear beneath her dress, and she pulled on the T-shirt. It would do.

"Stop splashing!" she shouted at the man. Then she dove down, her eyes open and stinging, looking through the green-hued water. She spotted a pale arm. The woman was sinking, and Beth came back up, took a deep breath, and then dove down again.

The woman was now unconscious, with her long brown hair flowing upward. Beth reached for her hand, the woman's arm slipping from Beth's grip, and so she grabbed the only thing she could get a grip on—a fistful of flowing hair. And she pulled.

Friesen Lake had claimed enough lives over the years, and it would not have this woman—not if Beth could help it. When she got the woman closer to the surface, she managed to get an arm around the woman's chest, and she kicked as hard as she could, their ascent agonizingly slow. Beth's lungs screamed, and she sent up a desperate, wordless prayer toward heaven just as her head broke the surface of the water and the sunlight, a babble of voices, and children's sobs collided with her like a wall.

Beth floated on her back, gasping for sweet, fresh air, and tugged the motionless woman along with her.

"I've got her!" the man gasped out, and she looked up to see both the shirtless *Englischer* and Danny reaching to grab

273

the woman. They hoisted her up onto the dock, just as she started to cough up lake water.

"*Danke*, Gott . . ." she whispered.

Beth stayed submerged up to her neck, the cool water caressing her legs. It felt wonderful to be back in a lake again—it felt like coming alive. But she also realized she was now wearing nothing but a T-shirt—very likely that *Englischer* man's shirt—and her underwear, and she had no way of modestly getting back out again.

"Elizabeth!" Beth heard Mammi's wavering cry, and she looked over to see her grandmother pottering along the path as quickly as she could, waving her arms over her head. "Elizabeth!"

Beth waved back, hoping Mammi could see her, but not sure if she could. Above, the woman vomited water onto the dock and the children cried and the man sounded relieved.

"Andrea, you scared us. Oh, my goodness. Don't move. Just rest. Oh, my goodness . . ."

"Beth?"

She looked up to see Danny above. He squatted down and held out a hand to help her up, but she shook her head. Her dress floated a couple yards away, a pink sodden swirl upon the water.

"I need a big towel or something," she said. "A sheet? A blanket? I need something to cover up."

"Right! I'll be back."

Danny disappeared again, and Beth moved her legs like an egg beater, keeping herself afloat and her head above water. This was one of the tricks her *daet* had taught her when she was a girl.

"*You've got to practice so you have the muscles to do this for a long time, if you have to . . .*"

Daet had swum across this very lake, and he'd flung his small self into the arms of an Amish woman who'd been waiting on the shore, and his future had changed forever.

"I've got a sheet." Danny appeared on the dock again and held out his hand. "I'll look away, and you can wrap yourself up."

The *Englischers* wouldn't be scandalized by bare legs, but even in her swim dress, she'd never revealed more than her knees down. The clinging T-shirt was another issue, though. She felt like her face was on fire as she hoisted herself up the wooden ladder and wrapped a sun-warmed sheet around her chilled body.

"Thank you!" the *Englischer* man exclaimed, tears in his eyes. "You saved my wife's life. Where did you learn to swim like that?"

"My *daet* taught me," she said. "I'm just glad I was able to help. Are you okay, ma'am?"

The woman nodded. "I got tangled in some weeds . . . Thank you so much."

Beth wasn't sure what else to say. She'd done what she could, and now she just felt embarrassed with all of that attention on her. Mammi was breathing hard and moving slowly, and Mary was running toward them.

There was a lot of excitement for the next few minutes. The *Englischer* woman and her family got into their vehicle to go into town and have her checked out by a doctor. That was a good idea, considering how much lake water she'd breathed into her lungs. It could cause other problems.

Mammi was in a panic when she finally arrived at the dock, breathless and worried, and Beth was grateful that Mary took over soothing her.

Beth looked over her shoulder once more, back at the

beckoning expanse of water. The glittering lake shone like diamonds, a beautiful, rippling surface that hid dangerous depths. For all of her life, her *daet* and *mammi* had warned her about those treacherous depths. There were similar depths in people, in families . . . in the stories that made them.

Danny brought Beth back to Mammi's house so she could change into proper clothes again, and when she came back down the stairs, she found him at the kitchen sink, wringing out her dress.

"You don't have to do that," Beth said. "I'll wash it. It'll smell like lake water now."

Danny put down her dress and turned toward her. His cheeks colored, and she felt bad for embarrassing him.

"Sorry," she said. "*Danke* for helping me."

"Of course." He shrugged, then he dried his hands on the front of his shirt. "Are you okay?"

"I'm not the one who almost drowned," she said, and tears sparked in her eyes in spite of her words. She didn't know why she felt like crying suddenly, but she did. Maybe it was the fact that a woman might have died today, or just her own simmer of emotions after finding out about her father's painful childhood finally pushing up to the surface, but her chin trembled and her eyes welled.

"I'm fine," she said, her voice shaking.

"Come here." Danny crossed the kitchen, and while she struggled to compose herself, he pulled her into his arms. He felt warm and solid and strong, and she rested her cheek against his shoulder while hot, silent tears soaked into his shirt.

He held her close, and she felt the tug of his shadowed stubble against her hair and *kapp*, and the scent of wood chips surrounded her.

"I was so scared for you," he breathed.

"I was okay," she whispered. "I was scared I wouldn't be able to get her to the surface."

He ran a hand down her back with comforting warmth. "Imagine if your *daet* had never taught you."

"She'd be dead," Beth said simply. Like Arden. Like others. Beth pulled out of his arms.

"I'm glad you're okay," Danny said quietly.

"Mammi told me the story of adopting my father," she said. Danny was the one person she could trust with this.

"And?" Danny had a wet patch on his shirt.

"And—" She licked her lips. "My *daet* was *Englisch* before Mammi adopted him."

Looking up into Danny's face, she longed to tell him everything—to spill out the story of her father's arrival to the Amish life in front of this earnest man, dump it out in its confusing, ugly mess and ask him to understand that there was beauty there too.

"What happened?" he asked.

"It's complicated." But she could trust him.

So she told him the story of her father's painful childhood before that fateful swim for shore and how her grandmother had rescued him.

"I don't blame her a bit," Danny said. "I would have done the same."

"Me too." She was glad to hear him say it, though.

"Now that you know, do you feel better?" Danny asked.

"In a way. It fills in the gaps for me." It told her why her father fought for her right to swim. It told her why her grandmother feared this lake and why no one would speak of the past.

His gaze met hers, and her smile slipped. Standing with this man, alone in her grandmother's kitchen, he suddenly didn't seem like the naïve boy who couldn't seem to put his thoughts together anymore.

Danny put a palm against her cheek, and she looked up at him, breathless. Then he lowered his lips over hers in a warm, melting kiss that made her sag against him. When he pulled back, he shut his eyes, and she could see the faint flutter of his eyelids, the moisture on his lips.

"I wasn't going to do that," he whispered.

"Me neither . . ."

He opened his eyes then and looked at her with such longing that it made her knees weak.

"I'm trying to decide if I can stay, Danny," she said quietly. "For you."

He didn't answer, and she took a step away from him, trying to clear her head from that kiss.

"Finding out that my *daet's* birth family was *Englisch* made a lot of things make sense," she went on. "I always thought I was rebellious or something. I love to swim, and I want to compete. I hate being hemmed in by lots of rules. I keep wanting to pursue more education. I know why we believe what we do, but I'm not sure that this is the life for me, and I finally feel like I know where those feelings are coming from. It's from my *daet's* side. I can't just commit to the Amish life. Not now."

"You don't believe in our ways?" he asked.

"It's not even about that," she said. "I do believe in many of our ways, but I don't think everything ends at our fence. And I see Tabitha Schrock—she was able to get that education and still work amongst the People. I think it's silly we can't compete if we're good at something. I think we should all be learning how to swim well. It saves lives. But modesty holds us back. My *daet* found ways around it, but it was a unique situation that let me learn."

"You're frustrated."

"I just——" She searched around inside of herself for the words. "I need to find my place, Danny."

"You deserve that."

But looking up at him, his heartbreak shining in his eyes, she couldn't leave it at that either.

"You'll always be special to me, Danny. Always. You're my first big hope and my first kiss." A lump clamped down on her throat. "You're special."

Danny pulled her closer and pressed a tender kiss against her forehead.

"So are you," he said gruffly.

If only she were less rebellious, less demanding, less questioning. If only she could be grateful for the love of a good man and simply settle into a happy Amish life with him. If only!

But there was something inside of her that wouldn't rest— not yet. It still looked toward the fence, toward the horizon, and longed to dive into that forbidden lake water and swim until she was faint. She was half *Englisch*, and she had to explore what that meant. Because she cared too much about Danny to make promises she couldn't keep.

30

Danny poured his pain into work that day. His *daet* asked him if he was okay a couple of times, but he didn't want to talk about it. There was no point. Beth didn't want the same quiet, disciplined Amish life that he did. He wanted her to be content with the restrictions they lived under, but she wasn't. Hoping she'd change wasn't fair to either of them. She was still looking for something that might take her far from here, and Danny had found his answers right here in Shepherd's Hill.

That night when he lay in bed, he felt like tears were on the edge of his throat, but he couldn't release them. Beth was more than special. She was woven into his past, and he'd been carrying her around with him all this time, even when he hadn't realized he'd been doing it. She was all wrong for him, but she was still knitted in there . . .

He didn't know what to pray for, so he didn't pray. Not really. He just opened up his aching heart to his Maker like a little boy holding up a cut finger for his *daet* to look at. He hurt, and he longed for something that would never be. But it still hurt, and he didn't know what to even ask Gott to do—

take away the pain? Take away his feelings for Beth? Help him accept things as they were? Give him another chance with her?

The next day, Danny dragged himself out of bed even though he felt like he'd hardly slept, although he had. His body ached, and he felt morose and disheartened. But he got up all the same, lit his bedside kerosene lamp, and dragged his Bible closer to him. He opened it to one of his favorite verses.

"Blessed be God, even the Father of our Lord Jesus Christ, the Father of mercies, and the God of all comfort; Who comforteth us in all our tribulation, that we may be able to comfort them which are in any trouble, by the comfort wherewith we ourselves are comforted of God."

Being comforted by Gott so he could be a comfort to someone else. Right now, that wasn't any salve on his torn heart. He closed his Bible and rose. There were chores to be done. He'd best get to it.

The family of the woman who'd nearly drowned came back to the ice house cottage, but they stayed out of the water. They were quieter too, and Danny had to wonder how that near-death experience had affected them. It had surely affected him.

The husband seemed more affectionate toward his wife, standing with an arm draped over her shoulder or leaning toward her when they sat side by side on the stumps set up by the fire pit on the beach. He didn't have his phone out anymore. The *kinner* were quieter and more thoughtful. They sat out by the beach bonfire as a family, roasting marshmallows and talking. Danny even saw them sitting out there together having worship an hour after sunrise.

Later that day, Danny sat with a pen and his Amish Market

stall application form. They needed a list of the items he'd sell, and he was giving that some serious thought. Before he applied, he needed to talk to some local women and see if they'd provide him with handcrafts to sell. He'd have to give them part of the revenue, of course. He'd need to do the math. Toby could help him out by crunching numbers. He was getting ready to take a break when he heard an engine in the drive. More guests, maybe?

He headed outside into the warm sunlight and spotted his brother's pickup truck. Zach was in the driver's seat, but he didn't have Meghan with him this time. Finally. Had he figured out that he needed to take care of a few things by himself, at long last?

Zach got out of his truck and just stood there for a moment, looking around slowly.

"Hey!" Danny called.

Zach spotted him then. "Hi."

Zach looked a little deflated, less cocky by far. He just stood there by his truck, so Danny headed in his direction. Zach looked like he hadn't gotten much sleep—his eyes were red.

"You okay?" Danny asked.

Zach shrugged. "I guess. What's going on over here?"

"A guest almost drowned yesterday," Danny said. "Beth Peachy saved her."

Danny looked over toward the *Englischer* family. They were eating a late lunch under the shade of a tree—hot dogs cooked on a propane stove, and what looked like macaroni and cheese. They were laughing. Someone dropped a hot dog, then shook it off before eating it anyway.

They were still keeping a pretty respectful distance from the water.

"Is Meghan going to teach you to swim?" Danny asked.

Zach shook his head. "We broke up."

Danny looked at his brother in surprise. The last time he'd seen them, his brother had been defiantly defending his woman.

"What? Seriously?"

Zach sighed, and all the fight seemed to have gone out of him. "*Yah.* Last night."

"What happened?"

The brothers walked in the direction of the woodpile—their old place where they could talk without being easily overheard by anyone. Zach crossed his arms over his chest and dug his toe into the dirt.

"I think we started out wrong."

"How so?"

"We didn't choose each other," he said. "I mean, we didn't choose to get serious. We kind of just stumbled into it. We were dating, of course, and we really liked each other. I was struggling to pay my rent, and I lost a job. She came to my rescue. She'd had a falling out with her roommate, and we both kind of thought—why not? Why not give it a try? So we moved in together."

"And you were fighting as a result?" Danny asked.

"A bit. I mean, we were just really different. Everything I did was weird to her. And she had her own ways that made no sense to me, but because she knew the *Englischer* life better than I did, she'd win every argument."

So they'd been at odds.

"Anyway, we came to see you guys that one time, and she said she agreed with Mamm and Daet, that living together without being at least engaged was a really bad idea. She was raised as a Christian, and she felt somewhat guilty about our arrangement. I guess I did too, but . . . I didn't want to get married."

"You still don't?" Danny asked.

Zach shook his head. "I wanted to date her. I'm not ready for marriage, and when I am, I'm not sure I want to marry Meghan."

That news would be crushing to Meghan, Danny had no doubt. She'd been going out of her way to get to know the Amish world and his family. None of it had been comfortable for her, but she'd done it.

"So you had one of those state-of-the-relationship conversations, realized she wanted marriage and you didn't, and broke up?" Danny concluded.

"*Yah.*"

"I had one of those too. With Beth. We want different things too, so I get it."

"I didn't realize you were dating."

"We weren't. Not really. Just spending lots of time together, and talking about everything, and holding hands, and . . ."

"And not dating," Zach said.

"Exactly."

"But she doesn't want more?"

"She's not sure if she'll even stay Amish. And I want someone who wants all of this as much as I do."

Zach nodded slowly. "I shouldn't have moved in with Meghan. It was a dumb money decision. It set us up for some huge expectations we weren't ready for."

"You're sure you don't want to marry her?" Danny asked. His parents wouldn't want him to encourage this, but if Zach was going to go *Englisch*, Danny didn't want to ruin his chances at love and stability. He could do a whole lot worse than Meghan. "We like her. We'd take the time to teach her about the Amish culture."

"*Nee*," Zach said, falling back into Pennsylvania Dutch. "This hurts, but it's the right thing."

"You're moving out, then?" Danny asked.

His brother nodded.

"Where will you go?"

"That's the question, isn't it."

"You could come home," Danny suggested.

"Another decision based on a tight financial situation?" he asked.

"Hey, living with a woman and living with your family are two different things. You belong here. You grew up here. But I daresay you'd need to stop doing those videos if you came back."

Zach's gaze flicked toward Danny, and he looked a little embarrassed.

"Probably," he agreed with a small smile.

"I'm sorry it didn't work out with Meghan, Zach," Danny said. "I really am. I know how much that hurts."

Zach nodded, and his chin trembled just a little. "*Danke*. I'm sorry about Beth."

"*Yah*, well, you know . . ."

They exchanged a rueful look, and Zach scuffed his toe into the dirt once more. Life was hard, and sometimes it really hurt, and that was when a family was so necessary. They might disagree about a whole lot, but at the end of the day, they still belonged to each other. DNA and a shared childhood did that.

Danny wondered if he'd made the same mistake with Beth. Had they somehow just fallen into intimacy over the years without ever properly choosing it? Maybe. And now when they faced really difficult things, it wouldn't work, regardless of their feelings for each other.

Their mother opened the side door and shaded her eyes. Zach waved, and she waved back.

"Mamm made pie," Danny said.

"Oh *yah*?" Zach brightened a little bit.

"Might as well come in and eat."

"*Yah*, I will," Zach agreed.

"Think about coming home, okay?" Danny said.

Zach nodded, and they headed back toward the house. Zach clomped up the steps first, and Danny looked back over his shoulder toward the Peachy house. It stood silent, and no one was visible in the backyard or on the beach.

He missed Beth already. Somehow, without ever actually choosing it, his heart had gotten entangled with hers. And even though this hurt right now, he wouldn't do it differently if he had the chance, because what they shared meant something. Even if it ended here.

31

Beth stayed away from the lake the next day. She longed to see Danny, and if she stood by the water, her gaze would move to the Lapp ice house and the woodpile, and she'd invariably see him. Then he'd see her, and regardless of what they'd said yesterday, they'd end up clapping back together again like two magnets. And right now that part of her heart was very raw.

He'd kissed her, and she'd kissed him back. But it wasn't just a kiss—it was realizing Danny had become a very important part of her world, and if she followed her heart and moved toward more freedom, she'd be cutting herself off from him forever. She could visit her family, of course, but Danny wouldn't sit here waiting for her. Nor should he.

"I think I'll make some bread today," Mammi said as they boxed up some of the dishes she didn't use often.

"I'll help you," Beth offered.

"You can go out and get some fresh air, dear," Mammi said.

Beth shook her head. "I'm fine."

"You don't need to babysit me." Mammi eyed her uncertainly.

Except Beth did need to be with her. Mammi couldn't stay on her own safely anymore. But her desire to stay in had nothing to do with her worries about Mammi today.

"It's not that, Mammi," Beth said. "I had a talk with Danny yesterday, and we agreed that we shouldn't court."

"Oh, Elizabeth . . ." Mammi cast her a sad look. "Are you sure? He's very nice."

"It's for the best, Mammi. And I think seeing him would hurt." Beth shrugged weakly. "So, can I help with the bread?"

"Of course, dear. I need you to fetch the flour. Are we out? Did we run out of flour?" Mammi looked around anxiously.

"We have four bags, Mammi."

"Are you sure? I don't think we have any—"

Beth opened the cupboard and pointed at two new bags of flour inside. "And there are two more in the cellar. We have plenty."

"Oh . . ." Mammi nodded. "I didn't remember we had any."

So Beth stayed indoors, and they made bread. Mammi had a way of making the fluffiest, softest bread that Beth herself could never seem to duplicate. It came down to Mammi's senses. She'd sniff at the bread dough and declare it "didn't smell risen enough." Or she'd measure out the sugar and salt by hand—no actual measurement besides her own eye. She just had a feel for what made the best bread, which made her recipes hard to copy.

Outside, the sound of a buggy's wheels drew Beth's attention, and she went to the window. It was Tabitha Schrock's buggy, and she pulled up and waved cheerily at Beth in the window.

"It's Tabitha," Beth said. "She must be checking on the cow."

Beth went to the side door, slid on her shoes, and stepped outside.

"Do you mind giving me a hand?" Tabitha called. "I've got a calf!"

No explanation beyond that, just mentioning a calf, and Beth couldn't help her curiosity. Besides, Tabitha obviously needed another set of hands here. As Tabitha tied her horse to the hitching post, Beth went around to the back of the buggy. There sat a very young Holstein bull calf. He blinked at her with those big, long-lashed eyes. This calf couldn't be more than three weeks old, toothless and knobby-kneed.

"Why do you have a calf?" Beth asked as Tabitha joined her and opened the door to the cage.

"He's my prescription for your milk cow."

Beth stood back as Tabitha tugged the calf toward her in the same way most folks around here transported newly purchased calves from the cattle auction. He leaned away and bawled out in annoyance.

"Come on, *boppli*," Tabitha said. "I've got a treat for you."

"Where did you get him?" Beth asked. "Did you buy him? Do we need to pay you back?"

"No, no, nothing like that. He was abandoned by his *mamm* on the Blank farm," Tabitha said, "And Jared doesn't want another bottle baby on his hands, so when I asked if I could use him to help a cow with mastitis, he was very happy to lend him out. When he's ready to wean, we'll send him back to the Blanks."

"That's smart," Beth said.

"*Danke*. It was a solution that presented itself," she replied, but Tabitha also shot Beth a grin. Tabitha seemed to know she was smart, and Tabitha still had that *Englischer* air about her. To Beth's eye, she was an interesting mix between her Amish upbringing and her *Englisch* education. It didn't always mesh, but she kept trying, which was rather endearing. Beth had overheard conversations about their new vet. Tabitha was slowly and earnestly fitting back in.

"Can you get me that crate?" Tabitha asked, pointing.

"*Yah*, sure." Beth went over and grabbed a wooden crate from by the shed and brought it back. Tabitha turned it upside down and used it as a step up. Then she wrapped her arms around the calf's upper legs and lifted him.

"Come on." Tabitha grunted. "You'll like this. I promise."

Beth put her hand up to help steady Tabitha as she carefully stepped down from the crate. In her arms, the calf settled down, and Tabitha carried the calf toward the stable.

"What's the plan?" Beth asked.

"Well, the antibiotics haven't done the job on Bessie's mastitis—not completely," Tabitha said through gritted teeth. "And we've given it a few days now since the last antibiotic dose, so it's time for a new angle."

"A calf?"

"*Yah*. Milking a cow doesn't work the same way a calf's sucking does. A calf will clear the milk out of an udder much more efficiently, and it will help the cow's body to regulate better. It comes down to hormones and pheromones and body chemistry."

Beth followed Tabitha toward the stable. Last night had been miserable, and today she felt hollowed out and empty. She'd come to Mammi's to make her decision, and she still wasn't positive which path to take. She couldn't stay in this limbo of *rumspringa* forever. Eventually, she'd need to decide which future she wanted.

"Are you okay?" Tabitha asked.

"*Yah*, I'm all right," Beth replied.

"Are you sure? You look like you lost your last friend."

It was a figure of speech, but not too far off the mark. She'd lost her best friend, at the very least. But she should have seen it coming.

"I, uh—" Beth swallowed. "I had to make a choice one way or another with Danny."

"Oh." Tabitha cast her a sympathetic look. "Don't tell me you broke it off?"

Somehow, talking about this with Tabitha was easier than with Mammi. Maybe it was because Tabitha expected less, or that Tabitha had also felt drawn to the *Englisch* world.

"Dragging on our relationship wasn't fair to him," Beth said.

"He's a good man, you know."

And Beth did know it. Danny was more than a good man—he was honest and decent and kind. He was stable, and he believed in this life so strongly that nothing seemed to shake him. He was a truly wonderful man.

"That's why it wasn't fair to him," Beth replied. "I'm not sure what I want to do with my future, and he's very sure about his."

"You want different things?" Tabitha asked.

Beth nodded, and she hesitated before she added, "I might leave." She hurried ahead to open the gate to the pasture. "The cow is in the pasture still."

Tabitha didn't answer, and while Beth knew that Tabitha had made a similar decision to leave her community about ten years ago, Tabitha had also returned. She'd disapprove of this, no doubt. But Tabitha didn't have *Englischer* family out there somewhere. It wasn't in her blood.

Tabitha was breathing hard by the time she passed through

into the pasture and bent, putting the calf down. The milk cow stood a few yards off, her head down as she grazed. She was doing a lot better, but like Tabitha had said, she wasn't fully healed. Her udder was still swollen, but the teats were no longer inflamed.

"Come on." Tabitha pulled on the rope around the calf's neck, but he refused to budge. She bent down and picked up the calf again, carrying him over to the cow.

Was Beth's confession going to be ignored? She suddenly felt a little foolish at having shared it. Maybe Tabitha wasn't the right person to talk to about this after all.

"I need you to block off the cow to keep her here," Tabitha said. "This might be prickly."

Beth headed around to the front of the cow, keeping a couple yards between herself and the big bovine while Tabitha put the calf down beside the cow and tried to pull his nose toward the udder. The calf balked.

Tabitha milked a couple of sprays of milk, then pointed the teat at the calf's face and sprayed. The calf startled, and his pink tongue came out, tasting the milk that dripped down his nose. Tabitha sprayed his mouth this time, then got on her knees and pulled the calf up to the udder. He fought less this time, and she managed to get his mouth to a teat. It took him a minute, but soon enough, he started to drink.

"There." Tabitha pushed herself to her feet and stepped back, crossing her arms and watching the calf drink with a smile on her face.

"That'll fix it?" Beth asked.

"*Yah*. We try not to bring a calf in because it uses up her milk, and obviously your *aent* has her here as a milker. But sometimes, the best thing we can do is bring it back to basics. A mama cow and a calf."

Beth remained silent, running those words over in her mind. *Back to basics.* What was basic for her? Was it an Amish life? Was it a life swimming and having a career? Was it finding the *Englischer* world her *daet* had left behind?

"That's what brought me home, you know," Tabitha said, finally turning toward Beth and giving her a meaningful look.

"Getting back to the basics?" Beth asked.

"*Yah.* I needed to get back to all the things that made me me, and I knew that I had to come home."

"I'm not sure what makes me me," Beth admitted.

"Sometimes you don't know until you've got some space from it," Tabitha said. "I shouldn't say that. No one wants me to say that."

"I'm glad you're honest with me." Beth gave her a small smile.

"Just be careful," Tabitha said. "There are some mistakes that can change your life forever, and there is no way to completely fix them."

Like Tabitha's marriage and divorce. Beth knew how much that had changed Tabitha's life. There would be no happy home with a husband and *kinner* for her. That was a sad thought, because whether Beth established herself as an Amish woman or an *Englischer*, she did want a family of her own.

And an image of Danny rose up in her mind, with his gentle eyes and strong hands and good work ethic, and her heart gave such a squeeze that it brought tears to her eyes. Was she willing to sacrifice Danny to find out if the *Englisch* world was right for her?

The calf was still busily nursing, and the cow craned her head back to sniff him, familiarizing herself with this new baby's scent. It boded well for an adoption.

Like Mammi and Daet. Like all the other families that had grown when a child needed a home or a home needed a child. But it once again left Beth wondering where she truly belonged.

Was it here amongst the Amish, who knew her best, or out there with the freedom to follow her passions?

32

Danny sat in silent support next to his brother as Mamm dished another piece of pie onto Zach's plate. Zach looked tired and sad. He had that red rim to his eyes that said he'd been crying at some point too. Maybe on his drive over?

Zach's phone lay on the table, and he glanced at it.

"She's not answering my text," Zach said.

"I'm so sorry, *sohn*," Mamm said gently. "I'm glad you came home. Home is the best place to nurse a broken heart."

"I think it's a bit unfair of Meghan to ask that we get married, just like that," Zach said.

"You were living with her, *sohn*," Mamm said.

"*Yah*, but we didn't move in because we were ready to get married."

"If you pick up the reins but aren't ready to drive a buggy, is that wise?" Mamm asked quietly. "I think she's got a good heart, and she wanted your relationship to be an honest one. If she's not the right woman for you, that's good to know, but you can't just move in with a girl and expect her not to think of the vows that would keep you together for a lifetime."

Danny glanced toward the window, his mind on Beth. He missed her. That was the problem, plain and simple. He missed her so much that his chest ached with it. It seemed to be pretty similar to what Zach was feeling too. Except Zach wasn't ready for a lifetime commitment, and Danny was. Maybe Danny had more in common with Meghan right now—two people who wanted the commitment of lifetime vows, but with partners who weren't ready for it.

Out the window, Danny saw a pickup truck drive up. He recognized it from before—the man who took a lot of photos.

"Zach," Danny said, nodding toward the window. "Do you know this guy?"

Zach leaned forward to get a better look and shook his head. "No, why?"

"Just wondering." Danny pushed himself to his feet and headed to the side door.

Outside, he stopped a couple of yards from the house. He was tired and emotionally drained. He didn't have the energy to dance around a curious tourist right now. The man parked and got out of his truck. He was tall and lanky and had a mustache that was just so *Englisch*.

"I've seen you around here before. Can I help you?" Danny asked. He put some bass in his voice—a message to the fellow if he wasn't here for friendly or business reasons.

"Hi," the man said. "I didn't introduce myself last time. I should have. I'm Ken."

He held out a hand, and they shook. "Danny. Good to meet you." He might be tired out today, but he was still civilized.

"Likewise," Ken said. "I should probably explain why I've been coming by here. When I was a kid, we used to vacation by this lake. I've got memories here."

"How long ago was that?" Danny asked.

"About forty years ago, I guess," Ken said. "Maybe a bit more."

"Before our time running the cabins," Danny said.

"Long before you, young man," Ken said, and he laughed at his own little joke. "Do you know much about the history of this lake?"

Beth sure did, and she'd been talking about her findings, so maybe Danny knew a few things at this point. Ken's gaze moved toward the water, and he had a look in his eye that Danny recognized now—a cross between longing and the respect that came with understanding the depth and danger of this body of water.

"I know a bit," Danny said. "Are you looking for some particular detail? I might be able to help."

"It's a long story, actually," Ken said, and he looked over at him uncertainly. "Are you busy? You're busy. Sorry—I don't mean to unload old stories onto you. If I could just take a look at the lake, I'd be grateful."

Ken obviously didn't want to get in the way, and Danny could see that this man wasn't here to cause trouble. Maybe he was here to find some peace of his own.

"I'm not busy," Danny said. "A friend of mine is really interested in this lake's history, so I might know a few things or could be of help. You never know."

They walked together toward Danny's family's stretch of beach—a little sandier than the Peachys' pebbled bit of shore. Ken shoved his hands into his pockets and took a deep breath as he looked out over the water.

"It's exactly the same," he murmured.

Danny stayed silent and looked toward the Peachy house. No sign of Beth.

"When I was twelve, my foster brother died in this lake," Ken said quietly. "Officially speaking."

Danny's heart skipped a beat. Was he talking about Beth's *daet*?

"What happened?" Danny asked.

"Our parents—my parents, I should say—took us out here for boating and camping. They had taken in a foster kid, and we were raised together. His name was Nelson." Ken was silent for a moment, and tears welled in his eyes. "My father died two months ago."

"I'm sorry."

"Thanks." Ken winced. "It means I can talk about stuff now that I couldn't talk about before. Things weren't right in our house. My parents didn't treat me and Nelson the same. Nelson was supposed to be grateful to be living with us, and he was supposed to show his gratitude by doing all the menial work none of us wanted to do. And my father was really harsh with him. He called it discipline, but it went way beyond that, if you know what I mean. I'm a father now myself, and I know the difference. My parents abused Nelson, and no matter how I tried to protect him, I couldn't stop it. But I still felt loyal to my parents. Do you know what that's like, when you know your parents are doing something bad but you still love them?"

Danny swallowed hard.

"No, you don't." Ken shook his head.

"What happened to Nelson?" Danny asked. He knew the story from Beth, but he was curious to hear what Ken would say. How much did Ken know?

"Well, we were fishing out there in the lake." Ken jutted his chin toward the water. "And this storm blew up, really fast, with very little warning. And Nelson told me he was going to make a run for it. I told him not to—that he'd drown—but he said he could make it. So with the waves rocking our little fishing boat, he tipped into the water and started to swim."

"There was a newspaper story about a boy who drowned."

"That's the thing," Ken said. "I told them he drowned. I said he went under. I lied. While I was paddling back to shore with my lie, I watched him swim. He disappeared from sight for a bit, but I saw him get to shore, and this Amish lady came outside and fished him out of the water. By the time I got the boat back to the shore here, my parents were more focused on me. No one saw Nelson or what happened to him. Just me."

"So you saw him get to safety," Danny said.

"I did, and I lied my face off for years because I figured he'd be safer with that Amish lady."

"You said your father passed away?" Danny asked, his voice tight.

"Two months ago. Mom died ten years ago—breast cancer. I guess that's what brought me out here. I know it's an incredible long shot, but I was hoping to find out what happened to Nelson." Ken turned toward Danny, searching his face hopefully. "Did you ever hear about anything like that?"

Yah, he had, and rather recently, too, but he wasn't sure how much to say.

"I might have," Danny said. "Look, I'm going to go talk to someone who might know something. Go have a piece of pie, and I'll come back in a few minutes and let you know if I was successful. Is that fair?"

"Can I come with you?" Ken asked.

"It's better if you don't. People around here are pretty private, and this is the kind of story that is more private still, you know?"

Ken nodded a couple of times. "Yep. I can understand that."

"Let me introduce you to my mother and brother."

And just then, Danny saw her. Beth walked down onto the pebbly beach by Iris's house and raised her head. He couldn't make out her face from this distance, but his heart skipped a beat.

Beth . . .

When Ken was settled with some pie, Danny headed back out and went straight to the Peachy house. Beth was no longer on the beach, but she did answer the door when he knocked. She wore a pink cape dress that brought out the color in her cheeks on this warm day. Her eyes didn't match the liveliness of the roses in her cheeks, though, and he had to stop himself from wrapping his arms around her right then and there.

"Hi," he said. Beth's eyes had that telltale red rim that his brother's had, and he realized she'd been crying. "Beth, are you okay?"

She nodded. "I'm fine."

So she wasn't going to admit to any more. Well, he'd had a miserable night too. He'd been walking around with his heart cracked open. Seemed to be a theme today.

"Can I come in?" he asked.

She nodded and stepped back. As he slipped past her, he could smell the pretty floral scent of her bath products. A smell that would stay with him, he was certain. He'd be an old man, and it would come to his memory.

The kitchen was empty; the house was quiet. He looked around.

"Where is your *mammi*?" he asked.

"She's resting upstairs."

That was probably for the best, because he didn't want to upset Iris. "I need to talk to you about something important. It's about . . . Well, I think it's about your *daet*."

"What about him?"

So he told her how Ken had been coming by and taking pictures, and the story he'd told about his foster brother who'd swam to shore in a storm.

"He's at your home?" she asked.

"In my kitchen. Having pie with my *mamm* and brother."

People were going to talk—starting with Ken. His father was dead, and he was starting to leak at the seams. His story was pouring out of him, and it wouldn't stop.

"What do we do?" Danny asked. "He's going to keep talking. He's looking for answers, and his father is dead now, so he feels freed up to look for this foster brother. He's going to keep asking around. I can feel it."

"I don't know . . ." Beth sighed. "I don't know!"

"You ask him to come by for a cup of tea," Iris's voice said behind them. "That's what you do."

Danny looked up, startled. Iris was at the bottom of the stairs, and he'd been so focused on Beth that he hadn't heard her descend. She'd obviously overheard what he'd said, and his heart threatened to hammer out of his chest.

"Mammi—" Beth started.

"He's the brother that Mose talked about," Iris said. "I heard about him plenty. He had a good heart as a boy, and he never let your *daet's* secret out. He's looking for your *daet* now, and he'll have to be told that Mose died. I think I'm the best person to do that."

"But, Mammi, your secret—"

"It was bound to come into the light," Iris said. "And I've been praying for some way to make it better. I think Gott answered. Don't you?"

Danny's gaze flitted between Beth and her grandmother, waiting for a decision.

"Go and fetch him, Daniel," Iris said firmly. "I'll put on some tea."

So Danny moved toward the door. He glanced at Beth, who still looked apprehensive. There was nothing left to do but what Iris had told him—to bring Ken to meet the woman who'd taken in his missing brother.

33

Tabitha pulled the brush over Fritz's glossy coat in long strokes. She never took a shortcut with Fritz's brushing. His side shivered in pleasure. This horse was also the most soulful animal she'd ever met.

She heard the stable door open, and she looked over her shoulder. A man's silhouette appeared in the doorway, and then Jonas's face became visible as he shut the door behind him.

"Hi, Jonas," she said, casting him a quick smile. "What brings you by?"

Jonas strode quickly down the barn's main aisle, passing empty stalls until he came to the big double-sized stall they used for Fritz.

Jonas leaned against the rail and watched in irritable silence as Tabitha brushed.

"How'd you know I'd be home?" Tabitha asked.

"I took a chance. I saw your *daet* outside and asked him."

Tabitha grinned. "I think my *daet* likes you now. This morning, he called you by name and not 'that Peachy boy.'"

"That's a big step." Jonas chuckled.

"Look how far we've come." She eyed him uncertainly. He

seemed different tonight—wound up. He tapped a fingernail on the railing.

"Okay, what is it?" she asked, putting down the brush. "You're stressing me out just standing there."

"I wanted to ask you about something."

"Sheep related?"

"*Yah* . . . Kind of." He stopped the tapping. "I've been trying to get my *daet* on board with starting out with some sheep, and he's been uncooperative."

Tabitha nodded. "Has anything changed?"

"It turns out he's willing to buy me a small herd of sheep and sign some land over to me—if I get married."

Tabitha stilled. Her stomach clenched. "Okay . . ."

"I hate that." Jonas pushed away from the railing. "I'm his son! I have a solid business plan. I've been educating myself on sheep farming, and we have a space in the local market for it. This is a good plan! But will he do it just because I've got a smart idea? No!"

"I'm sorry," she said. "Maybe he'll soften up with some time."

"*Nee*, he won't. He and my *mamm* already contacted that miracle-working matchmaker in Ohio. They want me to meet some of the women she's suggested."

Tabitha had heard of that matchmaker too. She'd been having wonderful results in setting up marriages. Some of the local women had been abuzz about how she worked, and rumor had it that she just had a sense about people. She could talk to a young man wanting a wife, and she'd have a sense right away about what kind of woman would be able to claim his heart. She could find good, solid men for the women in search of husbands too. It was a gift from Gott, they said, to be able to have that kind of discernment.

"It isn't right to push you toward marriage if you don't want it," Tabitha said. Would the matchmaker notice if the single man was being bullied into it?

"I know. This is my point." Jonas walked away a few steps, then turned back.

"And your *mamm* is going along with this?"

"She's the one who contacted the matchmaker!"

They wanted him married already.

I get it. He's sweet, handsome, and deserves a wife.

But if Jonas got married, this friendship would be over, and she couldn't bring out the words to encourage him to do it. She just looked at him, her heart aching.

"But sheep are a good idea," Jonas went on. "No one else is selling sheep products at the local market. Sheep cheese is delicious and really popular. Plus the wool, Tabitha. There is a whole market for virgin wool that can be spun into yarn. I could partner up with someone who wants to dye and spin wool—you don't have a hankering for making yarn, do you?"

Tabitha smiled, but she wasn't sure she managed to look natural. "I don't have that kind of time with my job."

"Right, right. But still, I'm sure there is some entrepreneur that will be on board. It's a good idea, Tabitha!"

"It's great."

"I'm so tired of being pushed around." He sighed. "So what do I do?"

She shook her head, then asked tentatively, "What if you moved away?"

"What?"

"What if you moved to a different Amish community and started on your own? You'd have more space to do what you want. You could buy land, raise sheep."

"Is that what you want? Do you want me to leave?"

Tabitha wasn't expecting that question. "It isn't about what I want." Her throat tightened. "What do *you* want?"

"I want to farm sheep. I want to hang out with you." His tone softened. "I don't want to get married, Tabitha. I don't want another woman. I want you."

Her breath caught in her throat. If she could redo her life, she wouldn't marry Michael and she'd find Jonas sooner. But they couldn't go backward.

"You can't have me," she whispered. "I'm divorced."

"So you just see me as a pal?" he asked, closing the distance between them. "That's all I am? A buddy?"

"You are so much more than that." Her voice shook. "But we're crossing lines here, Jonas. You know I can't marry."

"I'm just being honest with you." His fiery gaze met hers. "I'm not hiding it anymore."

His parents were trying to encourage him to marry. Did Tabitha really want to hold him back from that? From having a family of his own and a wife to love? Did she really want to keep him from taking that next step in his life because she would miss him desperately?

"It doesn't change facts, though, does it?" she shot back. "I understand where your parents are coming from. I had my chance at marriage. It's only fair that you get yours."

"With who?" he demanded. "Some woman I don't know? Some woman I'll probably disappoint?"

"Who says you'll disappoint her?" Tabitha shook her head. "You're smart, you're business minded, you're moral and decent." She swallowed hard. "You're very loveable, Jonas."

Jonas didn't answer. He turned away again, and she was left staring at his back. Why did he come here, for her permission? For her blessing? To talk him out of it?

"I don't want things to change just yet." Jonas turned back. "I want to just keep on like this—you and me being good friends, pursuing interesting jobs, and talking about anything and everything. I want to keep seeing you every day."

"It works for me. I love this too," she said, waving her hand between them both, but then she felt a pang of guilt and sighed. "But, Jonas, it isn't fair to you."

Jonas must know what she was talking about because he didn't argue or play dumb. He didn't pretend this was about sheep anymore, because it wasn't. Tabitha knew that. And so did Jonas's parents. They wanted what was best for him.

"Jonas, do you want to stay single for the rest of your life?" Tabitha asked. "Do you want to live with your *mamm* and *daet* and farm with them until they get old and you take over? Do you want to get your own place, be friends with me, and just end up being an old bachelor? Do you want to never have a wife and *kinner*?"

Jonas was silent.

"Sometimes that is just how life unfolds," Tabitha went on. "That's what my life will look like. I'll be okay. I'll find wonderful ways to be involved in our community, I'll have my career, and I'll be a favorite *aent*. I'll have friends, and I'll take care of my *daet* as he gets older. It's going to be a full life, so don't feel sorry for me. But do you want to choose that?"

"Do I have to choose now?" he whispered raggedly.

She nodded. "It looks like you do."

Jonas rubbed his hands over his face. "I do want a family of my own."

"I thought so," she said.

"And if you hadn't married Michael, I would have asked you out for a Sunday afternoon drive."

Tabitha swallowed against the rising emotion. If she weren't divorced and she was free to be courted, she would have accepted. She could imagine a courtship between them—a traditional Amish courtship, with buggy rides and visiting with each other's families. She could imagine holding his hand and stolen kisses when they passed through the covered bridge. She could imagine his solemn proposal late one evening when they were alone, and her equally solemn acceptance.

"But I did marry Michael," she said woodenly. "And I can't ever get married again while my ex-husband is alive. It's just how things are, Jonas."

"Sometimes people leave the Amish faith for each other," he said.

"I already did that. Never again," she said.

Tabitha picked up the brush again and moved to Fritz's other side, brushing his coat with a renewed strength. She'd had choices, and Tabitha had chosen the wrong man. A marriage could go wrong. It happened when a woman chose the wrong *Englischer*, and it happened when a woman chose the wrong Amish man too. And while no one thought it would happen to them, it did.

"So the matchmaker—what did she say?" Tabitha asked.

"She sent a short description of three different women who would be happy to meet with me," he replied.

Of course they would be. Jonas was a catch! She knew it—the whole community knew it, and Tabitha was holding him back.

"What will you do?" she asked.

"I don't know yet." He heaved a sigh. "I wanted you to tell me to stand firm and wait until I felt certain."

"I can't tell you what to do. This is a decision you have to make for yourself, Jonas," she said.

But she was willing to let him go. She'd have to. He needed to move on, and she needed to contribute here. Gott had provided her a new group of friends in the older widows, and she could feel Gott's nudge there. She could minister to them as much as they would to her. That was provision. Jonas was temptation.

"I won't be upset with you if you do what you have to in order to get married," she told him.

She was avoiding saying the words *cut me off*. But he'd have to. He'd have to nod at her on Service Sunday and treat her like an acquaintance and nothing more. He'd have to pretend that she didn't know him as well as she did and that he didn't know her.

"I wish you hadn't married him," Jonas said quietly.

"Me too."

Oh, how she wished she hadn't! If things had been different, she might have connected with Jonas, and a beautiful little courtship could have ensued. Right now, they could be newlyweds, keeping house, planning a future of their own. Getting excited about sheep farming together.

Tabitha met his gaze. "Pray on it, Jonas."

He nodded. "That's the best advice yet."

She smiled. "You're a good man, and while I want to keep everything just like this for my own selfish comfort, you deserve a loving, devoted wife."

"*Danke*."

Jonas gave her a wink, but his smile was sad, as if he knew this was a good-bye. She knew what he'd choose—he'd go find himself a wife. He hadn't come to talk to her because he didn't know what to do. He knew exactly what to do. He'd just wanted her blessing on it.

After Jonas left, Tabitha turned back to brushing Fritz,

but the tears wouldn't stay buried. She leaned her face into Fritz's warm side and started to cry. Fritz shuffled, and he nickered a soft, low, comforting sound. When she lifted her face again, she saw her horse looking at her with his deep, soulful eyes.

"You'll stay with me, right, Fritz?" she asked. "You're not going to leave me, are you?"

He nickered again, and she wiped her eyes and continued brushing once more. Gott would provide another friend for her, some companionship, some comfort. In fact, maybe Gott already had in the form of this loyal horse and the widowed quilters. She'd be a good veterinarian for the farmers in their community, and she'd be a friend to those widowed women. She'd make sure everyone's lives were a little sweeter because she'd come home. Sometimes answers looked different than one imagined, and she had to be grateful for Gott's provision, whatever form it took.

34

⁂

"A re you sure about this, Mammi?" Beth asked as her grandmother put the kettle onto the stove. Her hand trembled with the weight of it, and somehow Mammi looked frailer than she had even hours ago.

"I am, dear."

"What can I do if he does something? I'm bigger than you, but not by much."

"Danny will stay too. He knows the story anyway. I'd rather people know the truth than their own made-up versions of it."

"And if he reports you?" she pressed.

"Then I will tell my story to the authorities as well." Mammi met her gaze evenly. "There is a time when everything must come into the light, and, my dear girl, I would prefer it happen before I see glory."

Such a change from when Beth arrived and the stories were locked away. Just telling the story to Beth had brought enough healing to make Mammi willing to tell others.

And Mammi didn't have much time left while her mind was still cooperating with her. The more she slipped into the past, the more confused she became, the less opportunity to clear her conscience. And a clear conscience was a relief the closer one came to the end of one's life.

There was a knock, and Beth went to open the door. Danny stood outside with a middle-aged man next to him. The man was lanky and tall with iron-gray hair and a mustache. He wore blue jeans, cowboy boots, and a blue plaid shirt. He gave Beth a polite nod, and Danny met her gaze questioningly.

"Come in," she said. "My name is Beth. I'm Iris's granddaughter."

"Pleasure," the man said. "I'm Ken."

Ken came inside, and Danny hesitated at the door.

"Come in too," Beth said in Pennsylvania Dutch. "Mammi wants us here while she talks to him. And I think it's only wise. I'm not leaving her alone with a stranger."

"*Yah*, that makes sense," Danny said, and he slipped inside and shut the door behind him. He stepped forward. "Iris, this is Ken. Ken was telling me the story about his foster brother, and . . . well, I brought him over. He's looking for more information, if you're willing to give it."

She could tell that Danny was speaking carefully, but Mammi waved them toward the table.

"Have a seat," she said. "The water isn't boiling yet, I'm afraid, but we can talk."

Beth waited until the men sat down, then took a seat next to Mammi.

"You're Kenneth?" Mammi asked.

"People call me Ken," he replied. "I heard you might have known my foster brother, Nelson."

"Ken. All right," Mammi said. "And I did know your foster brother. But we called him Mose."

"Mose . . ."

"He needed an Amish name, dear, so that people wouldn't question where he came from." Mammi fixed the man with a direct stare.

"You hid him?" Ken asked. "Did he . . . did he stay with you?"

"He did."

"Did he tell you about how my parents—" He swallowed hard.

"*Yah*, he told me about the abuse, dear," Mammi said gently. "And he told me about your kindness. The abuse wasn't your fault. You know that, right?"

"On some level, I do," he said.

Mammi nodded sympathetically. "He said you begged him not to run away before he tipped the boat and you both went into the water."

"I did, but I kept the secret," Ken said gruffly. "I saw him get to shore, and I saw you help him."

"I kept the secret too." She smiled sadly. "I took him in, and I hid him. I didn't want to send him back to that life of abuse. I accidentally witnessed some of it, so I knew what was happening in your family. When I asked him what name he might like, I gave him a few options. He liked the name Moses, and we called him Mose, and I drove him out to Indiana, where we settled for several years."

"So Nelson—you raised him Amish?" Ken's eyes widened.

"Yes, dear."

"Is he—is he here?"

Tears misted Mammi's eyes. "No, dear. He passed away six months ago. But he married, and he had three children. Beth is his middle child."

Beth's heart pattered hard in her throat. She tried to swallow

313

against it. Ken's gaze flicked toward her, and he looked a little stunned, like he was still taking it all in. Did he understand what Mammi had said, or was he still processing?

"What happened to him?" Ken breathed.

"He died of a heart attack," Beth said. "The doctor said it was instant."

"Your father . . ." Ken seemed to be catching up now.

"*Yah*. My *daet*," Beth said. "My *daet* was Mose Peachy— the boy Mammi fished out of the lake that afternoon when the storm struck and he swam to safety. I didn't know about his history until very recently. Daet never told us. He wouldn't speak of his childhood."

Ken's chin quivered. "I'm very sorry for your loss."

"*Danke*."

"It sounds like he lived a happy life," Ken said.

"My *daet* was the happiest man you could meet," Beth replied. "He loved us so much. He adored our *mamm*, and he taught me and my brothers how to swim. He laughed a lot, and he joked. He had lots of friends. People liked being around him because he made them happy."

"Nelson was hilarious," Ken said softly. "When it was just the two of us, he'd have me in stitches." He was silent for a moment. "I've been looking for him ever since my father passed. I felt like I owed him something. I never told his secret—not once in all these years. I saw him make it to shore, and I never breathed a word."

"That is a terrible secret for a boy to carry," Mammi murmured.

"Yes, ma'am, it was." He nodded. "I loved my parents, but I saw a side to them that was ugly. That was very confusing for me. I kept making excuses for them. There weren't any more foster children, and there wasn't any more abuse. So

314

it was almost like it didn't happen. Except it did, you know? The minute I turned eighteen, I joined the army just so I could move out."

"Did they ever hurt you?" Mammi asked gently.

Ken shook his head. "Not like they did Nelson. When Nelson died—or when they believed he died—it scared them. They thought they'd be blamed. They were scared I'd say something. It was an awful time of secrets and guilt."

"Did you get married?" Danny asked, speaking for the first time.

Ken nodded. "Married and divorced. I have three kids too."

"I'm sorry about the divorce, dear," Mammi said. "Did you do your best?"

"Yes, ma'am."

"Did you love your children well?" she asked.

"Yes, ma'am. I learned a lot about what not to do from watching my parents. I did better than they did."

"Good." Mammi smiled. "Life can be harder than we expect, but Mose talked a lot about you. And I'm proud of you."

Ken's face crumpled then, and he wiped tears from his eyes. "Are you serious?"

"I am." Mammi reached out, and he reached back, clasping hands. "Gott brought me a little boy to love, but I heard about you, and you were in my prayers too. I think you've turned out to be a good man, Kenneth."

The kettle started to whistle, and Mammi released his hand and pushed herself to her feet.

"I can get it, Mammi," Beth said.

"It's fine," Mammi replied. "Maybe you can get the mugs."

Beth brought the mugs, sugar, and spoons to the table, and Mammi stayed there by the stove, a frown on her face.

"Mammi?" Beth said.

Mammi turned and looked around the room. "I do apologize. I think I forgot the time. I have to pick up Mose from school."

Beth's breath caught in her throat. Mammi was confused again, and Beth looked warily toward Ken. "She gets this way sometimes. I'm sorry."

"It's okay," Ken said with a slight shake of his head.

"Mammi, you don't have to get Mose," she said.

"It's a long walk. I need to go." Mammi headed away from the stove and toward the side door, whisking past Beth before she could catch her. Behind her, the kettle started to whistle again.

"Mammi, Ken is here to see you," Beth said, raising her voice.

"Who is Ken?" Mammi demanded.

"Me," Ken said, and he lifted his hand in a little wave. "Hi."

Mammi nodded slowly, then headed toward the stairs, walking slowly upward, her hand on the railing. The kettle continued to whistle, and Beth watched her go. When Mammi safely reached the top, Beth exhaled a shaky breath.

"Alzheimer's?" Ken asked.

"Dementia," Beth replied, and she pulled the kettle off the heat. "It's been getting worse. And every time she slips into the past, she's worrying over Mose . . . Nelson." The name felt foreign in her mouth. "My *daet*."

"She loved him well, didn't she?" Ken asked.

Beth and Danny both nodded. Mammi had loved her son very well. She'd done everything for him. She'd raised him to tell the truth, to be kind, to be respectful, and to love Gott with all of his heart. She'd taught him to be loving to his wife and to be wholeheartedly affectionate toward his *kinner*. And considering the abuse he'd endured before she found him, that was a miracle in itself.

"I'm glad he had that," Ken said, his voice tight. "He deserved a mother like that—one who would love him so much. He deserved that. I'm glad he found it."

"My grandmother never got married," Beth said. "So your Nelson was a gift to her too. She poured all her love into the raising of him. My *daet* loved his *mamm* very much. He had nothing but praise for her."

"So Nelson—" He paused. "Mose, I should say . . . Things turned out okay for him?"

"More than okay," Beth said. "He was very happy."

"I've worried all these years that my parents broke him. That I had—" He swallowed hard. "I worried that I had done harm to him by not helping him more. I tried, but I didn't know how, and I didn't go to the police either. I should have. I just worried that because of my cowardice, he would have never been okay again."

"You were a child, Ken," Beth said quietly. "You were a child too. And you did your best. Gott did the rest. Okay? My *daet* was happy and loved, and Gott made up the difference."

"He really believed in God and all that." It wasn't really a question. For a moment, there was silence around the table.

"Are you a Christian, Ken?" Danny asked.

"No." The answer was short. Clipped.

"Mose was," Danny said, and the two men exchanged a solemn look.

"And it sure seemed to make a difference for him," Ken said.

"My *daet* was always telling people about Gott," Beth said. "Gott is real, and he does help us. If Daet were still alive, he'd invite you to church."

Ken smiled faintly. "And if he were alive, I'd go."

"Consider it anyway," Danny said quietly.

Ken pushed back his chair. "Maybe I will. Thank you for this. It's answered a lot of questions for me, and it's given me some peace."

"I'll walk with you," Danny said, and he looked at Beth, his dark gaze meeting hers.

But Beth's heart was beating fast, and her thoughts were tumbling over each other. Daet had told them over and over again how very blessed they were to have been born Amish, and until she looked into Ken's face as he recalled his childhood, she hadn't really appreciated how much misery her *daet* had come from. She knew that not all *Englischers* experienced that kind of pain, but Daet had escaped a home filled with abuse, guilt, and pain—a hell on earth. And the Amish life had shown him love, stability, and faith for the first time in his life.

Daet had given her the best he knew how. He'd given her an Amish faith and a trust in Gott. And this life she'd taken for granted was the kind of peace that his foster brother could only dream of. She'd been questioning everything that worked!

"I'll see you in a while?" Danny asked, hesitating.

She nodded hurriedly. "I'll check on Mammi."

Danny cast her a reassuring smile and headed with Ken back outside into the sunlight.

Mammi came back down the stairs, carrying her purse this time.

"I have to get Mose," she announced. "I'll be late if I don't hurry."

And this time, instead of just seeing confusion and a battle ahead of her, Beth saw the depth of love that Gott had given her *daet* after his escape. Even when her mind betrayed her, Mammi's heart was fixed stubbornly on her son.

Her family had hidden the details of her father's adoption, if it could be called that. But they had never hidden the most fundamental truth. This family loved each other, and they loved Gott. Gott had made up the difference. He'd filled in the gaps. He'd miraculously healed a damaged boy's heart, and he'd provided Mose's *kinner* with a soft place to fall.

"Mammi!" Beth said, catching her grandmother's arm. "We're going to make some tea and toast, Mose's favorite."

"Are we?" She frowned.

"*Yah*. We're making tea and toast. You should have some too. You must be hungry."

"Oh . . . Does Mose want tea and toast?"

"Come on. The water is hot. Let's steep some tea."

And standing in that kitchen with her bewildered grandmother, Beth didn't need to go any farther to know where she belonged. She belonged right here in the community that her *daet* had loved so dearly. All that *Englischer* freedom couldn't hold a candle to the gift her *daet* had given her in raising her Amish. She looked out the back window at Danny's receding form as he and Ken headed back toward the Lapp property, and her heart yearned toward him so powerfully that it brought tears to her eyes. She belonged with Danny.

She just wasn't sure if Danny would still feel the same way.

35

Jonas stood in the field next to a newly filled cattle feeder. Even when the cattle were grazing, Jonas and his father liked to provide a little extra for the cows that had just delivered calves. They needed the nourishment.

The wagon bed was covered in loose straw, and the horse flicked flies away from his ears. Calves kept close to their mothers, and a few yards off, a newborn calf nursed eagerly. That little heifer would have to be tagged, and he made a note to come back.

The sun was high and the cattle were doing well, but Jonas's heart was far from peaceful.

"Gott, I don't want another woman!" he said out loud. That was a pure, honest fact! And he wasn't hiding the truth from Gott. Gott knew his rebellious, wandering heart.

A cow mooed at him in response, and the herd plodded over to check out the new food.

Somehow, out in the field he felt closer to Gott—a little like David in the Psalms. Out here, he could see the depth of meaning behind the words "The LORD is my shepherd."

Perhaps it was in a field like this one that David had first sung his song about Gott's providence.

But Tabitha was not available. She couldn't marry again. He was feeling far too much for her, and it was getting out of control. He wanted to do the right thing, but his heart kept yearning toward her.

"Gott, sweep her out of my heart," he prayed aloud. "Take away these feelings for the wrong woman. Help me to see clearly to find a proper wife, a marriage partner that I can grow old with. Please, Gott, just take away these feelings. Please."

He waited, wondering if Gott would answer like a thunderbolt. But there was nothing. Just the mooing of a cow for her calf and a little leggy newborn that went running in circles. Jonas rubbed his hand over the back of his neck.

He pulled the matchmaker's letter out of his pocket and opened it once more. There were three eligible women—all who would be sweet, moral, and wonderful, he was sure.

He did want to be loved. He did want someone to care when he got home, to cook him a meal, to tell him about her day. Someone to give him sweet kisses, and he'd laugh at her jokes. He wanted a woman to provide for and love. He wanted to parent a houseful of *kinner* with a sweet wife at his side. And maybe when he imagined that woman, he was thinking about Tabitha Schrock, but he'd best change that now, because Tabitha could not fill that role.

Sometimes a man had to simply take a step forward and do the right thing. The right thing didn't always feel good. Sometimes it downright hurt, but Gott always blessed a man when he had the bravery to do it. So he looked down at the little list of women the matchmaker had provided, and this time he changed his prayer.

"Gott, lead me to the right woman," he prayed. "I'm ready to start looking for a wife." It couldn't be Tabitha, and Jonas would have to be okay with that.

He was ready to face the pain of a severed friendship and the uncertainty of a new relationship. It was time.

"*. . . he leadeth me in the paths of righteousness for his name's sake.*"

If Jonas just kept moving forward in the right direction, his heart would catch up.

Wouldn't it?

After Ken had driven off, Danny stood on the beach looking out at the lake for a long time, his emotions tumbling around inside of him. A family of geese paddled in a line, the babies honking at their mother. The scene was much more peaceful than his heart. So much had happened over the last few weeks, and this story about Mose Peachy's adoption still had him turned upside down. No one expected these things to happen in their own community.

But under the shock of it all, he had a certainty that buoyed him up, and he finally had words for it. He'd been wondering how to explain the complexity of his feelings for Beth Peachy, and it finally fell together in his head. He loved her.

It wasn't just attraction or flirtation. It wasn't a hope or dream. It was something more basic, more fundamental. He loved her, and that wasn't going to just go away. He wasn't going to get over her. She wasn't going to stop being a part of his very foundation.

He stood there on the beach, biting his bottom lip, his brain spinning. There was a bedrock inside of Danny that pointed him in the right direction, and it was pointing to Beth. Even if she was a risk.

"What's going on?" Zach called from the doorway of the house.

Danny turned back. He knew what he had to do. "I'll explain in a bit. I'll be back."

The walk back down the path was faster than the walk home, and Danny even broke into a jog a couple of times. The lake sparkled in the afternoon sunlight, and he looked over that wide expanse of water that had separated him from Beth, that had guarded secrets, and that had cradled his own adolescent anticipation for the next summer's visit with the girl who filled his heart.

Gott, guide me, he prayed.

Beth came outside as his shoes hit the pebbles of their little stretch of beach, and she shaded her eyes.

"Is everything okay?" she called.

He saw Iris kneeling in the garden, picking small zucchinis that she put in a bucket, Goldie lying on the grass in the shade of a tree. Iris looked up at him questioningly.

"Hi, Iris," Danny said. "I just wanted to talk to Beth a bit, if that's okay."

"Of course, dear," Iris said. "Is Kenneth all right? Beth said you walked him back."

So Iris was back in the present.

"*Yah,* Iris, he is. He wants to visit again."

"That would be nice," Iris replied.

Beth crossed the lawn, and they moved together toward the beach and a little bit of privacy. Beth looked back at her grandmother a couple of times, and when she was satisfied the woman was fine, she turned her full attention to Danny.

"I'm no good at writing letters, Beth," Danny said. "I

could try again, but I still wouldn't do justice to what I'm feeling."

Beth blinked at him. "What?"

"Beth . . ." And now that she was in front of him, looking up into his face with that wide, warm gaze, he found himself floundering for the right words. He swallowed. "I can't say it in a flowery way. I can just say what I'm feeling. And I love you."

"You do?"

"It's not the kind of love that turns into pretty letters. It's the kind that puts some muscle into chopping wood, if I knew that wood was going into your stove. It's the kind that drives you into town, just to get some time with you. It's the kind that walks over here twice a day just to hear what you're thinking about. Beth, I love you. It's not reasonable. It's just a fact, and I know we said this wouldn't work, but what if I love you with all of your questions intact? What if I loved you even if you questioned some traditions? I can handle that, so long as you never question what I feel for you."

Beth just stared at him, and in those heartbeats of silence, he couldn't think of anything else to say, so he took her face between his two hands and lowered his lips over hers. That seemed to say things better anyway. She sank against his chest, and when she pulled back, she whispered, "I love you too."

"*Yah*?" he asked hopefully.

She nodded. "*Yah*. I don't want to explore beyond the fence anymore. I've seen what my *daet* gave me when he raised us Amish. He gave us the best he could. My family heritage isn't out there with the *Englisch*. My family heritage is the one Daet chose for me—the one he was loyal to. Meeting Ken opened my eyes to a few things. Daet chose this life, and I'm choosing it too. I won't always agree with everything, but if you're willing to talk it all out with me, I can make a life while remaining Amish."

"I'm so glad." Danny swallowed. "And maybe the bishop will let you swim. When the story gets out about your *daet*, and when they consider the drownings, maybe teaching people to swim will make sense to the leadership."

"Do you think it will?" she asked.

"It makes sense to me."

She smiled then. "And you're very traditional."

Yah, he was. But their traditions were supposed to serve the community, not the other way around.

"Because this is the thing," he went on. "We talked before about courting and all that . . . but the truth of the matter is, I've loved you for years. I don't want to discuss courting." Her face fell, and he hurried on. "I just want to marry you, Beth. That's what it boils down to. I want to spend the rest of my life with you. No more time away."

He looked down at her—her faint freckles across her nose, the pinkness of her lips, her long lashes, and the frank expression on her upturned face.

"*Yah*," she whispered.

"Wait." Was she saying what he thought she was saying?

"I'll marry you, Danny." Beth nodded excitedly. "I know I'll have to get baptized, and I know we'll have to spend some time courting, but *yah*. Danny, I want you to be chopping wood for me, all right?"

"I can try and write you a love letter," he said with a low laugh.

"Don't bother." A grin tipped up her lips. "You're better this way anyway."

"What about your grandmother?" he asked. "Is she going to live with your *mamm*?"

She nodded. "That's the plan. Maybe Mamm will agree to put off selling Mammi's house if you and I were to move into it."

"And I can open my stall in the Amish Market. I knew I needed to get my own business rolling, and now I know why."

"It sounds like we have a future all mapped out," she said, and she smiled up at him.

Danny gathered her up into another kiss, but Goldie's cold nose interrupted them. He looked over to see Iris staring at them with eyes wide and a hand in front of her mouth.

"Mammi," Beth said, "can you keep a secret?"

"I doubt it," Mammi said.

"Well, you can do your best." Beth looked up at Danny once more with a sparkle in her eyes. He wanted her to stay as happy as she was in this moment, and he'd do everything he could to make that happen. "We're getting married."

Danny and Beth walked together toward Iris, Goldie padding along next to them.

And Danny felt like everything had settled into place—his heart beating with the same rhythm of the waves that lapped the shore behind him. She loved him, and he loved her, and he couldn't wait to make her his wife and set about chopping that wood for the woman who filled his heart.

EPILOGUE

Beth Peachy put a cardboard box in the center of the kitchen table. Mammi had asked her to bring it upstairs, and Beth was curious about what was inside, but Mammi had ordered her not to peek. So she hadn't. Mammi was in a good place right now, and it was nice to enjoy her grandmother's good days.

Danny was busy getting his stall set up at the Amish Market. He'd be selling wood carvings, handcrafts, and Amish-made toys for *kinner*. The toys would be a first for the market, and he was certain they'd sell well. Beth hoped they did, because they had a wedding coming up in five weeks. It was rushed—she'd admit that. But in other ways, her and Danny's wedding had been a long time coming.

The church leadership were still discussing the issue of swimming lessons in the community, but considering that Beth had saved two lives in Friesen Lake since her arrival, they had agreed that she could swim so long as she used her modest swim dress and didn't do so in mixed company. It was a start, but Beth was hoping to convince them to let her teach some girls to swim too. It was a matter of safety.

Ken had come to visit this afternoon, and he now sat

opposite Mammi, a generous slab of cherry pie in front of him. He'd come to visit once a week since that first time, and every time he came, he brought a little gift—flowers, a box of tea, a bag of oranges—for Mammi. Today, Ken had brought a package of chocolate chip cookies.

"These are some of Mose's playthings," Mammi said, pulling a baseball mitt and a ball from the box. "He loved playing baseball with the boys."

Toys? Beth looked at her grandmother in surprise. After all the talk about Amish toys around here lately for Danny's stall, she hadn't thought to ask after her *daet's*. Ken reached into the box and pulled out a wooden horse.

"My cousin carved that for him," Mammi said. "And this is the matching buggy. It's a little broken now, but it was too fragile for a boy his age anyway."

Ken handed the buggy over to Beth, and she turned the carefully carved toy over in her hands. The spokes in the wheels, the axles—they were all perfectly carved and polished to a shine. One axle was broken, though, and so was one shaft.

"Have you seen that before?" Ken asked her.

"*Nee*, this is the first I've seen it." The buggy was well made, and she could imagine her father as a child playing with it, learning the Amish ways with toys. The carved horse was in better shape.

"He was lucky to have you, Iris," Ken said. "I had video games and Tonka trucks, but I didn't have what Nelson—I mean what Mose had with you."

"I'm glad that Gott sent you to find me," Mammi said. "I'd been praying for some way to make my mistakes right. And Gott sent me you."

"You didn't make any mistakes, ma'am," Ken said. "You saved his life."

"I lied, dear."

"You saved his life."

"Well . . ." Mammi's cheeks pinked. "I can meet my Maker with a clean conscience now. No secrets, Kenneth. They eat you up from the inside. Tell the truth loud and clear. It heals the soul."

"Yes, ma'am."

"We usually don't call people ma'am here," she reminded him. "In fact, it sounds just like our word for mother—*mamm*."

"Maybe it fits either way, then," Ken said. "If you don't mind."

"Oh, Kenneth." Mammi reached over and squeezed his arm. "I think I like it after all." She was silent for a moment. "I should have looked for you."

"And ruin Mose's chance at this life?" Ken shook his head. "You made the hard choice, but it was the right one. I was okay."

"Are you really okay?" Beth asked. "We worry about you sometimes. You've become part of our family, so we think we have the right."

Ken shot Beth a grin. She liked that he understood her humor, and he'd quickly started to feel like an uncle, albeit a very *Englisch* one.

"I really am okay," he said. "I'm much better now that I've met you." He turned back to Mammi. "I read what you asked me to read."

Mammi had asked him to read the Book of Matthew, and Beth was surprised that Ken had agreed. Mammi had taken Ken's Christian education on as a personal duty. Any boy of hers would know his Bible, and she was treating Ken just like her own.

"Good," Mammi said. "What did you think?"

"I think that Jesus shouldn't have let them kill him," Ken said. "The Pharisees were just jealous of his popularity with the people. That was all. And he could have stopped them—that's what I think."

"He could have, but he had to open heaven's door," Mammi said, then she was silent for a moment. "Kenneth, dear, you took risks for Mose because you loved him. We'll do an awful lot for the people we love. How much more would Gott?"

They talked over that pie . . . deep thoughts, deeper questions, and a love that spread over the foibles and mistakes. Beth sat there at the kitchen table, watching as Mammi and Ken discussed theological issues and formed a deep and lasting bond between the two of them. Mammi was helping Ken, but Ken was helping Mammi too. Beth could tell that they were healing each other's emotional wounds together.

Beth got to watch firsthand as Gott redeemed lies, deceptions, and best efforts. Gott was still here, working through their muddling and errors, getting Daet's foster brother into a home where Gott's presence filled up the cracks and crevices.

When they'd finished half a pie between them and their talk was winding down, Ken pushed back his chair.

"I should get going, Iris," Ken said.

"Can I pray for you first, Kenneth?" Mammi asked. "I used to pray for Mose before he left home, and then for Mose and his family after that. It would be a comfort if you'd let me."

"Okay," Ken said with a shrug.

"Close your eyes, dear," she said softly.

Ken smiled affectionately, but he obeyed, and Beth bowed her head as well.

"*Herr* Gott," she prayed, shutting her eyes. "Protect Kenneth. Guide him, bless him, open his eyes, and show him what he needs to see. Send angels to protect him, and put your hand on his shoulder. Save him in your kingdom, *Herr Gott*. Amen."

As the prayer ended, the side door opened and Danny came in. He stopped short when he saw that they had been praying. Beth slipped away to meet her fiancé.

"Are you done for the day?" Beth asked.

"*Yah*, at the market I am. I need to help Daet still, though." Then he looked past Beth to the toys on the kitchen table. "Is that a wooden buggy?"

"It used to be my father's," Beth said. "Maybe you could copy it—make some for your shop."

"You read my mind." Danny grinned and gave her a peck on the lips. It was as far as he'd go with other people around, but she knew how much Danny loved her, and in a few short weeks, she and Danny would be moving into this house together as husband and wife.

Ken and Mammi finished their farewells, and Ken gave Danny a friendly nod as he came to the door.

"I'll see you later, ma'am," Ken said to Mammi.

Always ma'am. Or maybe he had meant the Amish *mamm* this time?

"Come again soon!" Mammi called, and the tall, gangly man headed out the door toward his truck.

"Hello, Daniel dear," Mammi said, turning to Danny. "Would you like some pie?"

Beth looked up at her handsome fiancé, and she felt a rush of love. With the truth finally out in the open, they'd grown closer as a family, and even made space for Ken and Danny in the middle of it all. The truth had set them all free, and with that freedom, Beth had rediscovered home.

331

"I'd love some pie," Danny said, and he gave Beth's hand a squeeze.

Five weeks and counting. Beth couldn't wait to take her vows before Gott and her community and become Danny's wife.

DISCUSSION QUESTIONS

1. How do you think that family stories shape a family? How do they shape the members of that family? How much do you think a family's history matters?

2. Do you have any family stories that have been passed down through generations? How have those stories shaped you?

3. Danny's brother left the Amish faith, and he has some good arguments for why he wants to live a non-Amish life. Which of his arguments did you agree with personally? Which did you disagree with?

4. One of the Amish rules that Danny disagreed with surrounded taking photos. How important have photos (old and new) been to your family? Do you think that having family photos is important? Why or why not?

5. Mammi has held on to a big secret for a long time. Do think that keeping secrets can harm a person over time?

6. Do you think that Mammi's secret needed to stay

hidden all those years? Or do you think she should have told her family the whole story from the start? Why or why not?

7. Beth feels like she can't make a decision for her future until her family trusts her with her father's story. What do you think would have happened if that story hadn't had any redeeming qualities? Would it have damaged her faith or her sense of self?

8. Not every family story is encouraging or uplifting. Some are traumatic, and some don't have any redemption in them that we can see. How do we deal with family history that we aren't proud of? Can you think of any Scriptural examples to encourage people in this situation?

9. In this book, God redeems even the hardest, ugliest family histories to bring people together again and to help them find healing. Have you experienced God's redemption in your own mistakes?

AUTHOR'S NOTE

When I started thinking through the story for *Still Waters*, I had a lot of questions about Amish people's attitudes toward swimming. Thankfully, I have a terrific author friend named Judy Stavisky who has some personal Amish friends, and she went to them and asked my questions on my behalf. From there, I was able to start plotting out this story. If there are any mistakes, they are not hers but mine.

I want to thank Judy for her friendship, and for her compassionate research. Her book, *In Plain View: The Daily Lives of Amish Women*, is a great book, giving readers a glimpse into the regular lives of Amish women, and it sits on my shelf here at home.

*Read on for a sneak peek
of the next book in*

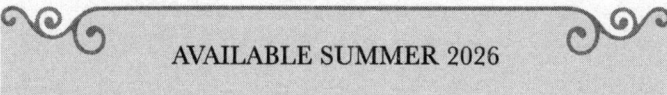

THE AMISH OF
SHEPHERD'S HILL SERIES

THROUGH THE VALLEY

AVAILABLE SUMMER 2026

CHAPTER ONE

The fact that Old Tom Yoder had invited Miri Schrock to help him with housekeeping during his illness was a bit of a joke. It wasn't that Miri couldn't keep house—she knew the basics as well as her sisters did—but no one thought of housekeeping when they looked at Miri Schrock. They thought of horseback riding and cattle wrangling. She'd even sewn a split into a few of her skirts so that she could ride bareback or jump a fence and still stay modest. Of course, she could only wear a split skirt when working on the farm. Just because the bishop hadn't spotted them yet didn't mean that they were exactly permitted. Thankfully, no one had told on her yet either—not Tom, nor Tom's grandsons who were working the farm for him. So for the time being, she was enjoying the freedom.

"I showed Tabitha the cattle that I suspect are ill," Miri said, peeking into the sitting room, where the old man was propped up in a hospital bed. Old Tom's eyes were shut, and he looked papery pale. He liked when she chatted to him about his cattle. If there was one thing Old Tom cared about, it was his herd.

Tabitha Schrock was the community's veterinarian. She

was Amish by birth, had left the faith and gotten her education, then came back home again and rejoined the community after a painful divorce. She was also Miri's cousin, and Tabitha had not made life for the rest of the family easy when she'd continued to come back and visit with her *Englischer* husband, flaunting her blue jeans and wedding ring.

"She said it was a good thing I separated the cattle we suspected were ill out from the rest," Miri went on, heading into the kitchen and raising her voice to be heard. "She wanted me to tell you that she had to take some samples and then get them tested at the lab to be sure what illness it is, but she thinks it might be contagious. Here's hoping we don't send anything home with your grandsons to their farm, right?"

Silence from the other room.

Miri washed her hands thoroughly with a thick bar of soap. Tom had asked her father for her help with housework and cooking because she was good with cattle too. He'd wanted someone who could run out and check things for him and report back, someone who could follow his instructions with the herd as well as make him some soup. Besides, Miri and Tom had gotten to be friends over the years. She used to ask him unending questions about cattle when she was a little girl, and he'd claimed that she was just like him when he was a *youngie*.

Tom's grandsons, Moses and Benuel, took turns staying overnight to help their grandfather with his personal needs, and Benuel would be arriving in a couple of hours. Right now, Moses was out on the farm somewhere doing chores and taking care of things.

"If it is contagious, we should get Moses and Benuel to wash their boots off really well before they go home, though," Miri called over her shoulder.

There was a tap on the screen door, and then it opened.

"Hello?" Tabitha called cheerfully.

"Come on in," Miri said, and she went to meet her cousin at the door. The shock of Tabitha's return had worn off, and most people were used to seeing her for veterinary calls. At first, Miri had felt conflicted about her cousin's return. Everyone did. But the fact that an Amish woman could hold this job—and do it well—gave Miri a secret thrill.

"Tom, Tabitha's here," Miri said, looking into the sitting room again. Tom hadn't moved. "Tom?" She turned back to Tabitha with an apologetic smile. "He likes being included in anything to do with the cattle, but he's sleeping. He's been resting a lot more lately."

"*Yah* . . . that's understandable." Tabitha looked into the sitting room thoughtfully. "I was going to tell him that the lab results will take a few days, but I also wanted to remind him to be careful to keep the sick animals away from the well ones."

"I'll let him know," Miri said. "And I'll tell Moses about it too. Did you see him out there after I came in?"

"*Nee*, I didn't."

That wasn't surprising. Moses was a man who kept to himself and worked steadily and with focus. He would likely inherit this farm when his grandfather passed away. Miri had gone to school with him when they were young, and she'd nursed a powerful crush on him at the time. But Moses was a man now, and while she saw him daily when he showed up for chores, she was no longer a blushing girl.

"Tabitha, what about my cows?" Miri asked, turning back to her cousin.

Mir had three head of cattle—a cow, a calf, and a heifer—all her own, and they stayed with Tom's herd. They could be recognized by their ear tags—hers being yellow, and Tom's being white.

"Yours are healthy so far. If you make sure to keep all the healthy cattle separate, they should stay that way," Tabitha said. She looked into the sitting room again, then frowned. "Is Tom okay?"

Miri headed into the sitting room and tiptoed up to his bed. Tom was always feeling too cold lately, and she had pulled a hand-stitched quilt over him earlier at his request. His German Luther Bible lay on the top of the blanket. His eyesight didn't allow him to read it anymore, but a man's Bible was as personal an item as was possible, and Tom liked to have its worn leather cover and well-thumbed pages close by. He always said he'd memorized enough of it for it to be a comfort without having to read a word.

The front window was propped open, and a family of songbirds twittered just out of view. A gentle breeze wound its way into the room, carrying the scent of cattle and freshly cut grass while Tom lay still and quiet.

"Tom?" Miri said softly. "Tabitha is here, and—"

He was very still . . . oddly still. Miri noticed his chest didn't rise and fall with his breaths like it usually did. There was no flutter of his eyelids, no twitch in a finger. Her heart hammered to a stop.

"Tom?" she said more loudly, and she reached out and caught his hand—it was cool to the touch. Her breath caught, and she struggled to suck in another lungful of air. Miri was here to help out during his final illness, but had the moment actually come?

Tabitha put her fingers against Tom's cheek, then pulled out a stethoscope, put the earpieces into her ears, and touched the chest piece to his sternum. She moved it to a different spot once, twice, three times. Then she lowered the stethoscope and shook her head.

Another gust came in through the window and lifted a stray tendril off Miri's neck. "He's died?" Miri whispered.

"*Yah*. He's died."

How long had she been chatting away with a dead man, she had to wonder? And yet it was a good day to die—quiet, fragrant, filled with birdsong and warm wind. This was the kind of day that Tom loved most, and it was only appropriate that he have this last taste of earthly beauty before passing on to glory.

Tears misted Miri's sight, and she swallowed against a lump in her throat. "I didn't know he'd passed. I was talking to him from the kitchen."

"It's okay."

"Even if he was dozing, he liked it when I talked to him about what was happening on the farm," she explained. "He said he preferred to know what was going on, and he liked to hear me prattle."

Tom had been declining for a long time, and it had suddenly sped up, which was why she'd been asked to come cook and clean for him while his grandsons took care of the rest of the farmwork. Moses was out there on the farm somewhere, and Benuel was due to arrive in a couple of hours to spend the night. . . .

Miri leaned over Tom once more, watching for breath, for movement. Tabitha had already checked, but she had to be sure. She touched her fingers to his wrist but felt nothing.

"Are you certain?" Miri asked. Mistakes could be made.

"There's no heartbeat, Miri."

If only he'd passed when his family were present. They would have wanted to be here, she was sure. But there had been no knowing how long he might have. Days, weeks—months, even. His daughter-in-law would often stop by during the day to see him and to give Miri a hand with washing up and by making a few easily digestible treats for the old man.

"All right," Tabitha said, her voice firming. "First things first. We need the doctor. He'll come certify his death and issue a death certificate."

"But you just checked his heart—"

"I'm a veterinarian," Tabitha replied. "I can let you know that he's passed away, but the government needs to know, too, and that's where a death certificate comes in. They need it for his will as well. A medical doctor needs to provide that."

"Right." Miri nodded, her mind spinning to catch up. "I have the doctor's number. It's with the medication."

It felt good to have something useful to do, and she hurried into the kitchen and opened the cupboard where Tom's medication was stored. She stood on a stool to see past the bottles and pulled out a business card for the doctor. Should she have noticed something was wrong? Should she have called the doctor earlier?

She stepped down from the stool, the card in hand. Tabitha's eyes welled with sympathy, and she folded her stethoscope over once, holding the tool gently.

"It's okay," Tabitha said. "It's just one step at a time. I'll help you."

"I missed something, didn't I?" Miri blurted out. "There must have been some sign that he wasn't okay, and I didn't see it."

"No, sweetie," Tabitha replied. "Old Tom knew he was dying, and he passed quietly. That's a blessing. No one was going to be able to stop this."

The sweet old man with his passion for his herd, his sage advice, and his patience for Miri's unique way of seeing the world was gone. Most older folks expected Miri to conform to the Amish ways—to find a husband, to devote herself to her home and to handcrafts. But not Old Tom. Tom had encouraged her to learn more about cattle, and he'd even allowed her to keep the calves she bought and reared in his herd. He'd been her friend over the years, and these past weeks, she'd gotten to know him better than ever before. And now he was gone.

"Okay," Tabitha said, "we have two things that need doing. First of all, one of us has to go call the doctor and get him to come out. And secondly, we need to contact Tom's family."

"Moses is here somewhere," Miri said. "He's probably in the west field today."

"Okay, so why don't you go find Moses and bring him back to the house?" Tabitha suggested. "And I'll go up to the phone shanty and call the doctor."

Miri nodded. "Okay. *Danke.*"

"Are you going to be okay?" Tabitha asked.

"*Yah*, I'll be okay."

All Miri really wanted was to get out of the house, away from these walls, and out into the sunshine and fresh air. She was better in a barn or a field. She felt more like herself, and that was where her talents waited. She'd go find Moses. As Tom's grandson, he could take over from there.

Miri was only the peculiar woman helping out with the housework, after all. And it looked like their need for her was at an end.

Patricia Johns is a *Publishers Weekly* bestselling author of more than fifty books. She writes Amish fiction featuring tight Amish communities, outspoken Amish heroines, and the handsome, rugged men who fall in love with them. She lives in Alberta, Canada, with her husband and son. Learn more at PatriciaJohns.com.

Sign Up for Patricia's Newsletter

Keep up to date with Patricia's latest news on book releases and events by signing up for her email list at the website below.

PatriciaJohns.com

FOLLOW PATRICIA ON SOCIAL MEDIA

Patricia Johns Author   @AuthorPatJohns   @AuthorPatJohns

Be the first to hear about new books from Bethany House!

Stay up to date with our authors and books by signing up for our newsletters at

BethanyHouse.com/SignUp

FOLLOW US ON SOCIAL MEDIA

   @BethanyHouseFiction